Copyright

All rights reserved

The characters and events portrayed in this book are fictitious. Any similarity to real persons, living or dead, is coincidental and not intended by the author.

No part of this book may be reproduced, or stored in a retrieval system, or transmitted in any form or by any means, electronic, mechanical, photocopying, recording, or otherwise, without express written permission of the publisher.

ISBN: 9798323448685

Cover design by: Erelis Design
Library of Congress Control Number: 2018675309
Printed in the United States of America

AUTHOR NEWSLETTER

Sign up to the Dan Stone author newsletter and receive a FREE novella of short stories featuring characters from the Jack Kane series.

The newsletter will keep you updated on new book releases and offers. No spam, just a monthly update on Dan Stone books.

Sign up to the newsletter at https://mailchi.mp/danstoneauthor/sgno14d1hi for your FREE ebook

Or visit the Dan Stone website at https: https://danstoneauthor.com

HIDDEN ENEMY

Book 3 In The Jack Kane Series

By Dan Stone

PROLOGUE

Kane moved through the darkness like a wraith, dashing between desks, around painted pillars and across soft carpet. He flexed his fingers around the grip of his Glock 19 handgun, the weapon compact and familiar in his palm. Long panel lighting flickered on and off overhead, and the whirring sound of electronics coming online buzzed behind the walls. Kane had cut the power twenty minutes ago when he killed the first Vertin Corp guard, and now, the auxiliary power generator had kicked in to keep the precious servers and company digital processes online. He paused, sinking low behind a knee-high pedestal set of drawers beneath a white desk amongst a sea of similar desks in the sprawling office facility.

The cut on his ribs throbbed and stung like a burn wound, and Kane reached for the survival tin at his belt, fished out a gauze, and pressed it to the knife wound beneath his shirt. He wore dark tactical trousers and a shirt, with an armoured vest and a length of static rope coiled over his shoulder. The survival tin contained a small knife with a serrated and straight edge to cut and strike a flame, a wire saw with key rings at each end, alcohol wipes, a tampon to either start fires or use as battle dressing, a fishing line and hooks, a condom that could carry a litre of water in an emergency, and a sewing kit for use on both clothing and flesh. The tin was a hangover from his days in the SAS, Britain's elite fighting force. Even though he had left the service years ago, Kane still always carried one.

"He's on the fourth floor," said a voice in his earpiece in a deep Texan drawl. "Doyle, Zelinski, Hernandez, get up there now."

Kane secured his tin back into its belt pouch and checked that the stolen radio was still clipped to his waistband. Kane had taken the body pack and earpiece from a dead guard in a hard hand-to-hand fight on a lower floor and could now listen to them homing in on his location.

"Echo one, over," said another American voice. "This is Kamil and Hoover. We are on floor four, boss. Proceeding to sweep office, over."

Kane rose, grunting from the pain. This was the end of the job, the last piece of a puzzle he and Craven had worked on for five long weeks.

It had taken them from New York to Palo Alto and now to Texas, following a trail of clues left by cyber thieves as they sought to recover an item of incredible corporate importance to their employers. Ceiling lights flickered again and then sparked into life, illuminating the office in a wash of golden artificial light. The entrance doors beeped and then shunked open on automatic runners to reveal two men in black fatigues and baseball caps. Both entered in military-style crouches, handguns held in two hands the way an instructor with some basic military experience had likely taught them. The guards scanned the expansive office space as they came in, but Kane could feel the fear pulsing from them as they stepped cautiously on the office carpet.

"Piece of shit killed Carl," said the same voice over the radio. "I'm gonna end his bitch ass."

Kane sighed at the crude turn of phrase and moved low and fast away from the desk, poised like a hunting animal. The chip was on the next floor. Kane had spent so long searching for the prototype chip, the innovative piece of IP worth tens of millions of dollars that had been stolen from his employer, and he had been tasked with returning it at all costs. He pressed his back against the door to a canteen. Inside sat brightly coloured stools, tables with low-hanging lights above them, coffee machines and free snacks designed to keep employees working longer, and happier. But there were no employees in the office at four o'clock in the morning.

The figures in black edged closer towards the canteen, which served as an atrium at the floor's centre. Kane watched their reflections moving in the tall glass windows and wondered if they even realised that the hyper-bright lighting gave away their positions. Kane edged again into the canteen wall until he faced the entrance doors, turned around the far side and raised his weapon. He shot the leftmost guard's knee out. The gunshot tore through the quiet office air, an explosion of sound that made the second guard jump in fright. Kane shot him in the shin as he spun around. Blood spattered the canteen walls, right across stencilled wording that read: *entrepreneurship, honesty, integrity*. Ironic that those words were the ethos of a company stealing chips from rivals.

Kane left the guards screaming and writhing in pain, clutching at their ruined limbs. But they were alive. He hit a green button. Kane ran through when the entrance doors slid open. In the corridor, he hit the elevator button for the fifth-floor, kicked open the stairwell door and pounded up the stairs. Less than a minute later, he waited behind the stairwell on the fifth-floor, peering at the lab floor through thin door windows. Clear windows fully encircled the laboratory from waist height upwards. Beyond the windows were machines, devices, blinking lights and technology Kane did not understand. All he knew was that his employer and Vertin Corp were competitors; both designed and manufactured tiny chips for mobile devices. If he returned the stolen prototype to his employer, they would pay him and Craven two million dollars. He needed the money.

Three men clad in black faced the elevators, weapons poised, waiting for the door to ping and for Kane to emerge from the elevator into a hail of bullets. The guards were disappointingly inept, perhaps former military personnel, but certainly not at the level of US Rangers, Delta, or SEALS. Kane kicked the stairwell door open and threw a flash bang grenade towards the guards. They turned, mouths agape, and then the grenade went off, emitting a thunderous bang and a cloud of smoke. The three guards fell to their knees, clutching their heads in shock, disoriented by the grenade's explosion. Kane shot each man in the chest, in the solar plexus of their Kevlar body armour. The bullets wouldn't kill them, but the blows would hurt like hell. The office fire alarm sounded, and Kane picked his way around the fallen men, clutching at their own chests, gasping for air.

Kane's boots squeaked on the lab floor, and he found the chip resting in pride of place inside a small silver case, its insides filled with foam to keep the precious piece of technology safe. He grabbed the case and, two minutes later, burst onto the building roof into a bracing gust of warm night air. A vehicle sped into the office car park, tyres screeching on tarmac and headlights casting a wavering glare against the building's shining glass front. A crescent moon shone in the sky like a scythe and stars lit up the clear, balmy night. Kane unslung the rope from his shoulders, fitted it to an aerial pole, attached the belay device, and walked backwards over the edge.

It took mere seconds for Kane to rappel down the side of the office building, and his boots landed with a crunch in a courtyard of shale on the building's west-facing end. Kane left the rope and made for the car park. Voices crackled on the radio as he moved out of range and Kane pulled the communication pack free from his waistband and tossed it and the earpiece into the patch of tiny stones.

"Hurry up," said a familiar voice. Craven frowned at him through the open driver's window of a black pick-up truck, the engine still running after his speedy entrance to the car park. "Those bloody weekend warriors will be out here any second."

Kane slipped into the passenger seat, and Craven stomped on the accelerator just as two men in black emerged from the building's front doors, weapons raised and ready to fire. They shot but missed as Craven gunned the truck through the entrance barrier, already smashed to ruin after Craven's bulldozing entrance.

"I got the chip," said Kane, tapping the silver case with his finger.

"Thank God for that. Now we can get the money and go home. If I have one more American breakfast, I won't be able to fasten my trousers."

ONE

The electric car hummed like a futuristic vehicle from a science fiction film from Kane's youth. He had hired the car at Seville Airport using a credit card in the name of Mark Wright, which matched the passport identity Kane used to enter Spain. He could never get used to driving cars without a combustion engine or a gearstick. The Peugeot 308 drove well enough, but it was like driving a hovercraft as it silently coasted across the city's roads like a phantom.

He drove through Seville on a pleasant summer morning as the city came alive under the rising sun's golden warmth. Danny sighed long and loud in the front passenger seat, and Kane glanced up at an old woman watering a thick bloom of bright flowers on her charmingly carved stone balcony. He drove past whitewashed walls and terracotta roofs, glowing in the morning sun.

"Why can't we just live with Auntie Barb?"

asked Kim from the back seat, her puppy dog eyes catching Kane in the rear-view mirror.

"She's not our auntie," Danny said and folded his arms across his chest. "Dad doesn't want us, and now Barb doesn't want us either. So, he's sending us to live in fucking Hogwarts for Spanish people."

"Watch your language in front of your sister," Kane said. "We've been through this a hundred times. Auntie Barbara has been sick again. She and Uncle Frank have moved to Seville to be close to the Hospital Universitario Virgen del Rocio for her treatment. You will board at your new school during the week and live with Frank and Barbara on the weekends."

"Will you be there on the weekends?" asked Kim, her brown eyes staring at him through the mirror again, washing over him with a tidal wave of guilt.

"When I can, princess, I promise."

"He promises," Danny said and huffed sarcastically.

It had been three years since their mother passed away, since Kane's time living in witness protection under a new identity had exploded like a fragmentation grenade. In those days, Danny and Kim lived a normal life, attended a normal school, played football and went to gymnastics. Since Sally's death and Kane's emergence from the programme, the kids had lived with Craven and his wife Barbara, first in Malaga and then at various other safe locations. After Sally's death, they constantly lived in fear, keeping an eye out for any potential threats. Government operatives had kidnapped them, and Danny and Kim learned to adopt alternative names like a fresh coat.

Craven wanted to live in Spain because he thought the climate helped with Barb's cancer, which it had. The air was a vast improvement on the smog and chemical-laced air in northwest England. As much as Kane wanted to enjoy life with Danny and Kim and live in peace under the Spanish sun, it was too dangerous for Kane to live with the children. People hunted him and would never stop. Governmental organisations, assassins, people with power and resources beyond belief, wanted Kane dead. He simply knew too much. His was a life spent living on that gossamer thin line between the real world and the world of secret intelligence, counter-terrorism, special forces, life and death.

Kane stopped at a red light. Locals with dark hair and melodious accents took breakfast outside a sidewalk café. The smells of churros and fresh coffee drifted through Kane's open window, making his mouth water. He turned and sped towards the city's exit road and caught a waft of spices and seafood from the Mercado de Triana. Kane sped along the dual carriageway, past palm and orange trees, before turning into the Yago school's sprawling gardens.

"You'll have fun staying here with other kids," Kane said as he parked the car. "It's only Monday until Friday, and then me or Auntie Barb will be here to pick you up for the weekend."

"What if they don't speak English?" Kim said, a fat tear rolling down her soft cheek. "What if the girls are mean to me?"

"There are English children here, too. It's a Spanish- and English-speaking school. They won't be mean to you, princess, and if they are, you must stand up yourself. Just like I taught you."

"You'd do anything to get rid of us," Danny said, fumbling with the door handle as he did his best to open it as violently as possible. "Mum would never have sent us away like this."

After more tears from Kim, and more belligerence from Danny, Kane left them in the capable hands of smiling school prefects in bright blazers and crisp white shirts. He drove away with a lump in his throat, heavy with regret, laden with guilt. Kim was nine and Danny was twelve. Kane hated that he couldn't simply take them away and live quietly somewhere. He had tried that before, once in Scotland and once in Morocco, and both times had ended badly. Though Craven and Barbara had offered to continue to look after them, he had booked them into the Yago school under new identities. Kane would live like a nomad, never staying in one place for too long—eluding his pursuers just as he had when he worked for Mjolnir, a splinter MI6 intelligence group. Barbara's cancer had returned last year, and though she was in remission again, Kane couldn't burden her with two children to look after.

Kane exited the school gates and headed east towards Craven's house. The money they had earned recovering the chip in the US would keep their lives going for a while, but it was an expensive business being a ghost, a grey man living off the grid and out of reach. Kane needed to work for his own sanity as much as for the money. His work, however, was specialist. He and Craven helped those who needed it most, using their skills to right wrongs, and sometimes to earn the money they needed to stay alive in a world that hunted them. So, Kane left his children at boarding school, even though parting with them tore at his soul like an eagle's talons.

TWO

Jess Moore left the football club offices at eight thirty in the evening after a long day spent arguing with financiers, investors, and accountants. She brushed her shoulder-length hair away from her face and tucked it behind her ears as her heels clip-clopped on the pavement leading to the Wessex Celtic Football Club car park. The unmistakable ring of an iPhone chimed in her bag, but she ignored it. Jess couldn't take any more conversations about bridging loans, shifting fixed costs, player wages and staff cuts.

She marched briskly past the overgrown hedges lining the pavement and flashed a wan smile at one of the youth team coaches coming in the opposite direction in his club tracksuit with a large bag of footballs slung over one shoulder. Her dad would stay inside, working until much later, drinking whiskey at the club bar with the bankers and investors, using his charm to tickle a few more millions out of them to keep the team alive. That was his skill, his super power—getting rich men to part with their cash and pour into the bottomless pit that was his lifelong obsession. This cursed football club. Andrew Moore made his millions through a bookies' shop he had opened in his twenties, which developed into a countrywide chain of betting shops, and then in the noughties, the online betting app and website which catapulted his self-made wealth into the stratosphere.

"Piss off," Jess mumbled as the phone rang again. She stopped, fished her keys out of the bag, and then grabbed the phone. *Dickhead* read the glowing display. It was her ex calling for the tenth time that week. She rejected the call and pressed the open button on her BMW key fob. The 3 Series' lights flashed, and she was about to open the passenger door to throw her bag in when she noticed two men resting against the car bonnet. She hadn't noticed them at first, her mind still shaking like a shuttlecock in a hurricane, figures and problems all hammering around inside her skull after a long day of complex meetings.

"Mrs Moore," the first man said in a slow Russian drawl. He straightened into his full height; he was tall in tight-fitting jeans and a black Versace t-shirt. He crossed tattooed, muscled arms across a broad chest, his face as angular and hard as a granite worktop. His eyes were the deep blue of a frozen river.

"Miss," she said absently, shaking her head, trying to process what the men could want. "If you are reporters, I've got nothing to say…"

"Not reporters. You should read your emails, Miss Moore. There is an offer there you should look at carefully."

"Offer?"

"For the team, for the club. To buy it. Solve all your problems, make you rich."

"I'm sorry, but who the hell are you?" Time slowed as the two men stood side by side, muscles shifting upon their lean arms, smiles and lifeless eyes dripping with malice and threat. She understood now. Phoenix Telecoms, part of the Phoenix Group.

"Just read your fucking emails. If you know what's good for you. We make good offer. Make you rich."

"Get away from my car or I'll call the police." Jess waved her phone at them and glanced towards the club doors, hoping that Kevin, the security guard, would come bounding, or at least waddling, to help her.

"Fuck police. Read emails and reply. Sell piece of shit club. Or we come back, and not gentle like this." He hawked up a gobbet of spit, spat it onto the tarmac and ran his eyes up and down her body as if he could see her naked.

Jess resisted the urge to shiver in revulsion. She stood strong, chin up and shoulders out as the two men swaggered away, gaits rolling like panthers. Once the thugs had gone, her lip quivered, and she unlocked her phone with shaking fingers. Things were getting serious. She dialled her dad's number, holding back tears.

THREE

"Is it working now?" Craven called, leaning around the doorframe.

"No, love," Barb shouted from along the polished tile hallway. "I don't think so, anyway."

"We're like the bloody Chuckle Brothers trying to sort this thing out." Craven turned the fancy doorbell over, its flimsy casing seeming fragile in his shovel-like hands. Kane had recommended Craven to pick up a video recording doorbell so that he and Barb could see who was at the door, or even approaching their door, before they answered it. It all worked via a phone app, and Craven didn't have a clue how it worked, how to install it, or use it.

"Leave that, Frank. I'll put the kettle on. If someone rings the doorbell, we can just look through the window before we open the door. Sometimes the old-fashioned ways are the best."

That was music to Craven's ears, and he

laughed, shaking his head. There was a gadget for everything these days. What was wrong with the simple doorbell? He had once bought a fancy vacuum cleaner that attached to the kitchen wall to charge up. The thing cost him over two hundred pounds and worked fine for six months, but then would break down every time he or Barb used it. When he'd eventually thrown the thing in the bin, Craven had realised that the vacuum cleaner seemed all modern and techy but was actually not an improvement on a simple dustpan and brush.

Craven lay the fancy doorbell on the window ledge and wondered how much the world had changed since he was a boy. When he wanted to meet a friend, they would arrange it on the landline telephone or in person the day before and meet at the allotted time and agreed place. Tough luck if you were late, or an emergency came up. Now, there would be three phone calls, WhatsApp messages, links to maps, and text messages to ask how far away he was from the meeting point. That was the way things were before Craven left the police force to begin this new life. Now the only people who messaged him were Barb, the Spanish bin collection company, and people who needed help. A special sort of help.

A humming electric car pulled into Craven's cobble-locked driveway, and he smiled when he saw Jack Kane behind the steering wheel.

"Better make an extra brew, Barb," Craven called back down the hall. "Jack's here."

"Place looks good," said Kane moments later, as he stepped out of the vehicle.

"It bloody well should. Cost us a small fortune."

Once they had agreed on the move to Seville, Kane had organised the house purchase through his intricate and untraceable network of companies and bank accounts registered in bizarre countries in the Caribbean and Asia. Craven couldn't remember what Kane had said at the time to explain that necessity, and he didn't really care. He trusted Jack to fix it so that the purchase wouldn't be linked to Frank or Barbara Craven, just in case anybody came snooping around.

The house was bright white with huge folding patio windows in the back and more glass than a London skyscraper. It had a swimming pool shaped like an egg-timer in the garden and two acres of manicured gardens covered with dark green grass, coarser underfoot than the grass back home in England's northwest.

"You should be safe here. Nobody can find you. Just remember to use the identification cards and credit cards I gave you last month. Barb's treatment is all covered by the trust set up in

Barbados and with what we earned from the last job, you should be able to live well here, Frank."

"I used to think a million dollars was a fortune. Now it won't even last five years. Not the way we have to live, anyway. The world's gone bloody mad. That reminds me, I've got a bone to pick with you."

"What, is it about the gardeners I arranged for you? They should be here once a week and receive payment automatically through one of our accounts."

"Not the gardeners. The new name you've given me. Samuel Shufflebottom. Fucking Shufflebottom?"

Kane laughed. "I thought you'd like that."

Craven shook his head and chuckled. Craven had laughed himself when he'd first seen the name on his Spanish driving licence and Revolut Visa card.

"Jack!" said Barb as they entered the open-plan living space. Barb still wore a scarf over her head. She was in remission, but her hair had not fully grown back since her last bout of chemotherapy. None of that mattered to Craven. To him, she was as beautiful as the day they first met. Kane pulled Barb into a warm embrace.

"I brought you something for the house." Kane handed her a bunch of flowers he'd kept hidden behind his back.

"At least it's not another bloody gadget," Craven said, and he went around the kitchen island to finish making the tea whilst Barb stood with Kane. They had found a shop a ten-minute drive away from the house that sold English tea bags and biscuits, which was a relief because Spanish tea wasn't tea as he knew it. So, he squeezed the teabags in each cup with a teaspoon and tossed the steaming bags into the pull-out bin. Although the tea wasn't up to scratch, the coffee available at the local coffee shops was outstanding, nice and strong and full of flavour. Craven preferred coffee, anyway.

"You look great," Kane said, grinning at Barb as he pulled away from her bear hug. "You've caught the sun, or it could be the Seville oranges?"

"It is lovely here, I must admit," Barb said, blushing slightly and fussing with her headscarf. "I've joined the local expat community club, and we play bridge on a Tuesday and go walking on a Thursday. But how did today go? Was Kimmy all right?"

"She was fine. A bit scared. Danny will take care of her. It's the only option. If things were different, I'd keep them with me, but..."

"I'll be there to collect them on Friday. I'll bring them to the plaza de... oh, whatever it's called, for an ice-cream. Danny understands, Jack. Things are the way they are, but it's hard on him and Kim. At least they're safe, though. They miss their mother, and they miss you. They know you love them."

Craven handed Kane and Barb their tea and took a slurp of his own, eying Kane over the mug's rim. Kane loved his kids; nobody could say otherwise. But he also loved action, the thrill of the chase, of problem solving and combat. He was born to do it, an expert, and more than once over the last three years, Frank had noticed the gleam in Kane's eye when he took down a target, fired his weapon, or defeated an enemy in hand-to-hand combat. Sometimes Craven wondered if, deep down, Kane was happier with their current situation than he had been working in a factory in the witness protection programme with his family around him. But that was a hard truth, and Craven blew the steam off his tea and banished the thought to the recesses of his mind.

Craven's phone vibrated in the breast pocket of his short-sleeved shirt. He placed his mug down on the island worktop, took the phone out, and squinted at the display.

"It's the number," he said. The number. A line set up by Kane's tech expert and old SAS buddy Cameron, which bounced around a dozen encrypted web-based phone exchanges across the world. It was a secret number, only made available to others who needed help by those who had used it before. The type of help beyond the police. Help only he and Kane could provide.

"Not again," Barb said. "You're not long back from the last one. We don't need the money now. Ignore it, take a break. Both of you."

Craven glanced at Kane, who gave a slight nod of his head.

"Yes?" Craven said into the phone. Barb tutted and marched off through the open patio doors and into the sun-drenched garden.

"Hello? Is that you?" said a man's voice, an older man, his voice a little shaky.

"Depends who you are and where you got this number."

"My name is Andrew Moore. A friend, a chap who owns a racing stud in Ireland, gave me this number."

"Do you need help?"

"Oh God, yes. My club, my daughter. Men are threatening us. Wicked men." The caller's voice cracked when he mentioned his daughter, and Craven set his jaw.

"Tell me all about it."

FOUR

"Sit down, Dad," said Jess. Her father paced his office for the hundredth time, wringing his veiny hands over each other, again and again.

"He called again this morning," said Andrew Moore.

"Mr Antonov?" Jess ground her teeth. The very mention of Phoenix Telecom's CEO made her blood boil.

"He increased his offer but warned me that things would get serious for us if we didn't accept it."

"Serious how?"

"I asked our accountants to investigate Antonov and Phoenix a little. They are a Russian business, part of the Phoenix group of companies owned by a man who is a known associate of the Russian President. I've also asked around about them and one of our first team players is Ukrainian. He says we should avoid

Phoenix like the plague. There have been reports that people who worked with Phoenix in Ukraine have died, and the company is linked to the war there."

"Hold on, Dad." Jess took her father by the elbow and led him to the leather couch beside his desk. The wide, Chesterfield classic sofa had been in his office for twenty years and was as cracked and wrinkled as Andrew Moore's face. It smelled of old leather and decades of stale cigarette smoke but was as comfortable as a morning duvet. He had bought and sold football players on that sofa, signed deals for shirt sponsorship, handed contracts to beaming youth team players, and bounced Jess on his knee before big games when she was a little girl. "This all sounds a bit far-fetched. Phoenix is just a shitty company with lots of money but without morals who want to intimidate us into selling our club. Your football club. The club you rescued from the ashes and sunk most of your fortune into. You took this place from non-league to the First Division. We can't just let these guys take it from us because of a few threats. Just because they have Russian accents doesn't make them the Russian mafia or whatever it is you think they are."

"Not the mafia." Andrew waved his hand and squeezed his eyes closed in frustration. "A company backed by the Russian Government.

Powerful and ruthless."

"We don't need to sell, Dad."

"You were at the meeting with our accountants last night. You heard the numbers; we are in real trouble this time. If we don't land a new shirt sponsor for next season soon and get an upfront payment, we won't be able to pay the players next month."

"We'll find the money. I have calls this afternoon with three companies interested in the sponsorship deal. We've been in tighter spots. Let's increase security around the ground, the offices and the training pitches in case Phoenix get heavy. We can ignore any calls from Antonov or his goons and ride this thing out. They'll get bored and move on to another club."

"But what if they attack the stadium or training ground, scare off the players? Or worse… what if they hurt you?"

"They won't hurt me, Dad." She sat beside him and hooked her arm around his.

"I've asked somebody to help us," Andrew whispered, fixing her with his red-rimmed eyes, the whites full of broken veins. His thin lips curled in on themselves and his top teeth nibbled at his bottom lip.

"Asked who?" Jess pulled away from him a little. She knew that look. It was the same as when he had sold their best striker two years ago to fund a new astro-turf training pitch. The same look when he had broken the news of her mother's death six years ago. It made her nervous.

"Two men, actually. They were recommended to me. They help people like us."

"If you think we're in danger from Phoenix, then we should call the police. Not some scammers who say they can protect us."

"And say what? That thugs are hanging around in the club car park and a company wants to buy me out of Wessex Celtic? What can the police do about that?"

"Dad, I'm worried. Who are these men you have asked to help us?"

"Do you remember John Kelleher?"

"The racing guy whose horse won your event at Cheltenham?" Moore Betting sponsored a few races around the UK flat and jump horse scene each year, and the flat at Cheltenham was Andrew Moore's pride and joy.

"Yes, that's it. His daughter got kidnapped, and these men helped to bring her back. It turned nasty, across country borders, and the police couldn't handle it. Kelleher heard about our problem, and he sent me their number. They have a confidential line for people who need help."

"Jesus Christ, Dad. It's just a business takeover. We don't need help. Especially not from a couple of jumped-up nightclub bouncers who want to charge us a fortune to look beefy and snarl at a few businessmen."

"They will be here tomorrow. Be nice, Jess."

"This is your call. You deal with these two chancers. I assume they aren't doing this for free? What are they even going to do?"

"Help us. Protect us. Protect you."

Jess smiled. Her father loved her, had always doted on her, and when she had told Andrew about the car park incident, he had almost burst with fear for her safety. She checked her watch, a Fitbit Jess used to check her heart rate when running and training splits. Jess owned other watches, expensive ones bought down the years, but the Fitbit was practical and reminded her to run, even on the most stressful of days.

"I love you." Jess leaned over and kissed her dad on the cheek. He was just doing what he thought best, and she wouldn't deny him his chance to protect her. Jess left his office and its old leather and cigar smoke and went into her own room, all glass, plastic, modern and business-like. She took her MacBook from its case and opened the accounts file, the red highlighted lines jumping out at her like an old pop-up book. They needed money or the club would fold. Everything her father had worked for his entire life, his dream and his passion, was at risk. He had always been there for her, even in the dark days, and she would never forget that. So, she dialled into another Zoom call with the accountants, ready for a day of fighting for the football club's survival.

The camera popped on and she saw herself, crow's feet at her eyes and criss-cross age lines on her top lip. She had been a model once, in what felt like a different life. She flashed a fake smile as the men in pinstriped suits dialled in, focused on the business numbers, and tried not to think about Russians, takeovers, and two men who had rescued a kidnapped Irish girl.

FIVE

Kane drove the Audi e-tron, hired an hour ago at London City Airport, out of London, heading westbound on the capital's busy ring-road. The Wessex Celtic football stadium was an hour's drive southwest of the city into the bread-basket of England's countryside. Kane still travelled as Mark Wright, a former Liverpool FC centre-back, and much to his displeasure, Craven travelled as Samuel Shufflebottom.

"I saw this lot play against Bolton Wanderers once," said Craven, eating a meat and potato pie purchased at a Greggs takeaway pastry shop close to the airport. "They were almost bankrupt until Moore took them over."

"I didn't know you were a football man, Frank?" said Kane.

"More of a Rugby League man, to be honest, not that my life as a copper allowed much time to watch sport. But a mate offered me a ticket to that Wessex Celtic game. It was in a directors' box, so there was free food and ale."

"What score was it?"

"I can't remember. I ended up getting pissed at the free bar."

"So, what do we know about the job?"

"The guy who called us is Andrew Moore. Got our number off John Kelleher. Moore's a self-made millionaire, owns bookies and a gambling website. He bought Wessex Celtic years ago, turned them into a proper outfit and they're in league one now. That's only two league promotions away from the Premier League, the richest league in world football."

"Didn't Liverpool win the Premier League a couple of years ago?"

"Yeah. Are you a Liverpool fan?"

"I was when I was a kid, but lost touch with the game over the years."

"Never had you pegged as a Scouser. Anyway, Moore bought the club and sank a ton of his own cash into it. New stadium, new training ground, buying lots of new players. They've done well. If they are knocking on the Premier League's door, then the club is worth a fortune. A company called Phoenix Telecoms, who want to take the club off his hands, have offered him a tidy sum."

"What's the problem with that?"

"Well, seems this Phoenix crowd is a shower of bastards. Russians, coming on heavy, threatening Moore's daughter, causing problems."

"The police won't help until something bad happens, and by then, it could be too late. Somebody could get hurt, or worse. Which is where we come in?"

"Which is where we come in. Moore wants us to help him with the Russians, protect him and his daughter, find out what they're up to and if they are a serious threat. Just in case it turns nasty."

"Why would it turn nasty? They make an offer, Moore refuses. That's just business. Why is Wessex Celtic so important to a telecommunications company? There are a dozen other clubs in that league, and many others in leagues above and below them."

"You are supposed to be the one who does the thinking, Jack. I do the organising. I take the jobs and make sure you don't get us killed."

Kane shook his head and tuned the car radio to a rock music station to avoid listening to any modern music, anticipating Craven's whingeing if a song released after 1995 came on.

Kane left the motorway at the turn for Ravenford, the hometown of Wessex Celtic. It was a large town between Salisbury and Bath, and they drove past fields full of yellow rapeseed, and wheat flowing with the wind like the sea. Upon entering the busy streets of Ravenford itself, Kane found himself in a large, busy town centre surrounded by suburbs. The football stadium rose like a crown above the shops, offices and factories to the left and right of the town's main street. It loomed above the town in a white dome, with a cantilevered, prefabricated steel roof and high terraces, and a rainbow of criss-crossed supporting steel girders.

"How many fans can the place hold?"

"About eighteen, maybe twenty thousand people."

Kane followed the yellow and black road signs to the Moorebet Stadium and parked the Audi close to a set of glass double-doors. Two tall men loitered outside the building, smoking and laughing loudly. Kane stepped out of the car and stretched his back, and Craven coughed to clear his throat, nodding towards the doors. A woman in a smart business suit and high heels opened the left door and came striding towards them. She had a severe but pretty face with dark hair and brown eyes. Kane guessed she was in her late thirties. She wouldn't have looked out of place in a top five consulting firm.

"Miss Moore," shouted one of the tall men in a thick Russian accent. "You check your emails yet?"

The woman stopped, startled by the voice. Her eyes jumped from the two men to Craven, and then back again. Craven was a big man, a head taller than most; broad-shouldered, big-bellied and bald. Of the two men Mr Moore was expecting, Craven looked the most likely to help in a dangerous situation. Kane was of average height and build, wore his brown hair in a non-distinct short haircut and had a normal, forgettable face.

Kane cursed himself for not waiting to get the intelligence report from his old friend and tech expert, Cameron, before coming to the meeting. It was careless and rushed. In the old days, he would have read the file in detail, known every potential contact's face and history, have reconnoitred the stadium for hours before the meeting. Perhaps he was getting old, or soft. Or both. He didn't know where the entrances and exits were, locations of CCTV, main road approaches, vantage points or routine movements in and out of the stadium. He had been sloppy.

"What are you doing here?" the woman barked at the tall men.

The Russians stiffened at her tone and ambled towards her. The blue-eyed man flicked his cigarette butt at the woman and sneered at her.

"Do as you're fucking told, bitch," he said. "Your time here is over. This is our time now."

"Don't talk to the lady like that," said Craven, striding around the Audi, pointing a thick finger at the man.

"Fuck you, too, fat man." The Russian pushed the woman out of the way, and she fell with a gasp onto the pathway. He reached out to grab Craven's outstretched arm and had not considered the quiet figure standing by the driver's side door of the Audi. Which was a mistake.

Kane darted forward and was between Craven and the Russian in two strides. Kane ducked beneath the Russian's outstretched hands and punched him hard in the solar plexus, sending the man stumbling backwards, gasping for air. The second Russian snarled, swung an overhand right at Kane and fell screaming to the pavement as Kane stamped his heel full force into the man's kneecap, shattering bone and ligament. The first Russian scrambled to his feet and charged at Kane, but Kane sidestepped, and hip threw him to the floor. He scrambled and then went silent as Kane drove his knee into the back of the Russian's skull. The sound of teeth breaking on the pavement made an audible, sickening crack.

"Get inside," Kane said. "If you have security, have them drive these two far away from the stadium, preferably to a hospital."

Kane held out his hand to help the woman to her feet, but she ignored his hand and got herself up as gracefully as she could in the circumstances. She brushed down her skirt and jacket and frowned at the two Russians, one groaning and gasping in pain, and the other unconscious.

"We're here to see Mr Moore," Craven said, smiling. "And as you can see, we don't fuck about."

SIX

Craven listened to Jess Moore ranting and raving in the stadium's reception area. She was furious, and shocked, at the level of violence Kane had laid down upon the ruffians. She shifted gears between letting Kane know of her disapproval and asking her portly security guard, Kevin, to bring around a van and escort the broken-up Russians to the nearest hospital. Jess Moore's voice boomed in the shiny tiled reception. Chrome bars, granite desks, and black tiling led to a grand staircase where, on the second-floor, the club's offices and access to the match day corporate hospitality boxes and dining rooms were located.

Kane stood with his hands in the pockets of his expensive suit trousers, his navy jacket open, and a crisp white shirt beneath. Craven rolled on the balls of his feet, his comfy Clarks loafers squeaking on the tiles. The hair-swishing, finger-pointing tirade only finished when a white-haired gentleman in a crumpled navy suit stepped out of a small elevator. His arrival softened Jess Moore's tone, and as she gave the old man the gory details of Kane's altercation, he smiled and held her hand.

"Better them than us, though?" the old man said in a voice as smooth as caramel.

"That's why we're here," said Craven, stepping forward and extending his hand. "I'm Frank Craven, and this is Jack Kane. I think we spoke on the phone, Mr Moore."

"Yes, we did. Thank you for coming," said Andrew Moore, and he took Craven's hand and shook it warmly, his skin as smooth as greaseproof paper, and repeated the gesture with Kane. "This is my daughter, Jess Moore. She runs the club, so you can come to her with any questions. Now, follow me please, gentlemen."

Andrew Moore led them up two flights of carpeted stairs. He moved slowly on bowed legs whilst his daughter held his arm. At first glance, the carpet seemed plush, but as Craven walked slowly behind the Moores, he noticed it was tarnished, with faded braiding on its edges and the middle of each step worn from use.

"We get an average of ten thousand people on this ground on match day," said Andrew Moore. "More if it's an FA Cup game. When I first took over, we'd be lucky to get a couple of hundred in the stands."

"You've brought the club a long way since then, Dad," said Jess, holding open a heavy door as they entered a wide room with four white cloth-covered tables and a view of the Wessex Celtic football pitch. "Which is why we need to ensure that we don't let just anyone invest in it. And that we don't allow anybody to tarnish your reputation." She flashed a hard stare in Kane and Craven's direction.

They sat around a circular table, and a young man in a black shirt and trousers poured them a glass of water and took orders for tea and coffee. They waited in silence whilst he poured tea for Kane, Jess, and Andrew Moore. Craven ordered a coffee, drowned it in milk and plopped two cubes of brown sugar into the white china cup.

"Mr Moore, please tell us how we can help with your current situation," said Kane, and smiled with his warmest grin; a fake smile, of course. Craven could count on one hand the number of times he had seen Kane properly smile. He supposed that was the price to pay for life spent around war, secrets and death.

"I've had various people looking to invest in the club down the years: builders, spivs from London, foreign investors, bankers, I've had them all. But I've never sold. Now this Phoenix company wants to buy me out. They came in and gave us a superb presentation, talking about how they planned to take Wessex into the Premier League within four years. How they would expand the stadium, increase its capacity, generate more ticket revenue and more lucrative sponsorship deals. All very impressive."

"Forgive me for being so blunt, Mr Moore," said Craven, easing himself back into his chair, "I don't understand. They've made a good bid, a bid that would make you a very rich man. Sure, they are coming on strong and making threats, but you can hire more security guards to handle that. So, where do we come in?"

"I'm worried they are going to hurt Jess or sabotage the club. These are ruthless men, gentlemen. I fear it is beyond Kevin and our security team."

"Why don't you want to sell?" asked Kane.

"My father made this place what it is today. Built it up using his wealth and his time. We won't let that go to ruin."

"Why does Phoenix want it so bad?"

Jess Moore stared at Kane, and he stared back. The dislike passing between the two was palpable, both as stubborn as the other, refusing to look away. Craven wasn't sure why the question vexed her so much. It was an honest one. Wessex Celtic was a league one team. It wasn't exactly Liverpool FC, or Manchester City...

it wasn't even Manchester United. Craven knew little about football, but he read the news and understood that investment in sports clubs was a notoriously reliable way for a rich man to lose his money.

"They haven't said," said Jess. "If they believe they can take Wessex Celtic to the Premier League, then they might get a return on their investment. The amount they are willing to pay is astronomical, so if they don't achieve that promotion, then..." She shrugged and took a sip of her tea. "It could also be sports-washing. If they are trying to improve their corporate image."

"Sports-washing?" asked Craven.

"Where a country or company based in a country with a questionable human rights record, or some other issue frowned upon by the rest of the world, buys a football club, or some other sports franchise to link their name to victory, popular players, and the shiny side of sport and deflect the public from their wider issues."

Craven remembered reading something about that in the news—issues linked to the owners of Chelsea FC and Manchester City. "Don't the league have protections these days against dodgy owners?"

"Yes and no. On paper they do, but if you have

enough money, grease enough palms and make the right friends, then you can wriggle through the rules. Salt Bae could get on the pitch after the World Cup, for God's sake. All because he stuffed some cash into the pockets of greedy FIFA delegates."

"I don't know who or what Salt Bae is, but it sounds like getting a seat in the House of Lords. Money talks more than reputation. One more question... what kind of state are the club's finances in?"

"The club's worth about fifteen million pounds," said Jess. "Our annual revenue is around twelve million. But costs are enormous. The stadium and training facility, player wages, it all mounts up. Our top players earn an average of ten thousand pounds per week."

"How much have Phoenix offered you?"

"Thirty million pounds to buy us out and own the club outright."

Craven blew out his cheeks. It was serious money.

"I'm no spring chicken," said Andrew Moore, leaning forward with his hands clasped together on the white tablecloth. "I want to leave something behind me, something people will remember me for. Not just my betting shops... the board and shareholders run that business now. I'm talking about something that means something to the working man. Most important to me is that Jess stays in control of this football club. I don't want to waste your time, and I can pay you for it, but I would very much like you to help us whilst we see off this Phoenix bid. If nothing nefarious happens, then great, you two get to home a little richer for doing very little, but if it goes pear-shaped, then my understanding is that you are the men to keep us safe."

"We'll do what we can, Mr Moore," said Kane, rising from his seat. "I assume you have conducted some due diligence on Phoenix Telecoms as part of their bid. Could you please share that information with us? We will also run our own checks. Here is a phone for you both." Kane passed a small burner phone each to Jess and Andrew Moore. "There's only one number in the contacts. My number. Call me whenever you need to. We'll stay close. Don't meet Phoenix without inviting Frank and I along."

"Thank you," said Andrew Moore. He sat back and exhaled deeply, a satisfied smile spreading across his wrinkled face.

"I'll see you out," said Jess. Craven and Kane followed her down the carpeted stairs and out through the large glass doors. The two Russians were gone, and there was nothing but a patch of dark blood staining the pavement to show they had ever been there.

"Thank you," said Craven as he left her on the tiled side of the doorway.

"What do you really think is going on?" asked Kane, turning to Jess before she closed the door.

She glanced up the stairs and then stared Kane straight in the eyes. "I think Phoenix wants this club to create a legitimate front for their activities in Europe. They want Dad and me out and judging by the thugs they sent to harass me, they aren't afraid to get their hands dirty."

SEVEN

Kane ate a dried-out chicken and stuffing sandwich he'd bought at a petrol station on the way to Jess Moore's house. He washed its cardboard taste down with a bottle of water and settled in for a long night. He and Craven had flipped a fifty pence coin for who would stay in the hotel to research Phoenix Telecoms, and who would stake out Jess Moore's house all night. That was necessary in case Phoenix sent any goons around to threaten her again. Kane lost the toss. So, he had stopped at a petrol station and bought two sandwiches, three bottles of water, an apple, and a large takeaway tea to keep him company through the long night.

He imagined Craven nice and warm in their hotel room, booked and paid for under the name Samuel Shufflebottom. Kane forced down another mouthful of his sandwich, which tasted like a camel's hoof, and imagined Craven tucking into a juicy steak and a pint of beer. Besides his own research, Craven would contact Kane's old friend Cameron to help dig up everything on Phoenix. Kane and Cameron had served together in the SAS, the UK's elite special forces unit, and now Cameron led a solitary life in Newcastle, in England's northeast. He performed various technological miracles: hacking, writing code, figuring out ways to bypass and manipulate new military grade tech, which seemed to pop up new innovations every month. Cameron, like a carpenter or a mechanic, made a living using his skills. His customers were shadowy figures who needed someone capable of manipulating the world's technological foundations. People like Kane and Craven. Cameron would trawl the internet and find infinitely more information a thousand times faster than either Kane or Craven could. Kane expected to have a detailed dossier by morning.

The Audi e-tron smelled of new car. The registration was barely two months old, and it came with more gadgets than some vehicles Kane drove whilst in MI6. He fiddled with the knobs on the lower right-hand side of the driver's seat and lowered the back of his chair to settle in for the night. Jess Moore's house was a large detached redbrick building in a cul-de-sac of six similar houses. Each had electronic black gates, a Victorian-style lamp-post to the right of the entrance and thick hedges running around the perimeter. Sycamore trees lined the pavements. A yellow Neighbourhood Watch sign fastened to one lamppost by two cable-ties told any potential burglars that the neighbours were vigilant. Kane guessed the house sat on about an acre of land, and in the waning daylight, the gardens seemed to be a mix of patio, footpath, grass and evergreen hedges.

A black box with the words HomeSafe in big white letters told thieves that Jess Moore's house was fitted with cameras and alarms, inside and out. HomeSafe provided a monitored alarm service. Once an intruder triggered the alarm, the cameras kicked in and the company could view a live stream of whoever had broken into the premises. They would also call the police and provide the footage as evidence of the break-in. It was an excellent security system for the average Joe and his family, but any serious person looking to infiltrate the house could bypass it in seconds. Jess did not own a dog, as far as Kane could tell, and despite the Moores' concerns, there was no private security at the residence.

All those factors told Kane that the Moores had never faced a genuine security threat before. Just like most people, they lived their lives blissfully ignorant of the world's dangers and Kane envied the peace that Jess and the rest of the world's innocents had. Kane watched the lights in the house turn on and off in different rooms as darkness fell, the sky covered with clouds shifting in silhouette beneath a sliver of moon.

He guessed Jess was roughly his age, perhaps a little younger. She was attractive, fit, and intelligent. Her dark hair and eyes shone, and he felt drawn to her the moment she'd stepped out of the club's doors. That initial attraction, however, quickly deteriorated when her mouth opened. She clearly disliked him, though he supposed the level of violence he had deployed against the Russians was severe for someone not used to it. However, Kane's training had instilled in him the brutal necessity of fighting with maximum force and leaving nothing to chance. No pity, no mercy. Jess was a businesswoman, successful and smart, and there was much to admire about that.

Guilt washed over him, and Kane pushed those thoughts from his mind. Even though it had been three years since his wife had died, it still felt like cheating to look at another woman, to feel attraction, to think of another woman's qualities. So, he cleared his mind and slipped into a meditative calm, just as he was trained to do, and kept his eyes fixed on the house and road into the cul-de-sac.

It was ten o'clock when the Mercedes E-class pulled into the street. The car came in slowly, alloy wheels glinting beneath the streetlights, blacked-out windows reflecting the yellow glare.

It came to a stop at a bend in the road opposite Jess's house and Kane slid down as low as possible in his seat, just peeking over the tip of the Audi's steering wheel. The Mercedes could be a neighbour returning after a late night at the office, or precisely what Kane watched for. An enemy.

A grating noise came from Kane's right. He turned away from the Mercedes as the iron gates slid open on their electronically-controlled hinges. Jess came striding from the half-open gates clad in black Lycra, save for a luminous yellow hi-vis vest. She paused, grabbed her left ankle and then her right to stretch her quads, then touched her toes three times to stretch her calves. She set the watch on her left wrist and set off on a brisk run away from her house, heading towards the cul-de-sac's exit.

Kane ground his teeth, calculating whether to follow Jess or stay with the house. If he followed her, someone might enter the building and lie in wait for Jess. But if he stayed with the house, then she was a target whilst on her late evening run. His job here was to protect the Moores from the perceived threat from the Russians, and Kane wished Craven was with him. In that case, Kane would have followed Jess Moore, and left Craven to watch the house.

The Mercedes' door opened slowly, and a stocky man in white tracksuit bottoms and garishly red Nike training shoes hauled himself awkwardly out of the driver's seat. He unzipped his white tracksuit top and tossed it back into the car, revealing a muscled chest and thick arms beneath a wife-beater vest. The man tapped a message on his phone, its artificial light shining on the sharp planes of his face for a moment before he tossed the phone into the car after his jacket. He set off at a brisk walk in the same direction as Jess, his thick arms pumping like pistons, a chunky gold chain on his wrist catching the streetlight as he went.

Kane cursed to himself and got out of the car. In the regiment, and when Kane worked for MI6, he would run ten kilometres three times per week, and swim three times per week. Fitness was a huge part of his role as a special forces operator and intelligence agent, and Kane had been amongst the fittest. He was never a man for the gym and lifting weights, so would split his time between running, swimming, and combat training. But since entering the witness protection programme, Kane's training had fallen by the wayside. He wasn't carrying much extra weight, or so he told himself, but he certainly wasn't fit enough to pass SAS selection again.

He followed the muscular man along the cul-de-sac, matching his pace, walking just fast enough not to jog. He passed the Mercedes and peered in through the blacked-out windows. It was empty, which made Kane's mind up. He had to follow the big man and leave the house unattended. He followed his mark out of the cul-de-sac, across a small roundabout covered entirely with small bricks in a herringbone pattern, and onto a long road lined with silver birch trees every ten paces. Jess was out of sight, but Kane kept pace with the Mercedes man, matching him step by step. His breath quickened and sweat broke on Kane's brow, his shirt clinging to his back as he kept up the pace.

A memory of SAS selection popped into Kane's mind, of a younger version of himself on a gruelling endurance march with a fifty-five-pound bergen on his back, shoulders burning, legs screaming at him to stop, sleep deprivation playing tricks on his young mind. But he had kept on trudging forwards to every checkpoint across the sixteen-mile march across Pen Y Fan's west slope in the Brecon Beacons, or the Fan Dance, as the SAS DS instructors called it. After ten weeks, including horrific jungle selection, Kane was one of seven men left standing from one hundred recruits.

In those days, Kane had been young, fit, angry, and hungry—eager to escape his bleak childhood and desperate to prove he was more than the fate life had dealt him. Now, he could barely walk a hundred yards without being out of breath. He turned into the lit entrance to a park, clambered over a wooden stile and followed a tarmacked walking path that wove between woodland and lakes like a twisting black snake. Kane promised himself that he would pick up his fitness routine once this operation was over. He wiped the sweat from his brow on his shirt sleeve, and as he turned into another sharp twist in the meandering path he realised he had lost sight of the Mercedes man. Then he heard a scream and Kane ran.

EIGHT

Kane thundered along the pathway, his shoes pounding on the tarmac as he raced towards the scream. His stomach curdled hot as he experienced a primal terror akin to the same kind of fear that courses through the mind of a driver of an out of control car. Kane ran beneath the park's lights, and around another bend to where two figures struggled underneath a dark underpass beneath a road bridge. They moved in the shadows like dancers, pushing and pulling each other. The bigger shadow lashed out and the smaller one yelped in pain.

"Stop!" Kane yelled to get the man's attention. The bigger shadow's head snapped around and he pushed the smaller figure out of the underpass and into the gloomy streetlight. It was Jess Moore, her dark hair dishevelled, vest ripped at the shoulder.

Kane slowed to a walk, taking deep breaths after running, trying to master himself before he closed in on Jess Moore's attacker. The big man emerged from the shadows, unmistakable as the Mercedes man in his vest and tracksuit bottoms, the gold chain as thick as a climbing rope around his wrist. Jess stared open-mouthed at Kane, surprise and fear playing out on her face as she tried to understand what Kane was doing there, whilst also stricken with terror after the attack.

"He tried to grab my phone," she said, voice catching her throat as tears flowed, though she tried to force them back.

"Get behind me," Kane said, breathing returning to normal as the big man strode towards him, hands curling into fists. He smirked at Kane, believing the smaller man dressed in suit trousers and white shirt must have stumbled upon the altercation whilst out for a walk.

"Out of the way, little man," growled Mercedes man in heavily accented English, so that way became "vay".

Kane took three quick steps forward and ducked low, aiming to swing an uppercut into Mercedes man's gut, but he saw the blow coming and shuffled backwards with the speed of a boxer. Kane gasped as a red Nike shoe flashed towards his head, and he blocked the head-kick with his elbow. An overhand right punch followed it up and Kane swayed away from the blow and was forced backwards again as another kick sailed barely an inch past his nose so that he could smell the dirt on the shoe's sole.

The man could fight. He was a different animal than the thugs outside the stadium. So Kane took a deep breath and set himself in a boxer's stance, light on the balls of his feet, wishing again that he was as fit as his younger self. Mercedes man grunted and came fast with another rapid flurry of punches and kicks, with some wicked elbow strikes thrown in for good measure. Kane blocked, ducked, and twisted away from the barrage, but a punch caught him on the ear, and a leg kick smacked into the meat of his thigh to deaden the muscle.

Mercedes man paused, setting himself again into a fighting stance, eying Kane carefully. He had withstood the furious assault, and Kane launched into an attack of his own. He swung a dummy punch and instead kicked the bigger man's calf and then kicked it again. His enemy winced at the pain and Kane circled around the weakened leg, limping slightly himself from his own dead leg. Another punch flashed at Kane's face, but Mercedes man was getting tired. He carried too much muscle to keep up the fierce attack, and Kane grabbed the thick wrist, pulled him in and used that momentum to throw the big man to the pavement.

Kane grunted as Mercedes man spun on his

back and kicked Kane's legs out. He fell upon Mercedes man and the two enemies writhed and snatched at one another, scratching, clawing and grasping for a hold. An iron hand clamped around Kane's forearm and twisted it savagely, so hard that Kane thought his bones would shatter. He reached up with his left hand and raked his nails down Mercedes man's forehead until he found the wetness of the man's eyes. Kane gouged his thumb deep, twisting and scraping until jelly gave way to gristle and bone and Mercedes man shrieked in pain and threw Kane away from him. The big man rolled off the pavement into the leaf mulch, clutching at his ruined eye. He howled in anger and came up with the cold metal of a knife flashing in his free hand.

Jess stifled a scream with her hand at the sight of steel, but Kane calmed himself. He let the adrenaline overtake him, transporting him into the familiar calmness of battle. The higher plane where Kane's guilty thrill of combat existed, where he found joy in the struggle between life and death. Mercedes man surged to his feet, left hand covering his devastated eye, dark blood oozing between his thick fingers, and his right hand clutching the wicked knife, its blade four inches long.

Kane didn't flinch from the weapon and didn't pause. With his enemy weakened and in shock, it was the perfect time to strike. The big man slashed with his knife and swayed away. Kane kicked his enemy's sore calf, and the Russian grimaced in pain. Mercedes man reversed his grip on the knife, showing his skill with the weapon, and came on in a series of short, brutal slashes. Kane timed his move, grabbed Mercedes man's wrist and dragged it down hard onto his knee, bending the joint beyond its range of movement. The knife clattered away. Kane pivoted and broke the big man's thumb with a snap. Mercedes man dragged his arm free and fled like a whipped dog, bent and limping. He hobbled beneath the underpass, casting furtive glances back at Kane and dripping blood from his dead eye.

In the tangle for holds, and when breaking Mercedes man's thumb, Kane had caught glimpses of tattoos on the man's shoulder and wrist. The designs etched into his flesh in faded black ink were familiar—a skull wearing a beret and a symbol of three interlocked triangles.

"Oh my God," Jess Moore said, bending over with her hands on her hips and shaking her head in disbelief.

"It's all right now," said Kane. He dusted himself down, tucking in his shirt which had come loose in the fight. His head ached and his thigh muscle was numb, but other than that, Kane thought himself lucky to have gotten out of the fight in one piece. Mercedes man was well trained and experienced in combat.

"He was one of them, wasn't he?"

"Yes, but he's gone now. Let's get you home." It wasn't just the accent that gave Mercedes man away as a Russian. The skull and beret tattoo was a symbol often used by members of the Spetsnaz, the special forces of Russia's military intelligence. The other symbol was also familiar, but Kane couldn't quite place it.

"Hang on a second," said Jess, standing up straight, arms folded over her chest. "What the hell are you doing here in the first place?"

"I parked outside of your house when…"

"You were parked outside of my house? What are you, a fucking stalker?"

"If you'd let me finish? I was outside your house watching in case anybody came to hurt you."

"I never asked you to watch my house, and I never asked you to get involved. You and your friend are like Laurel and bloody Hardy. Whenever you turn up, there's trouble. Just keep away from me."

Jess ran off into the night before Kane could get a retort out. She hadn't even thanked him for rescuing her from the attack. She was stubborn, belligerent, and ungrateful. But there was also something about her, the way her mouth curled slightly at the sides, the fire in her eyes. She was a pain in the arse, but Kane had to admit that Jess Moore stirred something inside of him he hadn't felt since his wife Sally had died. Guilt washed over him then, as though, in some way, his thoughts about Jess betrayed Sally's memory.

Kane made the long walk back to the cul-de-sac with his hands stuffed into his trousers, remembering the good times with his family, and trying not to think about Jess Moore. He wondered how Danny and Kim were getting along at boarding school, but that only slapped him with a fresh wave of guilt. Kane tried the door of the Mercedes and found it unlocked with a spare key in the sun visor. He drove it five minutes away and parked the vehicle in the car park of a sprawling retail park, searched it, and called Craven to check in as he walked back to the Audi.

NINE

McGovern tutted. She parked her Tesla in the third row, thirty metres from the entrance, as the first row of parking spaces was already occupied with BMW and Mercedes coupes. McGovern wanted to park as close to the office as possible, and usually found a spot in the first row, less than five metres from the entrance. She paused, enjoying the precious cool air-conditioning for another ten heartbeats before opening the door and stepping out into a wall of dead hairdryer heat. It was still only nine o'clock in the morning, but the heat was already stifling. Her new Dubai marina apartment in the high-rise Damac Construction complex was as cool as a winter breeze, as was the car, and the office would also be as chilled as a refrigerator once she was inside. Her life so far in Dubai comprised of shifting from one air-conditioned environment to another.

She made the dash to the office complex in

heels, doing her best to maintain an element of decorum whilst also not wanting to drench her freshly-ironed shirt in unwelcome sweat from the baking sun. A whoosh of icy air met her inside the swinging office entrance doors, pouring down from an overhead fan, and she waited there until it sent a shiver down her spine. An Emirati man in crisp white robes bustled from a ground-floor office and McGovern made way to allow him leave the building. She adjusted her clothes, making sure her shirt sat properly on her lean frame, punched the elevator button and waited for it to take her to the ninth-floor, where her new office awaited.

It had been a year since McGovern left the British Government—plucked from the midst of an in-depth, mind-numbing, and demeaning investigation into her conduct. The investigation was long and tedious, manifesting into various governmental committees, and interviews with fat-bellied and red-faced mandarins. Bureaucrats with no experience in the intelligence world pored over her files, evidence of the various operations she had instigated and conducted, as well as evidence from operatives and colleagues. Any investigation into MI6 conduct was a delicate affair. MI6, or the British Secret Intelligence Service, was the foreign arm of British Intelligence and therefore any sort of public airing of its dirty laundry was both taboo and impossible. Instead, there were internal joint committee meetings, lots of redacted documents and cursory overviews of operations and directives that nobody was permitted to talk about in any depth for fear of leaks leading to international incidents.

McGovern sat in her reclinable faux leather office chair and relaxed into its ergonomically-designed seat. She laid her encrypted laptop out on the clear white desk and opened it up. A small device connected to the laptop via a secure Bluetooth connection scanned her retina and the computer kicked into life. She stared at her reflection on the black screen for a moment, checking her lipstick and foundation which was liable to melt in the heat. McGovern's jet-black hair shone in the reflection; the roots touched up at a salon in the Dubai mall for an extortionate price. The laptop monitor clicked into the pale, backlit home-screen view and hid her face with its artificial light. McGovern sighed. She was fifty-three, single, and her career was over. McGovern's work defined her. She had devoted her life to it and come within a cat's whisker of rising to the very top of the intelligence community tree.

She remembered the day clearly, a blustery autumn morning of wind and crumpled wet leaves in the streets leading to Vauxhall House, the home of MI6. A representative of the Intelligence Services Commissioner had barrelled into her office, a little man with a high street suit too big for his stunted frame, and demanded her official equipment. They immediately revoked her systems access and, after a dressing down from a sour-faced politician, they escorted her from the premises. Before leaving, a sallow-faced policeman cautioned McGovern to secrecy and explained potential charges. She signed yet another non-disclosure agreement before returning to her London apartment. She had sat for hours, numbed, staring out the window and pondering a life lost to an unfulfilled career.

Visions came to her in that moment of peace, staring out of her office window at Dubai's gloriously sun-drenched harbour. Herself as a girl, excelling at school and university, but always a loner. She recalled parties she hadn't received invitations to and get-togethers she only found out about the morning after. McGovern had dated, but never for longer than a few weeks. Her slim figure and high cheekbones attracted men, but her driving, cold ambition did not. By her mid-twenties, she had made it into the British Government as an assistant, then as personal assistant to the Minister of Defence, then onto various security councils and eventually on to the glorious echelons of MI6 itself. In tandem, her personal life dwindled away to nothing.

Work was McGovern's life; her mother and father were alive and lived in Lincolnshire but she lost touch with them a decade ago. Too many unreturned phone calls. Unreturned by her. Nothing else mattered but rising to the top, achieving power, getting respect and authority. She had come so close to running her own, independently- funded splinter MI6 group. No accountability, no oversight, tasked with working in the dark, murky depths of the most dangerous counter-intelligence. The kind of operations nobody wanted to hear or know about. The splinter MI6 group pre-emptively eliminated terrorist cells based on intelligence, rather than waiting for an attack to occur. Her teams were judge, jury and executioner, and she pulled the strings. Until the last job, the last thread of a botched mission that McGovern had to tidy up before the gilded door opened to her new role. Running her own division of MI6. The thing she had worked her entire life for. That last mission failed spectacularly. Now she was out, investigation not complete. McGovern plied her trade in a different country, performing the same role, but for a different master.

McGovern's life teetered on a precipice of finality the day the man came to her. Her last meeting with the Intelligence Services Commissioner ended with talk of gross misconduct, crimes committed, shame brought upon the British Government, the most severe of consequences laid out before her. Every day after that, she'd lived with the sword of Damocles hanging over her head. Then he found her. A knock at her London apartment door prompted her to scramble to clear away empty bottles of wine and unwashed dishes. A man, tall and well-spoken in a tailored suit with a heavy limp, entered her home and offered hope, a chance to use her skills for a different purpose. Not quite a poacher turned gamekeeper, or so she told herself. Not a traitor, not working for the bad guys. He introduced himself as Mr Hermoth, the CEO of an organisation providing solutions to governments and companies in need of certain services.

The Balder Agency ran networks of mercenaries, assassins, hackers, and advisors deployed to whomever paid their fee. Mr Hermoth pitched it to her simply. How had she known which side was right and which was wrong in her old life? Did the goat herder in Afghanistan whose wife and son were incinerated by a British attack consider Britain and the USA as the good guys? Did the African mine labourer forced to work in unthinkable conditions believe that the vacuous pop stars who wore conflict diamonds in their teeth were on the right side of the war that ravaged his country? *Perspective,* Mr Hermoth had said, *is a strange thing.*

McGovern flew out to Dubai the following day on a private jet and had run three operations for Balder since, quarterbacking them effectively and efficiently from this air-conditioned office. Successful operations with top-level operatives—first taking out a target in Baghdad, then running an observation mission on a government agency in Hong Kong, and finally, the assassination of a subversive African union leader who had upset the wrong people on his country's governing junta. Her salary was five times what she had earned in MI6, her apartment three times the size of her old London shoe box. She had everything she could want: power, wealth, the job she excelled at. But a hole remained, an emptiness in her soul hollowed out like a canoe the day they escorted her out of Vauxhall House.

A knock at her office door snapped McGovern from her daze.

"Yes?" she called in her usual clipped manner.

"Morning, ma'am," said the young man who opened the door halfway and stuck his smiling head in. He was tall and fit, one of the company's many former military personnel. "Coffee?"

"Yes, please. Americano, no milk."

The young man smiled again and closed the

door. There was a coffee shop on the ground-floor level of the next building over, and every morning, one of the office staff would go on a coffee run for the ten people occupying the ninth-floor. They were mainly intelligence gatherers, monitoring satellite images, snooping on government systems via Trojan horse hacking code, passing on messages and orders to field teams, and working to keep the cogs of Balder's worldwide network operational.

McGovern opened her email account and skimmed through the usual day-to-day correspondence until she hit the red flagged messages. These were the important emails with details of new jobs the Balder Agency had taken on to service their high-paying clients. She skimmed through the details of a mining operation in Sierra Leone in need of help with United Nations red tape, but she didn't have the appetite to run a bribery sting. The next opportunity was an undercover sting against a Chinese intelligence operation in Hong Kong, which sounded more trouble than it was worth. She opened the next file and almost fell off her perfectly adjusted office chair.

A name and a face flashed up on the laptop screen. McGovern scanned the file, realised she was holding her breath, and exhaled. A Balder client was experiencing trouble in the United Kingdom. Someone had impeded a business transaction of high importance to the client and the troublesome man needed to be removed. She clicked to accept the job, her finger trembling on the touchpad as she clicked and emailed Mr Hermoth. McGovern closed her eyes and smiled, but the face remained before her, the same face that haunted her nightmares since the collapse of her career. A nondescript face, plain and boring. A cheap haircut, brown eyes and a forgettable face. Jack Kane. The loose thread McGovern had been tasked to clean up and remove, to clear the path to start her own MI6 operation. The man who had ruined her life.

Kane had surfaced, and a client requested Balder to eliminate him. McGovern laughed at the irony that it should be here, working as a failure, a tossed out piece of MI6 garbage, that she should have the chance at vengeance. To right the wrong, to correct the blot on her copybook that had ruined her stellar career. To destroy Jack Kane.

TEN

Kane sipped at hotel breakfast tea whilst Craven slowly clicked through the various steps on his laptop to connect to Cameron's secure video-calling platform. Lately, the old detective had made a conscious effort to improve his ability to use technology, so Kane stayed silent as Craven's thick fingers clicked keys one at a time, hovering above the keyboard as he whispered curses under his breath.

Kane returned to the hotel once a red sun had crept over the suburban rooftops around Jess Moore's cul-de-sac, believing further attacks were unlikely once the morning broke and the pavements and roads kicked into life. Kane briefed Craven on the night's activities, and Craven wasn't surprised that Phoenix had sent a heavy to Jess Moore's house, or that Kane had fought the man to bloody ruin.

They ate breakfast in Craven's Travelodge hotel room fifteen minutes away from both Jess

Moore's house and the Wessex Celtic stadium, or the Moorebet Stadium, to give the place its official name. Andrew Moore lived further out of town, but the club's security team was monitoring his home. Andrew was the most likely target for any unsavoury characters, but the security firm had two men on his address and had installed a heavy network of monitored cameras that sent a live feed back to their headquarters.

"It smells like something died in here," Kane said, moving to open the hotel window the fraction its safety mechanism would allow. Craven's room smelled of feet and farts, like a teenage boy's bedroom after months of no cleaning, old football boots, half-eaten sandwiches, and damp shower towels.

"It's that pie I had yesterday," Craven said, running a hand over his belly. "Didn't agree with me. Tasted good though."

"Maybe you should eat more salad and fruit?"

"Do I look like a fucking rabbit?" Craven shot Kane a look of pure disgust, and Kane stifled a laugh. "Here we go."

A black square flashed up on Craven's laptop screen and he clicked to accept the secure call. The square fuzzed and then cleared to reveal a ghostly mask staring down at the camera. Cameron always wore a mask to cover his disfigured face. It was as white as porcelain, with one eye painted black and an unnervingly blank expression. Kane and Cameron were once part of the same SAS squad, where Cameron had been the team's technical and communications expert, as well as its sniper. A rocket-propelled grenade incident in Afghanistan destroyed Cameron's face and inflicted terrible injuries upon his body and mind, forcing him into an honourable discharge from the army.

"Good to see you, brother," said Kane. Memories coming back to him so thick, he almost raised his hand to waft them away. Waiting in barracks playing football, chess, basketball or working out. Jokes and pranks within the regiment. Visceral, nerve shattering combat. And then Cameron's bloody, pulped body, crawling from the dust and rubble of a blown-up helicopter and destroyed building.

"Kane. Craven," said Cameron, his voice muffled slightly by the mask. "Gotten yourselves into a shitload of trouble again, I see?"

"Nah," said Craven, after taking a big gulp of instant coffee from a small, white hotel room cup. "Just a business transaction gone tits up and a few heavies. Nothing too serious. Not like the shit Kane got into in America."

"What happened in America?"

"Nothing much," lied Kane, wincing slightly at

the memory of his injuries. "So, did you look into Phoenix Telecoms for us?"

"I did, and you might have bitten off more than you can chew this time."

"I did a bit of research myself," said Craven, "whilst Kane was off watching Jess Moore getting dressed through her bedroom window. They're a Russian company linked to loads of other companies in the Phoenix group. There are lots of articles in the papers about their links to the Russian President, and the shady characters who run the company."

"Why were you watching a woman getting dressed?"

"I wasn't," Kane sighed. "That was Craven's idea of a joke."

The mask tilted to one side as though puzzled, then the shoulders below it shrugged and Cameron's mouse clicked three times out of view. "So I'd heard of Phoenix before, mainly because of their activities in the Middle East, Africa, Ukraine and around the Baltic states. Not corporate activity, that is; military activity."

"Military?"

"Yes, the Valknut Group. You would have come across them, Jack, if you were still working for MI6. Since your day, a new, non-governmental layer of military force has emerged in various parts of the world, and Valknut is the largest. Even a cursory look at recent wars in Ukraine, Syria, Libya, or Central Africa throws up their name like a firework display. Accusations of war crimes, rape, torture and robbing civilians."

"But what's that got to do with Phoenix?" asked Craven.

"The Phoenix organisation finances Valknut, and the CEO of Phoenix, Dmitry Sidorov, is also said to be the head of Valknut."

"The name Valknut is familiar," said Kane. "What does it mean?"

"It's a symbol. Three interlocking triangles originating in Norse mythology, linked to myths and legends and carved into ancient runestones. It's the logo of various modern companies around the world, like a Swedish Forestry company and the Mongolian Bank. More worryingly, however, the symbol also has links to white supremacist groups, and far right groups."

Cameron's mask flicked off screen and was replaced by various images and different interpretations of the Valknut knot and its three triangles, from ancient stone carvings to modern day graphics.

"The man I stopped from attacking Jess Moore last night had one of those tattooed on his wrist," said Kane. "Along with a Spetsnaz skull and beret."

"Kane's been in two fights already," said Craven. "We've only been here a day and he's sent three men to the hospital."

"Be careful, Jack. If Phoenix is coming on heavy, then they are using Valknut soldiers. Valknut's commanding general is Yuri Balakin, former lieutenant colonel and Spetsnaz GRU unit brigade commander. Fought in the Chechen wars and loves Nazi memorabilia."

"So let me get this straight..." said Kane, setting his cup down on the small round hotel room table. "Phoenix Telecoms are looking to buy Wessex Celtic Football Club. They are part of a wider Phoenix Group of companies who finance and are intertwined with the Valknut Group, a mercenary army?"

"Yes. It took time to find the details on Phoenix, like following a trail of breadcrumbs in a forest full of hungry mice. It doesn't exist as a single incorporated entity but exists as a monstrous network of businesses all interacting with the Phoenix Group, such as Phoenix Telecoms, or Phoenix Management and Consulting, and any of another dozen companies. Phoenix is registered in Argentina and has offices in Hong Kong, St Petersburg, Barbados, and Peru. Valknut is a private army, well-funded, deployed and backed by the Russian state in many of its recent conflicts."

"They must be rich bastards," said Craven, "so what the fuck do they want with a shitty English League One football club? No offence to Wessex Celtic intended."

"Trying to sports-wash Phoenix's track record with the cleansing glory of football? Using that as a stepping stone to a more legitimate presence in pan-European business?" suggested Kane. "But that doesn't explain why they want it bad enough to bring soldiers here to threaten and bully the Moores. The man I fought with last night was skilled. Certainly could have been a Spetsnaz operator, and the tattoos show he was."

"One element of my research might suggest a good reason," said Cameron. "Valknut has deployed heavily in the Central African Republic and Mali. They offered regimes in the region security and military support in return for diamond and gold mining contracts to Phoenix and other Russian-backed companies. So, they have a lot of dirty money to invest. What is better than a football club? Pass the football club ownership tests, which we all know various oligarchs and regimes have done already despite human rights issues, and then funnel funds into the club via Phoenix Group sponsorship deals. Buy players, build a new stadium, gain credibility for ever bigger business deals."

"That all makes sense to me," said Craven, opening a small, sweet biscuit from the hotel room tea tray. "Sort of, anyway. But why Wessex Celtic? Why not Chelsea, or Liverpool, or Aston Villa football clubs? They are already in the Premier League."

"Maybe a League One club allows Phoenix to fly under the radar, get in small and grow the club. Funnel their diamond and gold money into the football club and wash it on the world stage?" said Cameron. "Maybe Sidorov loves football and wants a piece of the glamour?"

"Could be any or all of those reasons," said Kane. "But sounds to me like the Moores are in over their heads here, and things could get worse before they get better."

"Why don't they just sell?" asked Craven. "Take the money and run?"

"The old man loves the club. He'd never sell unless he had to. He wants to leave a legacy for his daughter to take over, for his name to live on." Kane had seen the determination in Andrew Moore's rheumy eyes, the look of a man who had built his own fortune and spent much of it on his passion. No matter how much pressure they applied, he wouldn't sell to Sidorov or Phoenix. But his love for Wessex Celtic was surpassed only by his love for his daughter, which was why Phoenix was applying pressure in that most sensitive of Andrew Moore's weak spots.

"Who are the Moores dealing with at Phoenix?" asked Cameron.

"We don't know yet. I think they mentioned a Mr Antonov. I'll get the details and send them on to you."

"Do, and I'll see what I can dig up. If we know who he is, and which arm of Phoenix he works for, I can take a look. Also, if the Moores have his email address, we can send him a nice email with some spyware and get inside his life."

"Thanks Cam."

"One last thing, lads. Don't underestimate Valknut. They are serious operators, a real black hat organisation. They have access to all the kit and weapons available to any national military army. Their personnel are veterans of countless wars around the world, and Balakin did not earn the nickname The Axeman knitting patterns on his granny's knee. Tread carefully."

ELEVEN

Kane and Craven met a wall of four security guards outside the Wessex Celtic's Moorebet Stadium—burly men in black combat trousers and tight black t-shirts with radios clipped to their shoulders. One even wore black leather gloves to complete the bouncer look. After a few growls and a radio call, Kane and Craven could enter and met Jess and Andrew Moore in the same room as the day before.

The fight in the park left Kane with an aching shoulder and ribs, and his head swelled behind his ear where Mercedes man had hit him with a knee or a punch. Kane couldn't recall the details of the scuffle blow by blow. He and Craven waited in a carpeted corridor that smelled of shake and vac powder, and Craven belched, trying to hide the sound by keeping his mouth closed but still sounding like a bear waking from hibernation.

They'd eaten breakfast at the hotel before leaving for Wessex Celtic. Kane ate a piece of toast and a croissant washed down with a small silver pot of tea. Craven, however, had stacked his plate at the help yourself buffet with eggs, bacon, sausage, fried tomatoes, beans, mushrooms and two pieces of toast. He'd even mopped up the beans with an extra piece of toast before drinking a pot of steaming coffee. Kane was surprised that Craven hadn't fallen asleep on the drive over.

"I've stepped up security," said Andrew Moore, his wrinkled face pale and drawn. "Thank goodness you were there last night, Mr Kane, or God only knows what might have happened to Jess."

The three men sat around the same table covered in a white tablecloth and sipped at coffee or tea. Jess Moore paced the room, her face as sharp and foreboding as North Sea cliffs. When she first entered the room, Kane sat up straighter and shot the cuffs of his white shirt. He wore a navy Armani suit and black shoes, which he'd polished at the hotel before breakfast.

"He shouldn't have been there, Dad," she said, shooting a withering look in Kane's direction. "I don't need some creepy bloke hanging around my house. Just put the security lads there, like we did at your place."

"If I hadn't followed that man into the park..." Kane began, but she cut him off with a squint and a sweep of her manicured hand.

"He would have stolen my phone. That's all he wanted. Instead, you ripped his eye out. I'm astonished that the police haven't arrested you. That's two fights since you got to Ravenford."

"Because the men involved won't report it," said Craven. "They don't want the police involved. They want to get you two out of this football club by whatever means necessary."

"Listen, I don't think we need your services any more. Dad, pay them whatever was promised. Let's get the police involved, step up our own security and make it crystal clear to Mr Antonov that we will never sell."

"Hold on, Jess," said Andrew Moore, smiling and trying his best to calm his agitated daughter. "Don't be so hard on Jack and Frank. We might need them yet. What have you been able to uncover since we met yesterday?"

"You don't realise the world of shit you're both in," said Craven. "We've flown here to help you, at your request, Mr Moore. With all due respect, Miss, but your attitude fucking stinks. You are up against a private Russian army who has set their sights on this football club. I'm talking about killers here. Veteran soldiers come to take everything you own. Your smart comments and mean stares won't be enough to stop them. You might find yourself dead in a ditch, or worse, and these Russians won't give two shits. So, I suggest you sit the fuck down and listen to what we've discovered about Phoenix Telecoms."

Kane cleared his throat, and Jess Moore plonked down into a chair, staring red-faced at Craven after his blunt appraisal of the situation. Kane gave the Moores a more professional overview of the Phoenix organisation and their close links to the Valknut Group, and the Russian Government.

"So, let me see everything you can find in your records concerning Mr Antonov. I'll also need logins for your email, and details of your phone network providers," said Kane after the briefing. "I'll get you trackers to keep on you night and day and set up some more robust surveillance. Mr Moore, can you call Mr Antonov and let him know your representatives will visit his office today to discuss his proposal?"

"I don't want to see Antonov," said Andrew Moore, shaking his head and glancing nervously from Kane to Craven.

"You don't need to. Frank and I will close out negotiations. I'll come back this afternoon with new phones for you both and the tracking devices. Until then, stay here."

Moore nodded appreciatively and Kane left the meeting room, followed closely by Craven.

"Mr Kane?" said Jess, just as he was about

to walk down the stairs. She walked down the corridor towards him, arms folded across her chest, eyes staring at the carpet. "I might have been a little hasty in my assessment of the situation. I'm sorry if I've been a bit of a bitch."

"It's fine," he said, and smiled at her.

"There's a home game here tomorrow. Why don't you both come as our guests? Kick-off is at three, so get here an hour before?"

"Sounds great, thanks," said Kane.

"You fucking fancy her," Craven whispered as they reached the bottom of the stairs and dug his elbow into Kane's ribs. "Like them a bit mean, do you?"

Kane shushed his friend and tried his best not to blush. He couldn't resist glancing back up at the first-floor, where Jess Moore raised a thin hand to wave goodbye. He curled his fingers around the business card Andrew Moore had passed across the table. Mr Antonov's card, with his office address and telephone number.

TWELVE

McGovern took off her headset and laid it down on the glass-topped table. She sat back in her chair and allowed herself a satisfied smile. A water display lit up the Burj lake outside the office windows, fountains jetting into the air in time to music and lit by a light show of green, blue and red. It was almost as though the show was staged to celebrate her work, and although that wasn't the case, McGovern allowed the feeling to warm her.

It had taken a day of conference calls with finance teams, mobilising aircraft, sourcing weapons, and finally assembling a team capable of seeking and destroying Jack Kane. A team of mercenaries, all ex-Mossad, Delta, and commandos, would leave Syria in the morning and fly to the UK on a hired jet. They would land just outside London, where vehicles McGovern had sourced from ex-British intelligence sources would meet the team with handguns, rifles, knives, night vision, body armour, fragmentation and stun grenades, and a host of other equipment she thought the team might find useful.

McGovern shifted through screens on her laptop until she came to the briefing she had written on Kane, which included files detailing his operations for the SAS, and as much as she could recall of his activity working for the Mjolnir sub-division of MI6. There were maps of deadly missions through tunnels, crashed Chinooks, assassinations, insertions behind enemy lines, high-value targets captured, regimes destabilised, and weapons technology stolen from enemy governments. She hit send on her secure email and the data winged its way to the team. They would be fully briefed on their target before wheels-up.

It had been a long but satisfying day. Clients who paid for Balder's services were confidential, so McGovern did not know who had paid for the hit on Jack Kane. It could be any number of former enemies, alerted to his re-emergence in the world three years ago. She didn't care. All that mattered was that he would pay for what he had taken from her. A life's work smashed to a thousand pieces by a man who was supposed to have disappeared.

McGovern yawned, closed her laptop and packed her phone and other items into her small handbag. Just as she was about to leave the office and head back to her apartment, her phone rang—the strange ringtone of a call coming in via satellite phone, the display reading simply *Private Number*.

"Hello?" she said, lifting the handset to her ear.

"McGovern," said a familiar voice, a clipped upper-class English accent. Mr Hermoth.

"Yes, sir?"

"I see you've dispatched a team to take care of the Kane job."

"Yes, sir. They'll land close to London tomorrow. Estimated time until target elimination is three days."

"Good work. This is an important client for us, so I'm going to lead the team myself."

"You, sir? The team I have put together is excellent, all experienced agents with vast experience in these matters."

"I'm going to lead the team. There is some personal unfinished business with Mr Kane. I'll meet the team in London. Let them know."

"Yes, sir."

"I'll be flying out from Riyadh in three hours, so I'll need a new passport, UK driving licence, phone and credit card."

"I'll get on it now, sir."

"Good. This time, Kane dies. No mistakes. We go full force, no matter what the cost."

Mr Hermoth hung up the phone, and McGovern sighed. She unpacked her things and got back to work. It was strange that the CEO of Balder was going to lead the team personally. He hadn't looked like much of a killer when she'd met him in London, but then they say that was what made a perfect agent, an ideal assassin. Someone who could move unnoticed, a grey man. Perhaps it took one to kill one. Or so she hoped.

THIRTEEN

Kane and Craven walked through Covent Garden in central London, its streets cleanly swept, with creamy grey stone buildings rising on either side of them. The smell of garlic roasted chicken swept out of a restaurant window and filled Kane's belly with hunger. A street performer with a painted face juggled amid a ring of eagerly watching tourists, and from somewhere in the tangle of shops, cafés, galleries and eateries, a violin and flute played a melodious song.

"I've always thought London was a shithole," said Craven, his mouth turned down like a man appreciating a fine wine, "but it's actually nice here."

"You think everywhere is a shithole," Kane replied, as he tried to remember if the address on Mr Antonov's business card was left or right at the top of the road. Kane had been in and out of safe houses in the UK's capital for years, reporting to his handlers at various locations around the sprawling tube train network.

"Most places are. York's nice. So is Chester. Everywhere else..." Craven shrugged and flipped his hand from left to right like a rolling sea.

"Antonov's place is just up here."

The train from Ravenford to London took an hour and a half on a relatively new Southwestern Railway train. Trains travelled from Ravenford to London every thirty minutes, and Kane wanted to be back on the train as soon as possible once this meeting was over. Visiting any large city in the UK was a risk for Jack Kane. Facial recognition software linked to the myriad CCTV cameras would pick him up and flag his location to many organisations who had his name and face on their watch list. So, he walked beside Craven with a baseball cap pulled low, taking care to hide himself behind Craven's bulk and the surrounding buildings wherever possible.

Cameron's search on Antonov had yielded no results to help steer Kane as to the businessman's history, which showed he was working in London using an assumed identity. Antonov's Phoenix Telecoms office was only registered five weeks ago, even though another Phoenix Group company had a different London address, which rang alarm bells. The Phoenix Telecoms office linked to the purchase of Wessex Celtic was only opened for that sole purpose with a shadowy representative with no background, no history of addresses in Russia or any other country, and a passport used to enter the UK issued only four months ago.

"Here we are," said Craven, pointing to a boiler-plate sign fastened to the concrete wall. *Phoenix Telecoms* was all it said, and Craven pushed the bell. It rang three times and clicked to signify that somebody was on the other end, but no voice came over the intercom. "Misters Shufflebottom and Wright, to see Mr Antonov."

The door clicked unlocked and Kane followed Craven through the heavy oak and into a stale-smelling corridor with old cracked tiles and yellowed wallpaper hanging on tired walls. Nobody came to meet them, and Kane glanced up at a black and white listing of people in the different offices in the building. Most were empty save a few names stencilled in 1980s-style fonts, and then Mr Antonov printed in Times New Roman in shiny black letters on a milk-white background—a fresh sign amongst the old and jaded.

"First-floor," said Kane, pointing at the listing. They marched up a set of creaking stairs and Craven knocked his heavy knuckles on the hollow-core door with Antonov's name on the front, in the same style and font as the ground-floor listing.

"Come in, please," came a Russian-accented voice from within.

Craven opened the door and entered confidently. Kane removed his cap and stepped into a freshly renovated room. A portly man with wisps of black hair hovering over his bald head sat behind an old writing desk, and a hulking man with brush stiff blonde hair cut short in military style stood behind him.

"Mr Antonov?" asked Craven.

"Yes, please sit. This my colleague, Mr Boban," said Antonov, gesturing to the glowering man over his shoulder, and then to two chairs sat facing his own. The portly man stood and shook hands with Kane and Craven, his grip firm. "You can speak with Mr Moore's authority?"

"We don't need to sit. This won't take long."

"So, has Mr Moore accepted our generous offer?"

"You can stick your fucking offer up your arse. Moore won't sell. Not now, not ever. Stop trying to intimidate him, or we'll keep sending your lads to the hospital. That's the end of it now. Piss off back to Russia and leave the Moores in peace. Any more threats or bullying tactics and we'll come back here to your shitty office and take it up with you."

A smile played at the corner of Antonov's

mouth and he shrugged, glancing from Craven to Kane as if to ask if that was it. Kane almost winced at Craven's brutal tone, but supposed it suited the occasion. Craven yanked the office door so hard that Kane thought it might rip off the hinges, and the two men stormed out, down the stairs and out of the front door.

"I'm not sure you spoke plainly enough," Kane said, shaking his head.

"He got the message. We didn't come all the way here to talk shite. Now, let's find a pub and get a steak and pint before we get back on the train."

FOURTEEN

Craven yawned and rubbed the back of his hand across his eyes, rubbing the sleep away. He finished the strong, sugary coffee and tossed the white Styrofoam cup into a bin on the walkway leading to the Wessex Celtic Moorebet Stadium. It was match day, with a little more than an hour to kick off, and fans thronged the place, wearing garishly coloured team jerseys, scarves, and bobble hats. The smell of frying meat from a burger van on the corner made Craven salivate, even though he had eaten a large fried breakfast at the hotel before leaving for the game.

He contemplated getting another coffee and decided against it. The inevitable need to urinate ten minutes later wasn't worth it, despite how tired he was from guarding Jess Moore's house all night. Craven had fallen asleep inside the Audi three times, so he had spent the rest of the night standing outside the car, freezing his nuts off. There had been time for a couple of hours' sleep at the hotel before breakfast, and without that, he wondered if he would even have made it to the game.

Kane was inside, talking to Jess and Andrew Moore in their fancy corporate box overlooking the pitch. Craven had gone in, shook hands and smiled, but had come outside to make a phone call. It was midday and Barb would be out of her check-up at the hospital in Seville, so he took his burner phone out of his pocket and dialled her mobile phone number.

"Hello, Barbara speaking?" she said after four rings. The engine rumbling in the background told him she was still in the car.

"Hiya Barb, it's me," Craven said, smiling at the sound of her voice.

"Frank! How are you, love? How's England?"

"Not as nice as Spain, I can tell you. I'm all right, running around trying to keep tabs on Jack, but we're both doing OK. How did your appointment go?"

"Fine, the doctor said I'm still on track. He took some blood to test, gave me a thorough check over and told me to come back in two weeks. So, all good."

"That's great, love. Let me know when you get the blood tests back, will you?"

"Of course, but how do I contact you?"

"Oh, yeah." Craven had forgotten the necessity to keep communications secure—operational security, as Kane called it. Kane changed the burner phones every day or so depending on how many calls they both made, and he didn't want to give Barbara's location away if some bastard had figured out how to trace this phone. "I'll ring you in a couple of days. We might be home by then anyway, nothing much going on here. Just a straightforward protection job."

"That's good. I'll be back at the house in ten minutes. My friend Georgia is minding the kids."

"Your friend from the bridge club? Good. How did Danny and Kim get on at school this week?"

"I picked them up last night and Kimmy was full of beans. I think she likes it. Danny was a bit sullen, to be honest. He says he is getting a bit of grief from the other lads about being new and all that."

"Thanks, Barb, I'll let Jack know. I love you and I'll talk to you in a few days."

"Love you too. Be careful, Frank."

The phone clicked off. Craven imagined Barb driving their car around the unfamiliar streets of Seville in her scarf, listening to her pop music on the radio. She would have been nervous about going to the appointment on her own, and Craven wished he'd been there to accompany her —to hold her hand when she was frightened, to tell her the cancer wouldn't come back and that she would be all right. He sucked his bottom lip and threw the burner phone into the bin with the coffee cup.

A shoulder barged Craven in the back, and he stumbled forward.

"Watch it!" Craven snarled, steadying himself and straightening his jumper.

"You watch it, you fat old bastard," said an accented voice.

Craven turned to see three shaven-headed men in bomber jackets staring at him. One wore a strap around an injured knee, and Craven thought he recognised the man from the scuffle outside the stadium. Each man had a sharp jaw, fierce eyes, and faces twisted in anger. Craven took a step back and raised his hands to show he didn't want any trouble, and then took two more steps backwards. Craven couldn't stand against three men. He wasn't highly trained like Kane; he was just an old copper.

One of the three men stepped forwards, feinted a punch, and Craven flinched. The other two laughed. Craven turned to walk away as fast as possible to where the security guards ringed the stadium entrance. A blow cracked off the back of Craven's head, filling his skull with white light. He stumbled again, and a fist hammered into his back. He grunted and doubled over, winded. Another fist in his ribs and Craven retched from the pain. He fell to his knees and tried to flail out with his fists, but an iron grip caught hold of his hand and twisted it savagely. Another fist clubbed Craven in the face, and he sprawled on the hard stone pathway. Kicks pummelled him, painfully thundering into his back and head, and then Craven slipped into darkness.

FIFTEEN

Kane stared out of the large glass window, watching the Wessex Celtic players warm up on the deep green pitch below. The stand stretched away between him and the grass, reaching all the way along the long side, with a similar structure on the opposite end, and smaller terraces behind each goal. Thousands of supporters filled the stadium, eating pies, crisps and hotdogs and sipping on hot drinks. Children thronged the pitch-side hoardings, wide eyes staring at their favourite players who ran, skipping and stretching only ten paces away.

"How many fans are here today?" Kane asked as Jess Moore came to stand next to him, her perfume soft and alluring.

"Could be twelve thousand. Not full to capacity. We won't know for sure until the gate receipts are in," she replied. Jess smiled broadly as she paused, casting her dark eyes around the stands. "Nothing beats game day. The buzz, the roar of the crowd, the tension, the elation, the glory and the suffering."

"Who are we playing again?"

"We? Are you a supporter now?" She smiled again and nudged Kane playfully with her hip. Her smile was wide and full, creasing her cheeks and revealing a set of straight white teeth. But it was the gleam in her eye that warmed him. "*We* are playing Plymouth Argyle."

"Are they good?"

"Mid-table. We need to beat them if we want to push for promotion."

"Craven says it was all quiet at your place last night?"

"Yes. I don't know what you and Craven said to him, but maybe Antonov got the message when you went to London? Hopefully, that's an end to it all now."

"Fingers crossed," Kane said, and tried his best to sound hopeful. In truth, he doubted a few harsh words from Frank Craven would put Phoenix off. They had already invested so much in the deal. They'd brought Antonov to the UK, setting up his office, and then there were the ruffians they'd either hired or flown in to intimidate the Moores into selling their beloved club. Anybody going to such lengths to get what they wanted wouldn't let words put them off.

Not in Kane's experience.

"The match will kick off in a few minutes. Look, the players are going back inside."

Jess left Kane's side, and she glided through the directors' box, working the room full of sponsors and business partners, guiding them out to their seats just outside the huge pane of glass that led out from the comfortable box, with its white tableclothed tables and bar, into their seats and the throbbing atmosphere of a football match.

Kane followed the line of men in suits and sat on a faded plastic fold-down chair with a square of cushioned leather to provide extra comfort for the important seats, rather than the hard plastic of the Joe Soap seats closer to the action. Kane turned, craning his neck to search for Craven through the shining glass window, but could see no sign. Craven's seat next to Kane was empty, and the big man was most likely supping as many free pints of lager at the bar as he could before it closed for kick off.

Kane flicked through a match day programme left beneath his seat, filled with statistics of the season so far, player profiles and advertisements. The stadium air was thick with hot drinks, fast food, freshly cut grass, and the sense of anticipation was palpable. Music blared over the tannoy and the team ran from the stadium's depths and onto the pitch in a long line, each player making the sign of the cross, pointing to heaven, or leaping high to head an invisible ball. The crowd cheered and Kane's chest leapt with the collective excitement of thousands of people elated to see their heroes preparing to do battle. A stadium announcer welcomed everybody to the game, the sound system slightly too loud and tinny for Kane's ears. The announcer read out the names of each player, and the crowd cheered each one, and when he read the opposition players' names, the crowd booed each one loudly.

The whistle blew for kick-off and the crowd roared, and then erupted into a chorus of football songs, but Kane couldn't quite pick out the words. Jess Moore apologised as she shuffled past four men in the row two beneath Kane and sat in the seat next to her father, surrounded by white-haired men wearing Wessex Celtic scarves above their black- or camel-coloured overcoats. Jess turned and tossed a scarf to Kane, flashing him a quick wink before turning back to the game. Kane slipped the scarf around his neck. Perhaps Jess was warming to him. He was certainly fond of her. Then the guilt came again: Sally's face popping into his mind, how beautiful she had looked on their wedding day, how sad the witness protection programme had made her, how his attraction to Jess Moore was cheating on her memory.

The ball skimmed over the goal's crossbar and the crowd stood for a hopeful moment with arms outstretched, believing for a glorious heartbeat that the ball would sail into the goal and send the net bulging, and then slumped with a collective groan back into their seats and the referee indicated a goal kick. A disturbance in the crowd below caught Kane's attention: a cry of fear, hands flailing, a surge in the densely packed seating. The heads around Kane all shifted to stare at the scene unfolding beneath them. A woman screamed, and people peeled away from the centre of the stand where men fought, bodies crashing together, fists flashing and folk trying desperately to get away from the trouble.

An average-sized man with chestnut hair, wearing glasses, stood at the centre of six men, pointing, setting the others to attack. A heavy-set steward hirpled down the steps towards the troublemaking group, reaching out for them across the seats. The man in glasses grabbed the steward's arm and broke it with a savage strike of his elbow. The surrounding people cried out, the steward fell to his knees screaming, and the man in glasses punched him in the throat. Kane stood. The six men weren't football hooligans or rival supporters looking to cause trouble. Their movements, vicious and calculated, gave them away as something more fearsome. The man with the glasses moved like a dancer, controlled, highly trained strikes, battering supporters and stewards down as though they were training dummies.

The man in glasses pointed up at the directors' box seating, and his men clambered over the seats towards them. More stewards came running from the stairwells, but glasses man leapt onto the concrete steps and set about them with ruthless skill and brutal force. One of the six thugs hurled a bottle of beer up at the directors' seating. It turned over in the air, spraying beer as it raced towards the higher seats. Jess Moore ducked and covered her head with her hands, and the bottle sailed over Kane's head and shattered the enormous glass window between the seats and the box with a smash like thunder.

Another bottle flew, and this one clattered into a white-haired man's head two seats along from Andrew Moore. The man in glasses had beaten four stewards to the ground, and the rest fled from him, seeking more help. The six men were close to the directors' seating, faces twisted with anger and violence. Kane cursed and leapt out of his seat. He ran down the hard steps, taking them two at a time, and leapt over the directors' box. He landed heavily between two rows of plastic chairs, falling over a row to land just before the six men.

Rough hands grabbed him, punching and

hauling Kane to his feet. He drove his knee into the closest man's groin and jammed his fingers into the next man's throat. The hands on his suit jacket fell away, and he swerved to avoid a punch aimed at his face. Kane ducked under it and punched his attacker in the stomach, connecting with corded muscle. Strong arms locked around his neck, squeezing him in a rear naked choke. Kane spluttered and winced as a fist cannoned into his solar plexus. The light dimmed. Soon, he would slip into unconsciousness, vulnerable to whatever blows the six men wished to rain down upon him.

Kane grimaced, braced his feet against the seat in front, and drove himself backwards. The pressure around his neck fell away as the holder tumbled backwards over the seat behind. Kane dropped to his knees, sucking in huge gulps of air, and crashed his elbow into an enemy's knee. The knee popped, and the man fell to the concrete. Kane leapt over the seats and drove the man who had choked him back to the ground. He stood quickly and drove the heel of his shoe into the man's throat, crushing his windpipe.

A punch cracked on Kane's skull and he raised his arms to defend himself. The man in glasses bobbed before him, fists raised, face calm. Slightly smaller than Kane, and of a similar build, he was fit and strong, with non-distinct features save for a scar that ran from his left ear down to the corner of his mouth. He came at Kane again, elbows tight against his body, chin down, throwing calculated strikes that Kane barely fended off before his enemy kicked him in the side of the head. Kane wavered from the impact and then caught the leg as glasses man tried to kick him again. Cries from above. Kane grunted and threw glasses man over the row of the seats.

Four of the six men were clambering over the lip of advertising placards between the regular seating and the directors' seating. Most of those seats were already empty as Jess ushered her guests through the door beside the smashed window. Kane grabbed one attacker by the belt and hauled him backwards. Another struck out and Kane blocked the punch with his elbow and punched the man four times in the ribs until he felt bones crack. Amidst the furious fighting, Kane was aware that the match had stopped, that everyone inside the ground stared, horrified at the disturbance, memories of old footage of football hooliganism in the 1980s returning unwanted to their minds.

A shaven-headed security guard stepped through the smashed glass; he held a small cudgel in his right hand. He ran down the stairs to where one attacker had made it into the directors' seating, and the shaven-headed man swung his bat. The attacker ducked beneath the wild swing, but he edged backwards. More security guards rushed through the window until the seats were filled with men shouting at the attackers.

Kane broke off from the fight. Police officers raced down the steps towards the disturbance and glasses man roared at his men who followed him as he leapt over the hoardings and onto the pitch. The crowd cheered, mocking the police who pursued the men across the playing surface, before the attackers disappeared into the opposite stand and away from the officers. Kane dusted himself down and hopped back into the directors' seating. Security tried to stop him at first, but Jess waved him through their red, taut faces.

"I cannot believe this!" Jess sobbed, tears running down her face.

Without thinking, Kane pulled her into an embrace, and Jess buried her face in his neck. Her phone rang, and she pulled away, answering the call with one finger in her opposite ear to drown out the noise of panicked conversation in the directors' box where a dozen men huddled around the bar, shaking their heads and tutting at the broken glass and carnage. Andrew Moore caught Kane's eye. He was as white as a ghost, a veiny hand clamped over his mouth in horror.

"Oh my God," Jess whispered, her phone and

hand dropping limply to her side.

"What is it?" asked Kane, worried by the look of numb terror in her wide eyes.

"They've set fire to our training complex. The whole place is on fire."

SIXTEEN

"Can you hear me?" said a woman's voice. Craven opened his eyes a fraction, and the light hurt his brain like a red-hot knife stabbing into his skull. He clenched them shut. He was dizzy, not quite whole, drifting somewhere between consciousness and sleep like a ghost.

A light shone as bright as a furnace, and Craven felt it hurting even through his closed eyelids. It came back to him, the attack, his falling. Craven forced his eyes open, and stared into a round face, heavy with make-up and a butterfly tattoo on the woman's neck. She stared into his eyes, pointing a small torch directly into his eyeballs. Craven turned away.

"I'm all right," he said, or tried to say. The words came out garbled. Craven realised he was sitting propped up against a wall, a bright yellow ambulance in front of him and a crowd of onlookers gawping behind the paramedic.

"You are not all right," she said, her voice gravelly as though she'd smoked a thousand cigarettes. "You have a concussion, and your ribs are bruised. You had a lucky escape, though."

Noise erupted from somewhere beyond the ambulance, and the paramedics' radio buzzed and crackled inside the vehicle.

"Hang on a second," she said, jogged to the ambulance, whispered into the handset, and ran back to Craven. "I have to go. There's an emergency inside. Stay there and don't move. Don't get up too quickly or you'll fall again."

The paramedic jumped into the ambulance, fired up the siren, and sped around the stadium's west side. Craven tried to stand, thought he was going to be sick, and sank down again. Half a dozen men came hurtling from the turnstiles, pounding up the pathway like sprinters. The front runner, a lean-looking man wearing glasses, slowed to a jog as his eyes rested on Craven. He stopped running and ambled to where Craven sat against the wall.

Craven tried to rise, pushing his hands against the floor and bracing his legs, but the pain in his head made him nauseous and stole the strength from him.

"You tell them to sell," said the man, speaking slowly with a thick Russian accent and wagging his finger at Craven. "Sell now or shit get much worse. Today is like game, like children playing. If no sale in three days' time, things get serious. You, the fat man who threatens us in London, talk like big man. Now you know. Tell them to sell."

He took off after his friends, running at full tilt to the junction where the stadium pathway met the road with traffic lights. The men raced across the road, weaving through the traffic, and disappeared. Policemen ran from the stadium in pursuit, their equipment-laden belts jangling as they tried to follow the Russians. But they were too slow. Even though the world wobbled around him, Craven forced himself to stand, and his breakfast did its best to crawl up his throat.

Craven stumbled towards the stadium, worry and fear turning over in his throbbing head like bowling balls. Maybe the visit to Antonov was a mistake, but it was too late now. Craven and Kane had kicked the hornets' nest, and though he didn't know what the Russians had done beyond the stadium gates, he knew the job had taken a turn for the worse.

SEVENTEEN

Dried tears stained Jess Moore's face like drought-stricken rivers running across her smoke-smeared cheeks. Blackened timbers dripped water into fat pools of water, the skeleton of a torched building drenched by gallons of jets from fire engine hoses. Tendrils of smoke drifted from the ruined training complex. A light breeze snatched the smoke away and pushed it out over the distant fields and rolling hills beyond Ravenford.

Andrew Moore shuffled slowly towards her, breaking off conversation with a bald fireman in a heavy black coat and rubber boots. Her father looked older today, stooped, diminished by the attacks upon his great love, his football club.

"The place is insured, Dad," she said, holding her arms out to him. "We can rebuild."

"That was Mr Gregory from the fire service," Andrew Moore said, holding her hands but stopping short of embracing her. "He says it was definitely arson. The criminals broke in through the windows and rigged the place with accelerants. The fire crew have been dousing it for hours and the place still isn't safe."

"Those bastards will stop at nothing to get this place." Anger flared deep inside her again. Jess had hopped between anger, fear, and despair since the awful fighting at the stadium.

"Has there been any contact from the Football Association?"

"Yes." Jess squeezed his smooth hands, bracing him for the news. "They'll fine us for the match being abandoned and the violence. The trouble was in our home end, so even though we know it was Russian goons, it looks like our supporters were in the wrong. So, it will be a fine. Possibly also docked points by the league."

"Good God." Andrew pulled away from her and buried his face in his hands. "We don't have the money for all of this. Where will we train? If we don't get an injection of cash soon, we won't be able to pay the players."

"Well, I won't be able to sell the naming rights to this place until it's rebuilt. But I have a new training kit sponsor coming on board this week, and we should get the first tranche of their payment within fourteen days. That will keep us going for now." She didn't voice her fears that the sponsor might pull out after the stadium incident. It wasn't exactly the type of activity a brand wanted associated with its name.

"But what then? What shall we do?"

Her dad stared into Jess's eyes, and the depths of sadness in his face shocked her. Andrew Moore had always been strong, a titan of UK business, a winner and a man people looked up to. A self-made man, a hero. Now, he looked like a frightened old man.

"We can't let them win, Dad."

"Maybe it would be easier if we just..."

"Don't say that, Dad. Don't even think it. We'll find a way. Jack says he can help. Let me talk to him, see what can be done."

"You've come around then? Can he and Mr Craven can fix this mess?"

"The police can't help us. They'll investigate this arson attack, but that will take weeks, perhaps months. There are cameras in the stadium, and we can provide footage of the violence, and the police will seek to charge the troublemakers. But how long will that take? We need urgent action."

"I don't think Phoenix will stop until they've taken our club. They've set their sights on it for whatever reason, and I don't think anything can stop them."

"Go home, Dad, it's late. I'll finish up here. We can talk again in the morning. I'll come over to you for breakfast."

Andrew Moore smiled sadly, looked again at the smouldering training ground, and shook his head. His dreams had crashed down around him, his life's work gone up in smoke. Jess waved to Kevin, head of stadium security, and he waddled over on thick legs and smiled at her father.

"Come on, gaffer," Kevin said in a thick Cockney accent. "Let's get you home. I'll drive you there and get you sorted." He winked at Jess, and she put her hands together in thanks.

She waited for a while, watching the fire crew do their best to make the fire-ravaged building safe. It was ten o'clock at night, and a crescent moon sat low in a clear, star-filled sky. Beyond the ruins, the astro-turf training pitches seemed strangely unaffected by the fire. White goal posts shone in the darkness like beacons of hope, that even through the chaos and the violence, sport continued. If the pitches were untouched by flames, then the team could train. They might not have their luxurious gymnasium, state-of-the-art canteen and chefs—no more ice baths and physiotherapy rooms—but they had the pitch, the goals, the footballs and coaches.

Jess reset her herself, straightening her hair and crossing her arms across her chest. The team could train the old-school way and get back to basics. Players would get changed in the car park, train on the astro-turf and work hard. That was it. Sometimes the old ways worked best. It might forge the team into a new, stronger version of itself with victory through hardship. Jess fished her phone from her handbag and dialled the head coach's number. Life would go on; Wessex Celtic would go on. She would never give up.

EIGHTEEN

Kane sat back in the driver's seat of the hired Audi outside Jess Moore's house. She wasn't home yet. Still dealing with the fallout from the training ground fire, he assumed. He stretched his bruised ribs and opened his jaw wide to check if the swelling behind his ear still hurt. It did.

The visit to Mr Antonov had backfired spectacularly. Rather than being warned off, Phoenix had stepped up the pressure to the point now where it was beyond a simple business transaction, with a few threats thrown in for good measure. The violence at the stadium was both planned and savage. The men involved were highly trained and capable of extreme violence. Craven lay on his bed at the hotel, badly beaten and concussed. Kane had found him outside the football ground, stumbling and bloody. The man in glasses had warned Craven that the violence would escalate if the deal wasn't completed in two days. Kane didn't doubt it.

The Moores had asked Kane and Craven to help them, but so far, they had done little to keep them safe. If Kane was going to fulfil the job's requirements, he would have to escalate things on his side—turn a defence and protection brief into attack and destroy. Attack was the best form of defence. That was the only way Kane knew how to handle situations like this. Full force, no mercy. But to do that would bring more chaos and more violence. Things would get worse before they got better.

A knock on the car window startled him, and Kane was relieved to see Jess Moore staring at him. He pressed the button on the driver's door to lower the electric window.

"Do you want to come inside for a drink?" she asked.

"I shouldn't," Kane said, his mind kicking into overdrive. Guilt flashed subconsciously in his brain, closely followed by a memory of Sally laughing at their family dinner table, kids beside her staring at Sally with loving eyes. "After what happened today, I'd better stay out here and keep an eye out."

"Just one drink? Come on. That way, if anybody tries to break in, you'll already be inside, right? It's been a long day, and I could do with the company."

Before he knew what was happening, Kane

was on his way out of the car and following Jess Moore through her electronically-controlled gate as it screeched open on iron hinges. Conflicting emotions fought inside him, warning him not to go in but at the same time urging him onwards. Jess was his client, but she was also beautiful. It had been three years since Sally's death, and even before that, they had separated. How could one drink equate to cheating on her?

Jess opened the front door and pressed her key fob to a white pad inside the hall. The alarm beeped twice, and she beckoned Kane to follow her. Jess clicked on light switches, and the hallway lit up to reveal an ivory-white painted staircase leading to the first- floor. A long hallway floored with black and white subway tiles like the entrance to a Victorian building led the way to the kitchen and living room areas.

The kitchen was ultra-modern, cupboards without handles, an island with a sink and a huge copper extractor fan above the sleek, black cooking hob.

"What's your poison?" she asked, opening a cupboard to reveal bottles of vodka, rum, whiskey, gin and accompanying mixers.

"I don't drink really," Kane said as Jess mixed herself a gin and tonic. "But I'll have a drop of whiskey if you don't mind."

"Good. Coke? Ice? Or ginger ale?"

"Just ice."

She made the drink and handed Kane a heavy whiskey glass patterned with cut-out shards. He sipped it; a nice Redbreast with fruity flavours.

"Can you and Mr Craven help us with this mess?"

"We can. When I arrived, I thought this was a simple job. Look after you and your father and make sure a few thugs don't get too heavy. But it's more than that. Phoenix has links to the Russian Government, and more worryingly, to a professional military organisation. You mentioned this before, and we agree. We believe they want your club to sports-wash their money and give them credibility in European business markets. They won't give up."

"So, what are you saying?"

"You have two choices. Sell the club and be done with it. You and your dad walk away rich, safe and happy. Or let me deal with it my way."

"But we wouldn't be happy. Dad couldn't give up the club. It's like his child, it's part of him, carved into his very soul."

"Leave it to me. I will arrange somewhere safe for you and your dad to stay, where nobody can find you for a week or so. Before you return, I will deal with the Russians."

"Deal with them how?"

"The only way they understand."

A silence passed between Kane and Jess. He swallowed the rest of his drink, the whiskey warm and tingling at the back of his throat, and she poured him another.

"What do you do, Jack? What is your profession?"

He shrugged. "This type of thing. Helping people, fixing problems."

"You can obviously handle yourself. How did you get into this line of work?"

"I was in the army for a long time. Then I worked for the government. Now I work for myself." He stopped short of saying *and my kids.* He still didn't know Jess that well, and Kane's training told him to trust no one, to give away as little about himself as possible. "But what about you? How did you get to be a serious businesswoman in charge of a football club?"

"Serious?" she smirked, eyebrows raised, mocking him. The lines at the corners of her mouth creased, and her dark eyes twinkled in the dim kitchen light. He noticed then that she wore a soft pink lipstick, and realised he was staring at her mouth and looked away quickly.

"I mean, competent, or smart, whatever the correct terminology is these days."

"Well, my dad is the owner. He was rich before

I was born, so I went to a private school, then a good university. Travelled. Went a bit mad, did some drugs, modelled a bit, partied too much. I was young, and then I grew up. Never settled down, no hubby or kids. Eventually, I went to work for my dad. That's it."

"So, tell me about these wild younger days. Sounds interesting."

She laughed and poured him another drink. They slowly sidled closer together, standing and resting against the kitchen island. More drinks. Eventually, they were standing so close that he could smell her perfume through the smoke on her clothes from the fire. He fixed her a gin, and as he handed Jess the drink, their hands brushed together, accidentally sending a pulse up Kane's arm. Another drink, then a kiss. She was disarming him with her eyes and her smile, and it was a mistake, but her lips were soft and her mouth welcoming. Jess pulled him close, and before Kane knew what he was doing, he was unbuttoning her shirt.

NINETEEN

McGovern lazed in her office chair, watching the surveillance footage on her laptop screen. It was Sunday, but that was a working day in the Middle East—not that it mattered to her. She worked every day.

It was as though Jack Kane had forgotten his training, like the knowledge and training packed in his finely-tuned brain had deserted him, flapping out of his consciousness like birds migrating for winter. He strutted around Ravenford as though he didn't have a care in the world. He'd taken a train to London and McGovern's facial recognition tracers had lit up like it was Christmas. London was the most surveilled city in the world, with over seven hundred thousand cameras covering its streets and buildings.

Kane would have been perfectly fine walking London's streets if nobody was looking for him. If the right sort of person wasn't actively trawling UK information systems for his face, known aliases, and those of his recent friends, family and accomplices. Many of London's cameras were privately owned, but it didn't matter to McGovern, not with the technology at her disposal. The computer geniuses outside of her office, all graduates of Ivy League, or global tier-one universities, ex-employees of the CIA, NSA, MI5, MI6, Mossad and so on, wrote the required complex code for her in a matter of hours. Once the code was deployed, there was nowhere for Kane to hide.

McGovern knew Kane was in the UK, which helped. Without knowing his approximate location, the code and search would have been useless. How could she track the entire world and all its complexities? But Balder's client had identified him in a pisswater town in the UK, Ravenford, and McGovern almost danced for joy as she'd found him on grainy CCTV outside a football stadium in his expensive suit and shiny shoes. Almost, but McGovern did not dance.

She sent the collated footage, locations, vehicle details, and close-up pictures to Mr Hermoth and the Balder strike team on the way to take Kane out. They would pick it up in an hour when their jet landed outside London. Before McGovern ate dinner at her desk, the team would be in Ravenford. McGovern clicked out of the footage and opened another screen, double-checking the video streaming from the strike team through their body cams. Sure enough, the systems check showed all was OK.

Soon it would be over. Revenge would be hers. Kane would be dead, and that fat, annoying former policeman who ran around after him. McGovern would finally close that chapter of her life and move on. The man responsible for McGovern's ruined career and shattered dreams within MI6 was in her sights. Perhaps there would be more opportunities within Balder. Maybe she could run her own division or country team? McGovern couldn't help but smile at the irony that she would be the one orchestrating Kane's demise. He didn't even know her. They were complete strangers. Yet she hated him like a cat hates a mouse, a pure hatred born of circumstance and necessity. She checked her watch. It wouldn't be long now.

TWENTY

Ravenford high street was busy come Monday morning. It was a bright start to the day, the sun already high in the sky at eight thirty and warming the back of Kane's neck as he searched the rows of shops for Craven's favourite bakery. People bustled past him with AirPods in, or noise-cancelling headphones on their heads like aircraft marshals. A woman with dyed blue hair and a nose-ring walked a scrappy little dog in a tartan jacket, and Kane had to dance aside to avoid its sniffing nose.

Cars rumbled slowly through the various sets of traffic lights guarding pedestrian crossings from motorists on their morning commute. Nobody made eye contact. Everybody focused on their own space, back to the drudgery of work after a weekend of rest. Those who didn't work would still be asleep, but these were the nine-to-fivers, the backbone of society who paid the taxes that underpinned society and its systems.

Kane found what he was looking for; he stepped inside the Greggs bakery and joined the queue behind three builders, each dressed in dusty, faded jeans, Caterpillar boots, and hard hats. He waited his turn, trying not to think about Jess Moore—the curves of her hips, the softness of her skin and the smell of her hair.

"Yes, my lovely?" said a smiley faced woman in a hairnet behind the counter, snapping Kane from his daydream.

"One meat and potato pie, and one cheese and onion pasty please," he said.

She packed the pastries up in paper bags and Kane paid her in cash. He made his way back out onto the busy high street and turned right towards the hotel. Craven was still in bed, still sore from his beating and not yet strong enough to make it down to the hotel lobby for breakfast, so Kane wanted to surprise him.

Kane had left Jess's house just after sun-up, calling Barb in Seville and catching Danny and Kim before they left for a week of school. Kim was full of excitement, eager to spend the week with her new friends. Danny, however, was sullen and barely spoke. Kane had to spend time with them both once this job was over. Quality time. Perhaps he'd take them away for a weekend, maybe do something to cheer Danny up.

Kane turned left into a side street where the hotel rose high above redbrick buildings with its silver metallic walls and garish Travelodge sign. He stepped off the pavement to avoid a puddle and onto the road, and he saw a movement from the corner of his eye. A glimpse of quick, lithe movement like a cat, swift and purposeful, balanced and graceful. An old reaction kicked in before Kane's brain had time to register the warning to his consciousness. He dropped the paper bag and darted left two steps just as a suppressed gunshot spat from the corner of an alley.

Gunfire in Ravenford? A dozen thoughts flashed through Kane's head in a heartbeat. Was it the Russians coming to crank things another notch? During an ambush situation, a soldier is trained to react in different ways based on the proximity and severity of the attack. The gunman was close, so Kane threw himself to the ground as another bullet sang over his head. He rolled on the hard, damp road and came up in a flat run, sprinting towards the gunman.

Kane held his breath, spied a man with dark hair holding a suppressed handgun ten paces away at the corner where the street led into an alleyway behind the high street shops. Kane made erratic movements, feinting left, darting right, and then leapt through the air. Another shot went off and pain surged in Kane's hip. He cannoned into the gunman, knocking his arms upwards as another bullet spat from the silenced weapon.

The two men fell heavily, scrambling with each other, fingers clawing and legs kicking. Kane used an Aikido grip to rip the gun from his attacker's hand and the dark-haired man punched him in the face and wrapped his legs around Kane's torso in the beginnings of a jiu-jitsu hold. The gun's grip was warm in Kane's palm. Its shape told him it was a Beretta, and he already knew the safety was off. The gun was low, pressed against Kane's body by the man's legs. Without hesitating, Kane pushed the suppressor away from himself a fraction and fired. The man jerked and gasped as a bullet punched through his abdomen. The pressure on Kane gave way. He raised the gun, jammed it beneath his attacker's jaw, and fired again. Blood and skull fragments slapped against the redbrick wall and the man sagged dead.

Kane rolled away, brought the weapon up as he fled into the shadows, and leapt behind a large, red dumpster-style bin. Another shot hammered into the wall above him, dusting Kane with brick fragments. No gunshot sounded, but the bullet's impact was unmistakable. A sniper on the rooftops. Kane cursed under his breath. He glanced around him. More bins, rubbish bags and rear entrances to high street shops. Kane took a deep breath and ran. Another bullet slapped into a black bin bag. He had to get out of the alley, or he was a dead man. He kicked open a set of emergency exit double-doors and dived inside the closest building.

Kane hit the floor inside hard, dragged himself to his feet, and groaned at the searing pain in his hip. He glanced down at the dark blood smear he'd left on the polished floor and ran along a cream corridor, followed it around to the right, passed a small empty canteen room and burst through a set of double-doors and into a women's clothing shop.

The shop was empty apart from three shop assistants who gaped at Kane as he limped through the rails of dresses and shelves of neatly folded jumpers. He tucked the gun inside his suit jacket and made for the front door. Kane staggered out onto the high street and saw three men waiting on the high street that he would have to cross to get to the hotel.

Everything stopped when he recognised a tall man in a perfectly tailored suit. A man who should be dead. Kane had watched him fall from a balcony at the headquarters of the Mjolnir agency in deadly battle.

It was Jacobs, the man who had deceived Kane into entering the witness protection programme. Jacobs who was also codename

Odin, leader of Mjolnir, the rogue agency responsible for Sally's death.

A dead man come for vengeance.

TWENTY-ONE

The high street saved Kane's life. Too many people marched along the chewing gum-stained pavement, oblivious to the danger but creating a human barrier between Jacobs, his men, and Kane. The pedestrians blocked any line of sight for them to shoot accurately. A bus pulled up in front of the clothes shop, brakes shrieking, and three men stepped off. Kane pushed past them and jumped through the folding doors before they hissed closed. Kane fumbled in his pocket and dropped some change into the plastic fare tray outside the bus driver's Perspex cage. He dragged himself along the aisle, leaning heavily on the yellow handrails, aware that he was smearing blood along the seats as he brushed past.

Kane reached the empty back seat and stared through the window as the bus pulled away and Jacobs limped into the road, staring after Kane with a granite-hard look on his face. As if things weren't bad enough with the Phoenix problem, how was Jacobs alive and what was he doing here? Jacobs must have found him somehow. Perhaps it was in London, perhaps at the airport? It could be any number of locations if Jacobs was looking in the right places, monitoring CCTV or passport control with facial recognition search programmes. Kane had destroyed Mjolnir three years ago. He was sure Jacobs had died in that fight, but his old enemy had returned like a nightmare, and at the worst possible moment. Kane sat heavily on the gaudy blue and red bus seats. The gunshot wound in his hip burned like fire, bled freely, and he needed to examine it before he lost too much blood. Kane had his survival tin in his jacket pocket, but he let the bus carry him from Ravenford high street, out onto a country road, and away from Jacobs and his kill team.

The gun beneath Kane's jacket was cold through his shirt, its butt jabbing into his stomach. He ignored the faces watching him from seats in front, turning every so often to fix him with wary glances. *Craven*. Kane had to get back to the hotel before Jacobs and his men got to Craven. Craven would certainly be on Jacobs' kill list if this was a revenge mission. Kane pressed the bell to show the driver that he wanted to get off at the next stop. The bus leaned into a wide turn and Kane stifled a groan as his body weight shifted and his wound pulsed more thick blood onto his waist.

The brakes screeched, and the bus slowed. Kane pulled himself to his feet, gripping the cold bar, which ran from the bus roof to its floor to keep himself from falling. His eyes blurred, and he lurched up the length of the bus like a drunk. The driver stared at Kane but said nothing as he stepped groggily down the iron-shod step onto the pavement. The bus pulled away and Kane looked around him. Across the road, he saw only bushes and a bridge across a babbling stream. Behind him, Ravenford high street and its shops and offices rose above the trees with flashing traffic lights and grey buildings. Kane took a deep breath and steadied himself, controlling his breathing. He had to tend to his wound and stem the bleeding, or he would lose consciousness. Craven needed him.

A brown sign stuck out from the bus shelter, pointing to Kane's left; arrow-shaped with the word *Library* in clean white letters. A 1980s-style building rose beyond an empty concrete pond, three boxy structures in dark brick and long, black framed windows rose from cracked and uneven paving slabs. A coffee shop sat within the right-hand structure and Kane made for it, ignoring the library entrance. The coffee shop would have a bathroom, food and drink.

He stumbled through the front door, taking

care not to smear blood on the handle and arouse any suspicion. A short woman in a yellow raincoat stood at the counter chatting to a waitress in a brown apron, and Kane waited patiently, fighting with himself to remain upright and appear calm. A DeLonghi coffee machine rumbled and hissed, and the woman in the raincoat took her latte and Danish and left the counter. Kane ordered a double espresso, an orange juice from the fridge, and an energy bar.

"Do you mind if I use the bathroom, please?" he asked, in his calmest voice, even managing a smile through the pain.

"Sure, it's just through that door," said the waitress, and returned his smile.

Kane moved slowly to the door, opened it and closed it smoothly behind him before collapsing on one knee. His breath became ragged, and he took off his jacket and shirt, taking short, sharp intakes of breath. Kane grabbed a fistful of blue hand towels from a wall dispenser and mopped up as much of the blood from his body as possible. He probed the gunshot injury with shaking fingers, and hissed in relief as he found an exit wound. The bullet had passed through the side of his hip, missing bone and passing through the meat of his backside. Kane closed his eyes, thankful for a slice of luck. If the bullet was stuck inside him, the wound would be a different story and he would need urgent treatment.

Kane fished his emergency tin from his jacket and popped it open. He took the alcohol wipe and cleaned around both entry and exit wounds. It stung like hell and a finger of blood pulsed from the hole in his front. Kane pulled out the needle and thread, gritted his teeth and, pushed the flaps of skin together at his hip, putting two crooked stitches in the entry and exit wound. It was a quick and dirty patch-up job and the pain was shocking, but nothing new to Kane. He stared at himself in the bathroom mirror, telling himself to take the pain, to use it to make him sharper and more focused for the work to come.

Once Kane tied off the stitches, his shaking hands pushed the bloody needle and thread back into the tin. He cleaned his hands with more hand towels and wiped the excess blood from his hip. Kane took the tampon from his tin, opened it, and pressed it to the entry wound. He folded over four pieces of hand towel and pressed them to the exit wound. He then bound a length of rolled bandage about his midriff to keep both sides of padding in place. It would do for now.

Kane washed his hands and face in the sink, put on his shirt and fastened his jacket to hide the blood. He pulled another wad of hand towels from the dispenser and cleaned his own blood off the floor. Kane grimaced, leaned on the sink, and took three deep breaths. He was pale and weakened. The espresso and orange juice would give him enough energy to make it to the hotel. It had to. There were too many enemies—Russian Spetsnaz operatives to stop, and a ghost from his past come to kill him. The pain subsided a little; the bleeding stopped for now. There was no choice, no time for hospitals, rest, or recovery. Kane had to go on the attack, or he and Craven were dead men.

TWENTY-TWO

Craven lay in bed watching Homes Under the Hammer on the hotel television. An Asian man from Birmingham had bought a rundown flat in Solihull, fixed it up with a new bathroom and boiler and made thirty grand profit. Craven sighed because, clearly, there were easier ways to make a living than working with Jack Kane. He reached for the remote, cursing as his bruised ribs objected to the movement. He clicked off the TV and tried to get up. The pain in his head had subsided after a night's sleep and a morning of rest. He turned and sat on the edge of the bed. Craven blinked twice to test his vision. Still no dizziness. He grabbed a bottle of Lucozade from the bedside table and took a drink.

The beating was a visceral and raw experience and Craven's pride hurt as much as his body. A punch to the face left his lip swollen and cut inside. Craven ran his tongue over the bulbous swelling inside his mouth and closed one eye.

His ribs suffered bad bruising but were not broken, and he felt an ache at the back of his head. He thought about calling Barb to see how she was doing. It was Monday morning, and she would have dropped Danny and Kim off at school for the week and would meet her friends for coffee and a walk in the city centre.

Craven reached for the burner phone next to the orange bottle of Lucozade, and the front door to his room burst open, almost smashing into the wall. Craven sat up straight and clenched the white duvet beneath him in both fists, suddenly fearful that it was the Russians who had come to finish him off. But Kane came barrelling through the door and closed it behind him. He stood with his back against it, panting, his face sheened with sweat and a pharmacy paper bag clutched in one hand.

"What the fuck is wrong with you?" asked Craven. His friend was as white as a ghost.

"Jacobs is here with a kill team."

"Jacobs? You mean Odin?" Jacobs was the man who had eased Kane and his family into the witness protection programme and worked as his handler for years, keeping Kane's cover a secret. But in the carnage and mayhem when Craven had first come across Kane, Jacobs had revealed himself to be the head of Mjolnir, Kane's former MI6 splinter agency. He had set Kane up and betrayed him. Jacobs was a bastard and a killer. "Isn't he supposed to be dead?"

"I saw him shot, but never saw his body. It happened in the confusion of the fighting at Mjolnir headquarters. It was chaos. He took a bullet and fell from a first-floor balcony. I just assumed he was dead."

"Assumption is the mother of all fuck-ups." Craven heaved himself from the bed and stretched his back gingerly.

"We have to move. Now. Jacobs is here to take me out, and he'll be looking for you as well. One of his men ambushed me in the lane leading to this hotel, so we can expect his team to be sweeping the hotel as we speak. I came in via the service entrance. His men are armed and skilled, and we have to get out of here sharpish."

"What about the job we're on? Everything is falling apart for the Moores. The attacks at the game, the fire. They need us, Jack."

"We can't help them if we're dead. Do you have some clothes I can borrow?"

"You want to wear my clothes? Mr Sharp Suit in my old gear?" Craven laughed. Kane was always well dressed, and Craven's clothes were way too big for his lean frame, not to mention they weren't in the least bit fashionable or stylish.

Kane moved to the bathroom and switched on the light. He took off his suit jacket to reveal a white shirt. The material was stained dark brown from the chest down. It took Craven a second to realise that the stains were Kane's blood. Kane pulled the shirt off slowly, peeling it away from where the blood had dried against his skin. Beneath the shirt was a bandage and what looked like a blood-soaked tampon. Kane took a shiny black gun from his waistband and laid it down next to the sink. A gun. Craven's stomach turned over with fear. Things were getting worse, spiralling out of control.

"I need a t-shirt, or a shirt and some trousers. I can't go to my room, it's too risky. Anything you have will do. But move fast and get dressed yourself. We need to be out of here in five minutes."

"Jesus fucking Christ, Jack. We need to get you to a hospital." Craven tore his eyes away from the ragged, awful-looking wound at Kane's hip.

"No time. Get the clothes, Frank. Hurry."

Craven pulled on a pair of jeans, a polo t-shirt and a knitted sweater. He went to the wardrobe and found Kane a navy polo, some chinos, and his belt.

"Here," Craven said and then averted his eyes as Kane dressed his wounds in the large bathroom mirror. There were two holes in his body, hastily stitched and beginning to scab. "Fucking hell, Jack." Craven left the clothes on the bath rail. "Do you need a hand?"

Kane shook his head, cleaned the wounds with medical wipes and then pressed large dressings over each one. He pulled off his trousers and socks and they dropped to the bathroom tiles with a slopping sound, smearing dark blood on the white floor tiles. Kane washed himself and pulled on Craven's clothes, gathering the extra material in the chinos' waistline with the belt.

"You got one of them, then?" Craven said, gesturing to the gun which Kane must have taken from an attacker.

"One. But there's more. Are we ready?"

Kane tucked the gun back into his trousers, crossed the room, and peered through the white netting beneath the heavy curtains.

"Ready. But we can't just run. What about the Moores?"

"I said nothing about running."

Craven stuffed their spare phones, credit cards and passports into a sports bag, along with a few items of clothing, and followed Kane out of the room, leaving the door to swing closed behind him. Despite being shot and losing a lot of blood, Kane did not limp or complain. He walked as though nothing had happened—purposeful and determined on his course. Craven still felt shaky after his beating the day before, and if he had his way, he would spend the day in bed recovering, drinking coffee, eating bad food and watching bad television. But it was time to fight. New enemies had appeared to add their threat to the Russians. So Craven ignored the pain in his head and ribs and followed Kane along the hotel corridor, past the elevator and into the stairwell.

TWENTY-THREE

Kane took the stairs two at a time, moving down from Craven's sixth-floor hotel room. He was certain that Jacobs and his crew were in the hotel searching for them both. They had to know where he was. The ambush location had been perfect. Two operators flanking Kane's approach to the hotel and a sniper at an elevated position, but they had missed, and Kane was still alive. He turned around the stairwell and down another flight of stairs.

"Slow down," Craven gasped behind him, and Kane glanced up at his friend's red face. "You move like a bloody whippet, but I'm old and my head's pounding like a jackhammer. Slow down a bit."

Kane took the chance to peek through the narrow glass windowpane in the door leading from the stairs to the fourth-floor. A cleaner pushed a heavy trolley along the corridor, and a tall man in a suit bustled past her and touched his ear.

"They are inside the hotel," Kane said. The ear touching was a rookie mistake, a giveaway from a man who thought nobody was watching as he adjusted his radio earpiece. "Stay close. They'll sweep each floor. If we're lucky, they've already swept the staircase."

Kane took the stairs to the next level below, and just as he was about to turn to dogleg down to the next floor, the door to the third-floor hotel rooms opened. A stocky man in a black suit poked his head through the opening and looked down and then up. His blue eyes met Kane's, and he froze. Kane lashed out with his foot, kicking the door as hard as he could. It smashed into the man's neck, driving him back against the doorframe. Kane removed his foot and kicked in again. The man croaked in pain as the heavy fire door crushed his throat. Kane released the pressure again, and the man stumbled forwards. Kane grabbed two fistfuls of his hair and smashed his face into the steel banister with a metallic thud.

The man crumpled to the stairs, tried to lift himself and went still after Kane stamped his heel into the base of the suited man's skull.

"Three more flights," Kane said, "and we'll reach the lobby. We go into the lobby and leave using the front door."

"The front door? Hardly as cunning a fox. Won't that leave us wide open?"

"It's more dangerous here, in the corridors and lifts. There will be people in the lobby... hotel customers. Jacobs won't kill us there. Too messy, too many eyes watching. So, we stroll out of the front door, and I'll find us a vehicle."

"What about the Audi?" asked Craven.

"That's burned now. We have to assume Jacobs knows the identities we used to enter the country. We'll use new ones from now on." Kane pulled the earpiece from the unconscious enemy and placed it into his own ear. It was high-end equipment, earpiece only, no bodypack or press-to-talk microphone. He patted his hands around the man's torso, found a Glock 19 in a holster on the man's belt and took it, belt and all, including a leather holder with a spare magazine. Kane removed Craven's large borrowed belt and strapped on the new one. He pulled off the enemy's suit jacket and put it on to cover his two guns. The jacket was too tight across the shoulders, but it would do.

"Rest in peace, Mr Shufflebottom. Can't say I'll miss you."

Kane continued down the stairs, listening to Jacobs's team over the communications device in his ear.

"Fourth-floor, clear," said a French accented

voice. "Bravo moving to floor five."

"Delta. Second-floor, clear."

"Where's Alpha?" asked a voice. Jacobs.

Kane and Craven reached the bottom of the stairwell and walked out into the lobby beside the elevators and across from the check-in desks. The lobby was a basic square atrium within the hotel building. Two thick pillars painted beige divided it into the central foyer, a seating area, and a corridor leading off to the hotel restaurant. Kane touched Craven's elbow and guided him towards the front doors, two big sliding doors that opened automatically.

"Alpha's down," said Kane. A tall man standing in the seating ahead turned sharply, his head jerking from side to side as he realised it was not Alpha's voice. It was Jacobs, dressed in tailored trousers and a pastel blue shirt with the sleeves rolled up.

"That's you, isn't it?" said Jacobs.

"It's me, you bastard. You should have stayed dead."

"And you should have made sure I was dead."

"I will this time."

"I've come for you, Lothbrok. Have you forgotten your old codename? I created you, made you what you are, and I'll be the one to take you down. Powerful men want you gone, and you'll die in this backwater town."

"You were behind Sally's death, Jacobs. All the time pretending you had our best interests at heart, whilst you used me to plot and scheme your way to the top of Mjolnir. I'm glad you're here."

"I was always at the top of Mjolnir, and you were always weak. Jacobs was just one of my many names, as you well know. I go by the name of Mr Hermoth now, or Kyle Navarro, or Jarod Hightower, and many more. You were never quite ruthless enough, Jack, just short of being able to do what it took to protect your country."

"Protect my country? Since I left the service, I've often wondered how many of our missions were in the interests of national security and how many served other purposes. Were we ever the good guys?"

"Don't be so naïve. There is no good and bad, no right or wrong. We did what had to be done. Just like I am now. You are a mess that needs cleaning up, a relic to be swept under the carpet and forgotten about forever."

Kane marched through the hotel lobby and Jacobs' head came up, their eyes met, and time slowed. Six tourists wearing shorts and bumbags strolled through the lobby towards the check-in desk. It was as though they walked on clouds, plodding on the hotel's plush carpet. His hate for Kane changed Jacobs' expression. His eyes hardened and his mouth set into a grim, straight line. Kane resisted the urge to pull his weapon and kill Jacobs where he stood. There were too many people around, and he didn't want an innocent person hurt in the crossfire. Instead, Kane winked and smiled as Jacobs' fists balled.

"Change to frequency one five zero," Jacobs said icily, eyes still locked on Kane. "Target is in the lobby. Take him outside."

Kane pulled the earpiece out and let it drop to the floor. He quickened his pace and slipped through the double-doors as a fat man in a baseball cap waddled through in the opposite direction.

"Bastards," Craven muttered, jutting his chin to the parked Audi, where a tall black man stood guard.

The hotel doors opened onto a small roundabout covered with bright flowers. The car park lay to the left, and to the right was the slip road out onto Ravenford's main street. Directly in front of Kane was a motor coach with the words Jameson's Travel written on the side. A long, silver shining coach with its doors open as a sweating driver unloaded luggage from a flip-up cabin between its front and back wheels.

Two men stepped out of the hotel doors behind Kane, and another came running from the hotel car park.

"Get on the coach," said Kane without thinking. He ran for the open door and leapt into the driver's seat. It bounced beneath him. He pressed a green button to close the doors as soon as Craven climbed inside.

"Please tell me you aren't stealing a fucking coach?" said Craven. He sat down quickly once he saw the determined look on Kane's face. Outside, the coach driver gesticulated wildly in protest.

Kane checked the dashboard and manual gearbox. He shifted the gearstick into first gear and stomped on the accelerator. Jacobs' men stared open-mouthed as the coach surged forwards and Kane swore under his breath as he failed to get to grips with the steering quick enough to avoid driving over the roundabout and crushing the finely manicured flowers. The coach shuddered and bumped Kane a foot into the air from his seat. He landed and wrestled with the steering wheel to get the unwieldy vehicle under control. A window shattered half down the side, and then another. Bullets hammered the coach's flanks like a drum and Craven shouted in terror. Kane glanced in the side mirror, where two of Jacobs' men fired suppressed handguns at the huge vehicle as it swerved and lurched erratically away from the hotel.

He ignored a red traffic light and turned the enormous steering wheel to guide the long vehicle out onto the main street. He over-steered, and as he tried to correct it, the back-end flew out and Kane wrestled with the steering to straighten the coach out. The coach's rear end slammed into a row of parked cars and the bodywork crunched and wrenched before Kane could pull it away. People on the pavement screamed and leapt out of the way, as Kane fought with the steering, trying to understand the responsiveness of each twist of the wheel. He wrenched too far to the right and the back-end slewed again and crashed into a delivery van. Kane cursed under his breath and finally steadied the coach. He sped up down the main street, moving into second and third gear as the coach picked up speed.

"Jesus, Jack. Now what?" shouted Craven, gripping onto the sides of his seat for dear life. "Are we going on a tour of Stonehenge in this fucking thing?"

"Don't worry, I have another car," Kane said, speeding the coach out of Ravenford and onto the winding network of country roads, which led to a patchwork of farmers' fields and suburban housing estates.

TWENTY-FOUR

Kane turned the coach into a farmer's field heavy with yellow rapeseed. He pulled it in behind a tall hedge, wiped the steering wheel and gearstick down, and had Craven do the same for every part of the vehicle he had touched. A rudimentary police fingerprint check would throw up warnings in the UK Police Ident1 system, and Kane could do without more attention.

"So, you just happen to have a vehicle stashed away somewhere?" asked Craven as they left the field, crossed the farmer's driveway and pushed through a gorse thicket to enter the winding suburbs close to Jess Moore's house.

"No, I took it from the man I caught outside Jess's house, the one who followed her whilst she went jogging," said Kane.

They found the E-Class Mercedes where Kane had left it in the retail park, locked, with the key hidden on the underside of the driver's side wheel alloy. Kane opened the vehicle and slid into the driver's seat, allowing himself a grimace at the pain from his gunshot wound. Craven climbed into the passenger seat and Kane gunned the car out of the network of streets and cul-de-sacs and out onto the main road. After fifteen minutes, he pulled into a service station so that he and Craven could decide on their next course of action.

"I'll go in. We have to be careful now," Kane said. He parked the car in the furthest corner of the service station, away from the cameras, which would cover every inch of the forecourt. He kept close to the building, noting the positions of the cameras high on the building's walls, and over at the four petrol pumps. Kane kept his head low, hand over his eyes to hide his face. He avoided the cameras and entered the petrol station. Kane bought two plain blue baseball caps from a shelf containing toys, hats, water pistols and board games. He grabbed a tea, a coffee, and two sandwiches, paid with his head down and returned to the car.

"Thanks," said Craven as he took the coffee and sipped at its steaming contents. He ripped open the cardboard sandwich box and took a bite of bacon, lettuce, and tomato.

"Everything I know, all my training, tells me we should abandon this operation. We should drive north today and take a flight from Liverpool or Manchester airport to either Germany, Greece, France or Portugal, and from there, get a connecting flight to Seville. But we can't just cut and run, we owe it to the Moores to finish the job."

"Our old enemy is here, tooled up with guns and trained soldiers, all here to kill you certainly, and me probably. Doesn't that make it even more dangerous? We might bring greater trouble down on the Moores rather than helping them."

"I can't leave here with Jacobs alive. He won't stop. There's no way he's working for the British Government, not after the fallout from Mjolnir and all the fucked-up missions he sent us on. I honestly believe that on half the ops I worked in those days, I was working for the wrong side. He must pay for that, and for Sally's death. I owe it to her, and to my old mates who died in the service."

"But we can't walk around in the open like we have been. So, what can we do? Do you think it's a coincidence Phoenix and Valknut are here, and now Jacobs is here as well?"

"Could be he picked my face up using a scanning system. But more likely, Jacobs and his men are working for Phoenix. It must be. It's just too much of a coincidence. Jacobs has contacts. After the collapse of Mjolnir, it would have made sense for him to set up his own operation, a mercenary intelligence agency working for the highest bidder. He would know who to contact to recruit rogue agents, men and women dismissed from governmental roles for breaking the rules. Too bloodthirsty, unable to follow orders, black hats. He knows where to source weapons and communications equipment and probably had accounts filled with money siphoned off from Mjolnir or access to its accounts that no one else knows exist. Jacobs can move like a ghost across borders, create new identities, charge fortunes for his particular set of skills."

"So how do we help the Moores, then?"

"Take it to a different level. Bring Jacobs and the Russians a war they aren't expecting. Do what the government used to pay me for. Rain down hell on our enemies and show them something they've never seen before."

TWENTY-FIVE

Jess Moore sat in her kitchen drinking her third glass of cool Sauvignon Blanc from a long-stemmed crystal glass. She rubbed the back of her left hand across eyes stinging with tiredness, and peered at the Excel spreadsheet on her MacBook laptop. Wessex Celtic was almost out of money, and no matter how many times she jigged around the fixed and variable costs, the club's existing funds would not stretch beyond the end of the month.

It had been a long twenty-four hours since the training ground fire. The players were given Monday off, and Jess spent the day making calls and sending emails to make the necessary arrangements to keep the training ground open and the club running. Team coaches and the manager filled their cars with footballs and training gear salvaged from the fire. Thankfully, the west wing, where they stored the actual football equipment, was saved from the worst of the fire's ravages. She had arranged for four Portaloos to be delivered on Tuesday morning and placed beside the training pitch, as well as a temporary truck container for the squad to use as changing rooms.

The coaches and players were all behind the club and what must be done. If anything, Jess sensed a greater sense of purpose about them, their resolve hardening in the face of tragedy. She hoped that steel would transfer itself into their performances on the pitch. Wessex Celtic was close to achieving a play-off position in the league, and only seven points off second place and automatic promotion. If the club were promoted, a cash injection from the Football Association and a clause inserted by Jess in each sponsorship contract to provide for an increase in funding would solve all their problems.

Jess drained her glass and set it down on the granite kitchen counter. The numbers stared back at her from the laptop screen, the summary double-underlined and highlighted in red by the accountants. Promotion and dreams of growing Wessex Celtic would fade like smoke in the wind if Jess was not able to stretch the club's finances beyond the next fourteen days. If she couldn't pay the players, or the club's debtors came on heavier, then the FA would punish Wessex Celtic. The club would go into administration, there would be points deductions, players would seek to leave at the end of the season and her father's dream would be in tatters.

The electrical and water utility companies agreed to allow the club to enter a payment arrangement and defer their bill out past the month. That, at least, was something. Jess had made calls to the travel partner in Ravenford, who provided coaches or air travel for away fixtures, and they had promised to look at their fees and come back to her. She had called the insurance company, but they seemed less than impressed by the request to review their premiums.

Jess closed the laptop and walked to the window, peeking out of the wide folding patio windows to watch the security team performing a slow patrol around her gardens. Her father had insisted on putting the team in place, paying for it himself to make sure she was safe. Kane and Craven worked on their security, but they were focused on investigating Phoenix and could not be expected to always monitor her house closely. Jess made sure that the same level of security was also in place at her father's house. If the Russians had the audacity to start a mini riot at the stadium and burn down the club's training grounds, then who knew what else they might be capable of in their quest to force the sale?

Jess pulled a blanket from a basket beside the windows and pulled it around her shoulders. She wondered again if it would be simpler to just take the offered money, to end all this stress and danger and walk away rich. Jess shook her head and went to the fridge to pour another glass of wine, telling herself that she would never sell. It would destroy her father's dream, and that could not happen. No matter what the cost. Even if it made more sense to sell.

Her mobile phone rang, vibrating on the worktop, and snapped Jess out of her tired thoughts. It was a private number, so Jess answered it nervously.

"Hello?" she said.

"Jess, it's Jack," said Kane, and she smiled.

"Are you coming to watch the house this evening?"

"Maybe later. We've had more trouble today in town, and I need to locate Antonov and the men he sent to cause trouble at the stadium. Can you try to pull the footage from the stadium CCTV?"

"Yeah, sure. I can have our IT guys look at it now. What are you looking for?"

"I need images of their faces, each of the men who were fighting at the stadium. They attacked Craven on the pathway leading up to the ground, and we obviously saw them attack ground staff below the directors' box."

"I'll get on it right away. How soon do you need

the images?"

"Quick as you can. If I have time, I'll call around later. Are the security team in place?"

"Yeah, there's ten of them walking around the front and back garden."

"Good. Don't go out running or anything like that, just stay at home. Call me if you need to go anywhere. Stay safe, Jess."

He clicked off the line, and Jess placed her phone back onto the worktop. He seemed genuinely concerned about her safety. Jess realised she had been wrong about Jack Kane. At first, she thought he was just an ex-army security guard looking to make some quick cash out of her father. But Kane was more than that. He was capable and professional, but he really cared. After they had spent the night together, Jess worried things would become awkward between them, that he would avoid her, or that she would want to avoid him. She missed Kane, which was strange because they hadn't actually spent that much time together, but his quiet, strong manner connected with her.

Jess opened her laptop again and got back to work. She emailed IT security, requesting the images, her fingers quick and deft on the keyboard. In ten minutes, she would follow the email up with a call. Until then, she flicked open the Excel spreadsheet of the club's finances.

There must be a way to find some money from somewhere.

TWENTY-SIX

Kane sat on the bed, its springs creaking and groaning under his weight. The small room smelled of damp and wet dog, but it would do for a night. He and Craven had driven an hour away from Ravenford in the Mercedes and found a bed and breakfast above the White Hart pub in a town called Great Hawksby. It was too dangerous for them to stay near Ravenford with Jacobs and his men trawling the town for any sign of them, so a pub B&B without Wi-Fi with only five regulars in the bar would do perfectly.

The gunshot wound hurt like hell, and Kane had bought some painkillers and more dressings from a local pharmacy, as well as replacement items for his emergency tin. He showered in the shared bathroom across the hall, cleaned his wounds and re-dressed them.

Kane lifted the Beretta 92 from the bed and checked the gun. It had fired four rounds of its fifteen-capacity magazine and Kane looked over the weapon, which seemed clean and in good order, and laid it back on the bed. Next, he checked the Glock 19. It was smaller, lighter, and easier to handle than the Beretta. The Glock also fitted nicely in the holster and belt taken from the enemy on the stairwell. The holster concealed the weapon from view—depending on clothing—and it had a full fifteen rounds, fourteen in the magazine and one in the pipe. That should be enough firepower to deal with Jacobs' men, for now.

Kane had two burner phones left from the bag he had brought over from Spain, and he took one out and dialled Cameron's untraceable phone line.

"Jack?" said Cameron's voice after four rings.

"Cam, we've run into a few problems, and I need your help. Again. Sorry to ask, mate."

"Don't apologise. Anything for you, Jack. What's going on?"

"Trouble with a face from the past and the Russians we are dealing with down here. The Russians have taken things to a new level, and I need some help with them. Craven is going to use the secure laptop to send you images of some faces at a football stadium. See if you can figure out who they are, so we know what we are dealing with. Also, I want to track down our friend Mr Antonov, the CEO of Phoenix

Telecoms. Find out where he lives so I can make this a bit more personal for him."

"No problem. Once Craven sends the images through, I'll get straight to it. If you really want to fuck with Antonov and Phoenix, there are other things we can do, you know? Things that don't involve violence."

"Like what?"

"Whilst you've been busy down there, I've been looking into Phoenix in more detail. Seems like Sidorov made a sizeable chunk of the Phoenix Group billions using their very own Tinba programme to steal from millions of people across the globe."

"In English please, Cam? Sidorov is the CEO of the Phoenix Group, if I remember correctly?"

"Sorry, mate. About a decade ago, Sidorov recruited the best hackers in Russia to build what's known as a Tiny Banker Trojan programme. He deployed it through Phoenix Telecoms call centres, of which he had already had hundreds of offices providing outsourced call centre services to businesses all over the world - services including telephone tech support. His call centre agents connect to victim companies' computer systems via their tech support access. From there, Phoenix established a man-in-the-browser attack, sniffed the company's network, and accessed their online banking."

"I still don't follow. Who in the browser? Sniffing?"

"Basically, Sidorov could hack into his clients' companies' computers and steal money from their bank accounts. When you need IT support in a business, the helping tech company will usually send you a link to click so that they can take over your desktop. Once inside an unsuspecting client's computer, Phoenix deployed their hacking programme, the Tiny Banker, to steal banking passwords and online access. Phoenix was so big and had so many clients that Sidorov only had to steal a few thousand each year from every client company to net himself a fortune. With that fortune, he bankrolled Valknut, and is now one of the richest and most dangerous men in the world."

"Jesus Christ," said Kane. The odds seemed to get worse and worse with every passing hour. "How did you find all of that out?"

"There were rumours in online hacker forums, and I followed the trail. But it gave me an idea of how to inflict a bit of poetic justice on the fuckers."

"I like the sound of that."

"I have built a nifty little programme to steal whatever funds Antonov and his arm of Phoenix have in the bank accounts. All I need is someone to send Antonov an email, which he is likely to open. When he does, it will ask him for a specific permission, but in a simple and unassuming way. Once he clicks to agree, we are in. It's a kind of Pegasus software programme. I can take control of his systems, access whatever accounts he has, and drain them. I'll transfer the money into one of your offshore accounts. You can donate it to a dog's home, keep it, or do whatever you want with it. I might also take a little slice for myself, as a sort of finder's fee."

"Can they trace it back to you?"

"Jack, please. Do you think my head buttons up the back? The programme self-destructs, and I can destroy it remotely if I need to."

"Well, let's see how much money Antonov has access to and drain the bastard dry. Good work, Cam. I'll ask Craven to send those images as soon as possible."

Kane clicked off the phone, filled up the small sink in his room and threw the phone in the water to destroy it. He dressed in the clothes borrowed from Craven and the jacket taken from the enemy in the stairwell, and went to knock on Craven's door.

"Hold your horses, bloody hell," barked Craven. Moments later, the door opened, and Craven stood there in his towel, scowling like a man stung on the arse by a bee.

"I've spoken to Cameron," said Kane. "As soon as we get the images from Jess, send them to Cam from the laptop."

"Yes, sir, no sir, three bags full, sir. Who made you the fucking captain of this operation?"

"What?"

Craven sighed and held his hand up to apologise. "You used all the hot water, so I had to have a cold shower. Then, I banged my fucking head on the bathroom door on the way out. My sore fucking head. This operation is a disaster. Sooner we get back to Spain, the better."

"I'm going out for a few hours with the car. It will be late before I'm back."

"Suits me. I'll get this email to Cameron and then I'm going downstairs for a few pints. Where are you going?"

"To pick up some burner phones and a few other bits and pieces."

"It's ten o'clock at night!"

"I'll go to the motorway services we saw close to the M3 motorway; they'll be open all night."

Craven squinted at Kane as though he could see into his soul, testing his truthfulness. "All right then. Be careful. I'll see you in the morning. I called Barb. She got the kids to school and she can pick them on Friday if we aren't home by then. Which I hope we will be."

Craven closed the door, and Kane made for the stairs. He felt bad lying to Craven, but he didn't want his friend to know that he was going to spend the night with Jess Moore. He wasn't sure why; it wasn't necessarily a bad thing. Unprofessional, maybe. Perhaps he didn't want Frank to judge him about Sally and the kids. He missed Danny and Kim and would call them sometime this week. As Kane jumped into the Mercedes, he promised himself that he would be a better dad when he got home, make it up to them for being away so much. But for now, he had to see Jess. He couldn't get her out of his head.

TWENTY-SEVEN

Kane woke with summer sun shining through the bedroom window, warming his back and cascading through the half-open curtains in a waterfall of light. He lay on his side, watching Jess sleeping. Her raven black hair fell over the pillow, glossy and thick, and her skin was milky smooth beneath the white sheets.

It was five thirty in the morning, and Kane slipped out of the bed and pulled on his clothes. He kissed his fingers and touched them to Jess's forehead lightly and left the room as quietly as possible. He opened the bedroom door, and it creaked on its hinges.

"Jack, wait," she said, her voice groggy from sleep.

"It's early. Go back to sleep," he replied.

"Stay for breakfast?"

"I can't. Today will be a busy day. I'm going to tie the Russians up in so many circles that they won't have time to bother you or your father."

Jess ran slender fingers through her hair and lay back on her pillow. "I've a busy day too. Meetings up to my eyes, all about costs and saving."

"Be careful. I have to go. I'll call you later."

Kane left the house, head down so that he didn't have to suffer the knowing stares from the security team patrolling the house. He jumped in the Mercedes and headed back towards the White Hart. Kane stopped for a takeaway tea at a service station, where he bought four burner phones at the cash desk. He arrived at the B&B before anybody in the place was awake and crept to his room. Kane checked his wounds and his weapons and waited until eight o'clock. Then, he drove to a retail park twenty minutes away and found a menswear outlet store. He used a credit card under the name Robbie Fowler to buy a new Italian suit, two shirts, and a pair of black shoes.

The suit fitted well, and the jacket adequately concealed the Glock and its holster at his waist. Kane felt a bit more like himself. Ready for action. He called into a home improvement store and bought some useful supplies and a workbag to store them in. Lastly, Kane bought a laptop, some more throwaway phones from an electrical store, four sets of communication devices, simple twenty-channel body packs, earpieces, and touch-to-talk lapel clips.

On the way out of the retail park, Kane spotted a drive-thru Starbucks. Though people queued in their cars for coffee like it was a McDonald's, Kane parked outside and took the new laptop inside. He ordered a large tea and a croissant and connected the laptop to the shop's Wi-Fi.

Kane wasn't a technical genius by any stretch of the imagination, but he had learnt some important basics whilst with MI6. He fired up the laptop and logged into a safe network set-up hosted by Cameron and his web of infinite complexity. There was a message in Kane's inbox with some information from Cameron. *Cameron, you are a legend.* The file contained a breakdown of each of the Russian men involved in the trouble at Wessex Celtic's stadium. Most were standard Russian army paratroopers and commandos, but the man with the glasses was different. He was a former Spetsnaz and GRU, a highly-skilled operative and close lieutenant of Yuri Balakin, Valknut's general and commanding officer. Kane clicked through images of Balakin and the man with the glasses in various war-torn countries, each wearing military fatigues and looking every inch like a veteran soldier.

The man with the glasses was Valery Ivanov— an orphan, raised in care homes across Moscow and sent to educational correctional facilities, or young offender institutions, from the ages of thirteen to eighteen. At eighteen, Ivanov joined the Russian army, and from thereon, most of his records were redacted. A hard man, and, from his pictures, a grey man, a perfect recruit for Russian special forces and then secret services. It was like looking into a mirror. Kane recalled fighting Ivanov in the stadium, a skilled combatant who was certainly holding back the full lethal force he was capable of.

Valknut was in the UK helping Phoenix close the Wessex Celtic deal. That much was clear now. Kane must take them down using the only method they understood. Violence. He opened another message from Cameron, and Kane almost fell off his wooden chair. Mr Antonov's Phoenix Telecoms corporate business account contained eight million US dollars, and Cameron had deposited the funds into Kane's various accounts around the world. Kane stifled a laugh of joy. That would really piss Antonov off, and his employers, when they found out their millions were missing. When the operation was over, Kane decided he would split half of that money between Craven and Cameron and set up trust funds for Danny and Kim with the rest.

Kane was about to snap the laptop closed when an idea occurred to him. A way to help Jess and Andrew Moore with one of their problems. He accessed one of his shell bank accounts registered to an office cleaning company based in Bolivia and transferred five hundred thousand dollars into the trading account and then sent a link via email to Jess Moore from which she could transfer the donation to Wessex Celtic.

The croissant was soft and flaky, and Kane washed it down with the last of his tea. He replied to Cameron, thanking him for the information and reminded him to send the location of Antonov's home address as soon as he had it. Phoenix had given Andrew Moore three days to close the deal, and that was up today. If everything went as planned, today would be a long day, but by the end, Kane's enemies would know they were in a war against a different sort of enemy.

TWENTY-EIGHT

"Tell me again what we are doing here?" said Craven, raising an eyebrow at Kane as they strolled along Ravenford High Street at eleven o'clock in the morning. "I thought we were supposed to avoid this place."

"We were," said Kane cheerfully, "but I changed my mind."

"Are we going anywhere in particular, or just out for a stroll amongst the trained killers and Russian special forces soldiers trying to kill us?"

"Just walking. Smile for the cameras." Kane looked up and waved at a circular CCTV camera outside the high street bank.

"Have you been drinking?" asked Craven, convinced his friend had finally lost his mind. They were supposed to be keeping their heads down. Multiple, extremely dangerous enemies were trying to kill them, and it seemed Kane was actively trying to taunt them. "Hang on a second. We are fucking bait, aren't we?"

"Like maggots on a hook."

"For fuck's sake. I had a few nice pints of Guinness last night, a good chat with the locals about Salisbury plain and Stonehenge. My head feels better today and my bruises are healing, and now you're trying to drop us right in the shit again?"

"Up to our necks. It's time to take a few pieces off the chessboard."

Craven shook his head and marched beside Kane, past the bank and a charity shop, across the road at a set of traffic lights and back down towards their parked car beside a recycling facility. Kane stopped, looked around again, made sure the town CCTV got a good view of his face and got into the passenger-side car door.

"So, where to now, Mr Happy?"

"Turn around and follow the signs for Swallow Mere. It's a wildlife park and forest about fifteen minutes away."

"You think they are going to follow us?"

"Without a doubt. Jacobs wants me so badly, he won't be able to resist."

Craven shrugged and pushed the ignition button to start up the Mercedes and headed out towards the wildlife sanctuary. He glanced at Kane, noting the determined look on his face, and decided against asking him to share whatever plan he had cooked up overnight. It would undoubtedly involve some sort of extreme violence, or a ridiculously reckless situation Craven would want to avoid like the plague. Sometimes, ignorance is bliss.

"Don't worry, Frank," said Kane. "When we get there, you are going to hide in the forest whilst I sit and wait for our friends. On my signal, you will call the police and let them know a gang fight has erupted in the sanctuary and that you have heard gunfire. The police will be there quick as a flash. They will still be on high alert after the trouble at the stadium and reports of the fighting in the streets around the hotel."

"Won't the police arrest us as well?"

"Leave that bit to me."

Craven frowned at him. "That's what I thought you were going to say, and it doesn't make me feel much better. Don't get us killed, Jack."

TWENTY-NINE

Swallow Mere covered four hundred acres of marshland twelve miles outside Ravenford. It had an adventure and information centre for kids on school trips and was a sanctuary for protected and rare birds. Ponds and small copse forests dotted the place, along with picnic benches and marked walkways for ramblers and adventurous dog walkers. Kane marched along a pathway covered with shredded wood chippings, and the sun shone through high branches swaying in the breeze. Oak, elm, ash and hawthorn hid chittering birds and a plethora of wildlife. Kane retrieved the Glock from his holster and checked the weapon.

Kane carried a plastic bag under his arm, a regular black bin bag bought at the hardware store earlier that morning. He dropped the bag behind a small wall made of natural stone that kept the wild ferns and gorse away from the pathway.

"Put this radio on, Frank," Kane said, and handed Craven a communication set purchased at the electrical store. They walked around the drooping leaves of a willow tree and Kane opened another radio set, popping the earpiece into his right ear, and fastening the pack to the back of his trousers. He clipped the touch microphone to his suit jacket lapel and helped Craven put his kit on correctly. Kane set both packs to the same frequency and tested both microphones and earpieces.

"So, we're going to split up then?" asked Craven, fiddling with the pack clip at the rear of his navy chinos.

"Only for a few minutes. I must draw Jacobs and his men in a little so I can take a few of them down. Then I have another surprise for them."

"Let me guess, I'm the bait?"

Car engines roared somewhere to the west, and tyres screeched on the road tarmac. "I'm afraid so, mate." Kane clapped Craven on the shoulder. "Sit on that bench over there and wait for my signal. Run around the willow tree and head for the car park when you hear it. I'll meet you there."

"Where will you be?"

"Out of sight."

"I should have taken a nice, quiet job when

I left the force. Something easy. Like collecting trolleys at Sainsburys or delivering packages for Amazon. Something safe. But here I am, waiting for a band of ruthless killers to come at me in a fucking bird sanctuary. What is it with these places, anyway? Didn't you meet Jacobs somewhere similar before?"

"Yes. It's an excellent location, wide open, lots of places to hide and close to roads and exit routes. Follow the plan. Wait for my signal and everything will be OK."

Kane left Craven and jogged towards the forest, slipping between two silver birch trees, stepping over fallen branches and through soggy leaf mulch. He made a quick call on his burner phone and slipped the handset into his jacket pocket. Cars screamed into the car park and Kane doubled back, flanking the car park through the dense forest. Two black Range Rovers hurtled into Swallow Mere's entrance and skidded into the car park before coming to an abrupt halt. Eight men in dark suits leapt out of the vehicles, one still strapping on a Kevlar bullet-proof vest. The rest were already wearing their body armour, three carried MP5 automatic rifles, and the rest drew handguns as they strode from the jeeps.

Jacobs limped purposefully from the lead Range Rover and drew a pistol from a shoulder holster. He checked the magazine and held the weapon low at his side. Jacobs barked an order Kane couldn't make out from within the woodland, and his team fanned out. Three men stayed with Jacobs following the pathway away from the car park, two ran wide around the left flank, and two more jogged in Kane's direction on the right.

"They're coming, Frank," Kane said, pressing his touch microphone. "Stay calm. They won't shoot you until they know where I am."

"Well, that's great comfort, isn't it? Your half-arsed hypothesis is that they won't just blow my head off when they see me sitting on this park bench like Forrest Gump? All I'm missing is a box of fucking chocolates."

Kane crouched in the undergrowth, the damp smell of rotting vegetation filling his nose. He left the Glock in its holster and instead took out a retractable Stanley knife bought at the hardware store. He used his thumb to slide out the thin, razor-sharp blade a thumb's length and waited. Footsteps came closer, crunching through the leaves, twigs and branches, with no care that an enemy might lurk in wait for them. They thought they came to ambush two outnumbered men, to work around their flanks and surround them in the park. They were wrong.

Kane remained crouched, a great hawthorn tree hiding him from the approaching enemies.

One peeled away, heading further right to take a wider approach to where Craven was waiting on the park bench. Kane assumed word had come through their comms that one or more of them had eyes on Craven. Kane waited until the nearer footsteps were so close he could hear the man's breathing and the rustle of leaves as he moved a branch out of his path. A brown loafer shoe appeared to Kane's left, followed by another. Then, a man in a dark suit moved past the hawthorn, moving low and efficiently, his MP5 held before him, ready to pounce like a stalking lion.

Kane shifted from his position, and a twig snapped beneath his shoe. The enemy froze in his tracks, his blonde-haired head whipping around and eyes widening in terror as he saw Jack Kane lunging at him from the shadows. Kane drove the Stanley blade underneath the blonde man's chin, into the soft flesh between Adam's apple and jawbone. It punched through skin, muscle and gristle without resistance and Kane pulled the blade free. He caught the enemy as he stumbled, clutching at the slim but deadly gash in his windpipe. Kane stabbed him twice in the groin and once more in the throat. The blows struck so quickly that only a bead of blood appeared at the blonde man's throat.

Kane lowered the dying man gently to the forest floor, slipped the MP5 from his shoulder and threw it over his own. He unstrapped a black, Zahal bullet-proof vest, and strapped it around his own torso. Kane checked the dying man's pockets and found an oval-shaped Range Rover key. Finally, Kane took a spare fifteen-round MP5 magazine from a leather holder clipped to the man's belt and set off through the woods.

"Here they are," said Craven through Kane's earpiece. "Jacobs and three others. Big fuckers."

Craven recognised Jacobs because the two met during the chaos in Warrington and Manchester three years ago, but in his guise as Kane's witness protection handler, not as the ruthless head of a counter-intelligence force gone bad.

Kane ran, swerving between the trees until he glimpsed a suited man kneeling behind a sprawling oak tree with a handgun held in two hands, pointed at Frank Craven. Kane slowed, moving swiftly but carefully, watching how he trod so as not to snap a fallen twig and alert his enemies. Months spent training in the Brecon Beacons and forests of Scandinavia had prepared Kane for woodland fighting, and then active service in the jungle made him an expert.

Kane trod so softly through the undergrowth that he moved like a ghost, like an ancient woodland spirit flitting through trees as old as time. The first the enemy knew of Kane's approach was two inches of Stanley blade punching into his temple. He died instantly and Kane let him fall dead beneath the oak tree, where his blood would soak the soil to nourish its deep roots.

"Mr Craven," said Jacobs' crisp, upper-class voice through Kane's earpiece. Craven had cleverly pressed his microphone to allow Kane to hear the conversation. "Long time no see. You have been keeping rather dreadful company these past few years and I'm afraid it has landed you in a spot of hot water."

"You look well for a dead man," said Craven.

"Yes, well. I thought I was dead for a while until I realised I was just in Syria. I am very much alive, and regretfully, I have orders to remove you from blocking the business arrangements between Wessex Celtic Football Club and my client."

"You mean you've come to kill me?"

"Remove you by whatever means necessary would be a politer way to phrase it. But sadly, yes."

"Best get to it then."

"Where is Jack Kane?"

"Who?"

"Really, Mr Craven? Please don't be so tiresome. Only Kane needs to die today. We both know you aren't really the threat here. With all due respect, you couldn't knock the skin off a rice pudding, old boy. So, tell me where Kane is, and you just might walk out of this mess alive."

Kane took the burner phone from his jacket pocket and threw it deeper into the foliage. It had served its purpose. He took the Glock from its holster and strode from the trees just as a wail of police sirens burst through the forests, calm like a grenade.

"Jacobs," Kane shouted, and as his enemy turned to face him, Kane shot him twice in the chest. The gunshots boomed like explosions, and the men surrounding Craven flinched involuntarily at the sound. Craven leapt up from the bench and ran in the opposite direction, away from Kane and around a clutch of trees from which Jacobs' remaining two operatives now came with weapons raised.

Six armed men faced him, and Jacobs writhed upon the grass, grasping at his body armoured chest and gasping for air. Chaos was about to erupt, and Jack Kane turned and ran for the trees.

THIRTY

Frank Craven looped his arm about a birch tree and paused, gasping for breath. He had only run for five minutes and already his lungs burned and his face glowed bright red. He pushed himself away from the rough bark and crashed through the undergrowth until he rounded the drooping willow tree and came within sight of the Swallow Mere car park.

Gunfire crackled and thundered like a firework display and Craven kept moving, forcing himself to keep running despite the objection in his lungs and legs. Police sirens wailed, growing ever closer and Craven had to stop again, leaning over to rest his hands upon his thighs to suck in huge gulps of air.

Kane came racing from the woods at full tilt, a stubby-looking machine gun over one shoulder and a gun in his hand. He wore a black bullet-proof vest and moved with the litheness of a man half his age.

"The police are coming!" Craven shouted, waving at Kane to join him quickly.

"I know. I called them on the burner before I threw it away," Kane replied, barely out of breath as he leapt over a small wall and picked up the black bin bag he had brought from the car. "Here, put this on, quick. Jesus, I need to get fit."

Craven ignored the last comment. Compared to Craven, Kane was as fit as a butcher's dog. Kane tossed Craven a bright yellow hi-vis vest and a blue cap winged with luminous yellow strips. He tossed Craven a set of secateur garden clippers and pulled on his own yellow vest and cap. Five men came sprinting from the forest holding weapons, followed by Jacobs, tall and limping behind them.

"Over here, Frank," said Kane and he ran around the far side of the wall so that the bracken and plants within shielded him from the charging gunmen. Three police cars roared through the gates to Swallow Mere, coming to a skidding halt as officers leapt from each door. Each copper wore black tactical gear and carried a gun: an armed response unit. Craven stood beside Kane and followed his lead. Kane's usually calm face changed to a panicked, fearful expression, and he ran towards the police officers, holding his own set of secateurs and waving frantically at Jacobs and his men.

"Over there!" Kane cried out as though terrified. "Men with guns! Help!"

The officers hurtled past Kane and Craven, assuming they were gardeners at work on the grounds.

"Stop, police!" the lead officer bellowed at Jacobs and his men. More officers ran from their Skoda Octavia police vehicles towards the threat.

Craven shook his head in disbelief as he and Kane waited for the police to leave them alone in the car park. Kane took a car key from his pocket and clicked it once. The lights flashed on one of Jacobs' Range Rovers and Kane jogged to it, opened the driver's door and slid inside. He closed the door halfway and looked at Craven as though puzzled by the surprised look on Craven's face.

"What are you waiting for?" said Kane. "Get in."

Craven jumped in the passenger side door and Kane calmly reversed the Range Rover and drove slowly out of the car park and back onto the main road.

"I can't believe that worked," said Craven, still unsure how a couple of yellow vests and some garden clippers had fooled the police.

"Well, it did. The police were full of adrenaline, warned that armed gangsters were involved in a gun battle in the park."

"Warned by you."

"Warned by me."

"So, they weren't expecting to arrest a couple of terrified gardeners."

"They'll arrest Jacobs and his men, and that should keep them busy for twenty-four hours. One piece removed from the board."

"Surely the police will keep them in custody on weapons charges?"

"Jacobs has contacts, and whoever he is working for will have him out by this time tomorrow. How do you think Jacobs and his men are so heavily armed? They have contacts here in the UK, people with access to weapons, intelligence and money. So, we need to act fast. Time to remove another piece."

"The Russians?"

"Cameron found Antonov's home address. Time to pay him a visit."

"Why didn't you just kill Jacobs when you had the chance? Why shoot him in the chest?"

"I only had time to get off a few shots. If I'd aimed for his head, I might have missed and I wanted him hurt. He'll be even angrier now, furious that we got away and that I shot him. His vest saved his skin, but Jacobs' pride was badly wounded. Angry men make poor decisions."

The Range Rover growled as Kane gunned the accelerator and sped along a dual carriageway. There was a glint in Kane's eyes, a look Craven recognised. A spark inside Kane caught fire whenever he was involved in deadly action. It was as though Kane came alive in the moments between life and death, when bullets flew, and Kane's skill and training moved him through the danger like a wickedly sharp sword blade. Kane thrived on that thrill, lived for the action. No matter how much Jack loved his children, Craven knew his friend could never leave the action behind. It surprised him that Kane had lasted so long in the witness protection programme. It must have eaten him up inside to live a life of peace.

"Should we expect more trouble at Antonov's place?" Craven asked, reaching into the back seat and finding a grey rucksack which he placed between his feet to search through later.

"Yes."

THIRTY-ONE

McGovern slammed the phone down and shot up from her chair. She paced the office, wishing for once that she was a field agent, that it could be her aiming at Jack Kane in the crosshairs of a rifle so that she could blow his brains out once and for all. It was early evening in Dubai, and the lights and music around the harbour began to light up restaurants around the glistening water.

She had spent the best part of an hour chasing around senior officials in the UK's Sussex police force and the Ministry of Defence, with little success. Finally, via a search through classified Balder databases, McGovern found a contact in MI5, who was also on the Balder Agency payroll and had finally found some success. Mr Hermoth, despite his aloof tone and blind confidence in his own field ability, had got himself arrested by the police whilst in the middle of a gun battle in a bird sanctuary. It beggared belief. Luckily, McGovern listened to the Balder team's comms frequency and took evasive action before the team got locked up for questioning by the local police.

McGovern heard Kane's voice over the radio, referring to Mr Hermoth as Jacobs, which she assumed was a former identity, and then the explosion of gunfire. Two more of their team were dead and besides trying to spring Mr Hermoth and the others from the cells, McGovern had also co-ordinated a clean-up team to get to the bird sanctuary and clean up the mess whilst the police were still trying to organise themselves. It was arduous work. In MI6, McGovern had access to a serious and complex organisation, resources and teams across the UK and the world who were available for this type of situation. Working privately was a different story.

The clean-up team was a private firm in Birmingham, who performed all kinds of surveillance work for Balder and other agencies around the world. McGovern shuddered to think which ones. They arrived at the scene within two hours and removed the bodies. She did not know how they had accomplished that rather delicate task right under the police's noses and within their yellow tape, but they did. The bodies were gone. Five operators, along with Mr. Hermoth, remained, and one of them suffered an injury while fighting Kane in a hotel stairwell.

The MI5 contact was on his way to Ravenford police station at that very moment to use his credentials and clout to free Mr Hermoth and the others. Then it would be back to searching for Jack Kane. Kane had revealed himself on Ravenford high street, parading like a cock in the henhouse, smiling up at the cameras for all to see. McGovern saw, or rather one of the team outside her office saw, his face and raised the alarm. McGovern flagged Kane's presence to Mr Hermoth, with the caveat that Kane's behaviour was off, like he was purposefully trying to let anybody watching know where he was, but Mr Hermoth ignored the warning and steamed on in.

"Come in," McGovern responded to a knock at her door.

"We've located the Range Rover," said a short young man with greasy, shoulder-length hair. He wore board shorts and flip-flops to the office every day.

Probably a Harvard graduate or some sort of computer genius, she thought.

"Where?"

"Heading to London on the motorway. ETA forty minutes."

"Keep following the vehicle and let me know where it stops. Also, notify our client of... no wait. I'll do that."

The tech bro nodded and closed the door behind him. McGovern went to her laptop and typed a message to her contact at the Phoenix Group—now known to her as the client in the Kane operation—to warn them of his impending arrival in London. Eleven urgent emails from Phoenix marked urgent found their way into her inbox, diverted by Mr Hermoth. The messages were curt, angry emails referring to a missed deadline and severe consequences.

McGovern finished the email and stretched her neck after another long day. Thoughts of the clean-up company in Birmingham and Phoenix clouded her mind, making her tired. At least when she worked for MI6, Mjolnir, and the other governmental departments McGovern had represented, she believed she was one of the good guys. Even when she green-lit clandestine operations, knowing they were funded by drug lords or military juntas seeking to destabilise their own governments, she had convinced herself that it was all for the greater good. That she worked for a government trying to do the right thing in the world.

The world, however, was dark. Even in those days, McGovern questioned how much harm she had done, how far she had shifted from the path of being a good guy. Perhaps that was naïve. In her experience, there are neither good nor bad organisations and governments, just people with different objectives and beliefs. McGovern was sure that the governments she had once toiled against considered that they were right and that Western governments were evil. It wasn't clear-cut. Even Jack Kane probably thought of himself as a good guy, but McGovern had seen his file. He was a trigger-man, a lethal asset deployed to obey orders he would never question.

McGovern ordered an espresso from the coffee shop beneath her office using the store's app. She rose and left the office, striding past the desks outside without making eye contact with anyone. She must chase her MI5 contact and hurry him up while keeping tabs on Kane's location. Perhaps erasing him would make her feel better about her new job and her new life. He was perhaps the last link to the disappointing end to her career. Rub that out and she could start afresh.

THIRTY-TWO

Kane parked the Range Rover two streets away from Mr Antonov's address in Chelsea. He and Craven arrived in London in the late afternoon, and the traffic was heavy on the M3 and M25 motorways. The bag Craven found in the Range Rover stolen from Jacobs contained a knife, a roll of duct tape, a length of rope and basic climbing equipment, hand-sized underwater breathing apparatus and some tech equipment Kane couldn't identify. It was a serious kit. The type of pack men in Kane's line of work brought on a mission when unsure of the lengths they might have to go to in order to get the job done.

"I've sent pictures of the tech stuff we don't understand," said Craven. "And Cameron has sent satellite shots of Antonov's house. It's a Georgian-type building, very posh. Like a terraced house, one in a long line of huge, three-storey buildings. The types where singers, celebrity chefs, and earls live side by side, with fucking basements fifty feet deep with swimming pools in them."

"Antonov has a swimming pool underneath his house?" asked Kane, imagining the expense and work involved with building the thing below ground in central London.

"How should I know? The pictures are all of outside."

Kane turned off the car and laughed. "So, what are we looking at, then?"

"Three storeys, no side entrances. Flat roof, doors front and back. Lots of windows. I can't see any Phoenix goons hanging around on the pictures, so maybe he's there all alone and unprotected."

"Don't bank on it. He will guess we are coming for him after what happened with the fire and the attacks on the stadium. It's a bit like the trick we played on Jacobs this morning. If Antonov is still living here, then it's because he suspects we'll come for him. So, there will be more Phoenix or Valknut men inside. If it's one of those Georgian duplexes, then there could be many rooms on each floor based on the original designs or knocked through walls and wide-open plan spaces. We can expect flights of stairs, cameras and perhaps even a celebrity-style basement."

"Well, I'm sure you have a plan."

"I do, and I'll fill you in on the way."

Kane and Craven left the car and made their way across three busy streets filled with expensive cars, women in sunglasses walking little white dogs, and men in Lycra jogging around London's streets with serious faces and huge headphones. Kane told Craven how he expected the evening to unfold, and Craven listened, adding only the odd huff or shake of the head at parts of the plan he found unpalatable. They carried a bag each. Kane's held the MP5, the Beretta and the spare ammunition, a set of body armour, the laptop, spare burner phones, plus the bits and pieces purchased at the hardware and electrical shops. Craven carried the bag found in the Range Rover over his shoulder and a larger bag containing their clothes and other belongings.

The two friends found a round, metallic table outside an artisan coffee shop fifty metres from Antonov's house, where they could sit at an outside table and watch the house. In his old life, Kane would have watched the place for twenty-four hours, built up an idea of the layout inside and of Antonov's movements. But he wanted to hit the place today, and so a few hours of surveillance would have to do.

Craven went inside to order a coffee and a tea, and Kane settled in to watch Antonov's house. It was almost five o'clock in the evening, so people would start returning home from work over the next two hours. Kane allowed himself a wry grin, wondering how Jacobs and his men were faring with the police. He had visions of angry faced mugshots, belligerent sergeants, long interviews, and wide-eyed constables examining the array of automatic rifles and handguns.

"This place is a bloody rip-off," blustered Craven, opening the coffee shop door with his shoulder. He set a black plastic tray down on the small table and handed Kane an almond croissant.

"Thanks," said Kane.

"How much for the drinks and two croissants?"

"No idea." Though Kane had an idea, they were in Chelsea, one of London's most upmarket areas, and sat in a fancy coffee shop. Not a Costa or Starbucks, but a privately owned place where the customers had beards, walked boutique little dogs, and the women all looked the same with pouting lips and cement flat foreheads.

"Twenty-five quid. We are in the wrong game, Jack. Bloody rip-off."

A long-bearded waiter with a sleeve tattoo and a black-and-white striped t-shirt brought their drinks and set them down on the table. Kane thanked him whilst Craven tried not to snarl, his face like thunder. Kane shifted his position, moving the Glock slightly from where its grip dug into his midriff. He sipped at the tea, which was a little bitter, so he added more milk from a small white jug.

"The coffee isn't even that nice," Craven said, folding his arms in disgust. "I've had better at roadside fry-up cabins."

They drank their drinks and ate the croissants, and Kane monitored Antonov's house. An hour passed, and Kane bought more drinks and a sandwich each. There wasn't much left in the counter refrigerator that late in the evening, so he picked a croque monsieur for Craven, thinking he would appreciate the cheese and ham and ignore the fancy name, and a chorizo roll for himself.

At six twenty, three black Mercedes jeeps rolled up at the traffic lights close to the coffee shop. Each had blacked-out windows, with the same big, alloy wheels, and drove menacingly close together like the convoys Kane remembered from his time in the Middle East. There, it was common practice to drive at top speed and extremely close together, because anybody trying to follow the convoy would need to replicate that speed to keep up, and therefore show themselves as a tail.

"They're not even trying to hide themselves," said Craven, finishing his sandwich. "Why don't these people ever drive a Ford Kugas, or Volkswagen Jettas?"

Kane laughed at that truth. The vehicles moved off as the lights turned green and pulled up outside Antonov's house. Two burly men jumped out of the middle vehicle and opened a passenger door to let Antonov out. He glanced up and down the street and then waddled up the steps to his front door. More guards exited the Mercedes jeeps, mostly muscled men in tight t-shirts. But then Kane sat up straighter because Ivanov, the man in glasses from the stadium was amongst them—the GRU Spetsnaz soldier, the Valknut special operator.

"It's time," said Kane, and so it was.

THIRTY-THREE

Kane didn't wait for the cover of darkness to attack. Eleven men poured out of the jeep convoy outside Antonov's house, all dressed in black, touching their suit lapels or ears as they set up a radio comms network around the house. To wait was to give them time to prepare and set up their observation points, settle down into a routine of patrol and guard. They expected any attack to happen during the night, with the house equipped with infrared cameras and night vision. Kane made it a point to never follow expectations.

"Keep an eye on the front," he said to Craven, and slung the rucksack over one shoulder. Before leaving and whilst drinking his tea and eating the sandwich, Kane transferred some helpful items into the rucksack found in the Range Rover. He had his survival tin as always, spare ammunition, the climbing rope, gaffer tape and the knife.

"Will do. I'll let you know if any more goons show up," Craven replied, fiddling with his earpiece and radio.

"I've set us up on the same frequency, so we are good to go. I shouldn't be any longer than twenty minutes. When I come out, we'll need to get away quickly. So be ready to move."

"Jack?" said Craven as Kane got up to leave. "Don't get killed. Remember, those bastards from the stadium aren't your everyday men. They were highly trained, and they mean business. They won't just let you waltz in there and get to Antonov. If it gets too hairy, get out. Think of Danny and Kim. This isn't worth them losing you. It's just a job."

Kane nodded and walked up the street. It wasn't just a job. Phoenix was a dangerous outfit, used to war and death through Valknut, its military arm. He feared for Jess and what Phoenix would do to her when tomorrow came and the deadline for completion of the football club sale expired. The men Kane had come up against were Valknut soldiers, which meant the Russians wanted the sale badly—bad enough to bring a military force into the UK with a willingness to use lethal force.

As he strode through the leafy London suburb,

he wondered if any of his old colleagues in MI6 were watching Phoenix. They must keep tabs on a company with such well-publicised links to both Valknut's private army and the Russian Government. Kane crossed the road and reached the end of Antonov's row of houses, following the bend of the road around to the street running next to the row of Georgian houses. As he walked, Kane glanced at parked vans and cars, and at the people walking up and down the pavements. None seemed suspicious, but an MI5 or MI6 covert surveillance team, by its nature, should not be easy to spot. He looked up, conscious that things had changed since his day. Back then, teams always performed this type of work, but these days, small drones could hover above a property undetected and pick up conversations and movements using heat-sensitive detectors. It was a brave new world, but for Kane, the old ways still worked best.

From the café, Kane had noticed that house number twelve on Antonov's street was empty. The blinds in each window were down, and though it was still daytime, a hallway lamp glowed faintly behind a downstairs window. A ploy used by householders everywhere to put off would-be burglars when on holiday. So, as Kane strolled down the street behind Antonov's, he waited until he came to a whitewashed building directly behind the empty house, checked that nobody was watching, and ran down its driveway covered with tiny white stones. He scrambled over the gates, down the garden and over the fence separating the two properties.

Kane crouched, pausing for ten heartbeats to check if anybody had spotted him or if any alarm had been raised. All clear. He ran to the back of the house and climbed up the back wall, using the drainpipe and window ledges as supports and handholds. Halfway up, he paused to catch his breath, one foot on a first-floor window ledge made of stone, and his arm around the plastic drainpipe.

The drainpipe groaned as Kane hauled himself up again, using his foot to spring off the window ledge and scramble for purchase. His right hand scratched on the plastered facing, searching for a hold whilst his left gripped the smooth drainpipe. His fingers clawed into flaking plaster, but a chunk of it came away, covering his face in a cloud of dust. Kane coughed, his heart leapt when, for a terrifying moment, he thought he would fall and break his back on the patio below.

Kane steadied himself, hanging from the pipe with his left hand, one foot wedged into the drainpipe's supporting bracket. He swung again, and this time, his fingers found a grip on the exposed brickwork and he could scramble up another two feet and grab the next window ledge. Kane hauled himself up and paused again, staring down at the street below. All seemed quiet, and Kane breathed a sigh of relief that he remained unnoticed, hidden as he was by a light covering of garden trees, and undetected because half of the pedestrians walked with their heads buried in their phones.

It was another twist and leap to grab onto the concrete sill beneath the roof tiles, and then Kane was crouched on the empty house's roof. The row of Georgian houses all had flat roofs, and most had a dormer window rising in a triangular wedge with south-facing windows. The dormer turned the top floor, which had originally formed a dark attic space, into another bedroom or living space for its occupants.

"Craven, this is Kane. Do you read me?" Kane said into his communications device.

"I can hear you, loud and clear, over," replied Craven, just as he would have spoken into his police radio.

"Any new arrivals or problems outside?"

"No, three goons at the front door. The rest have gone inside. I'm sure I recognise a couple of the bastards from the football match."

"I'm going in."

THIRTY-FOUR

Kane ran along the flat rooftop, keeping low and hidden from anybody at street level. He leapt over a waist-high dividing wall between two properties and raced along the rooftops until he reached Antonov's house. Kane dropped to his knees in the dormer unit's shadow and took the bullet-proof vest from the rucksack. He strapped it on over his shirt and took out the knife. There was a risk that entering the property would set off a security alarm and Kane could find himself faced with half a dozen Valknut soldiers inside the house. Cutting power would kill the alarm but would instantly put Antonov's team on high alert.

The point of Kane going in straight away and in daylight was to catch them off guard and hit them whilst they were still setting themselves up before Antonov settled down for the evening. Kane peered through the dormer window into a top floor room with a dark wooden floor and gym equipment resting on foam mats. There was also a running machine, exercise bike, sets of weights and workout benches. By the look of him, Kane doubted Antonov used the room much.

Kane took his knife and began working to scrape out the clear grouting around the dormer windowpane. The window was locked from the inside, so there was no way to pick the lock from the outside, and smashing the window would undoubtedly raise the alarm. So Kane slowly whittled away at the rubbery plastic, using the knife's point to pick away the adhesive until he could rip the seal from the glass. The knife was a standard military-issue survival knife—the one Craven had found in the Range Rover. It had a serrated back edge, a blade slightly longer than Kane's hand, an iron crosspiece and a plastic grip. The point and edge were razor sharp, and, in a few minutes, Kane had picked away most of the grouting from the windowpane.

The glass was heavy, triple-glazed glass, and as the sealant came away, Kane forced the knife around the edge, careful not to crack the pane and not to let the window fall inside and smash on the wooden floor. The knife slipped behind the window and Kane leveraged it towards him until he could slip his hands around it and slide inside. Kane dropped lightly onto the floor and lowered the pane, arms stretched high above his head. The glass rested back into its frame, and Kane searched the white plastic housing for any sign of an alarm wire but saw none.

Lemon cleaning products filled the air in the gymnasium room. The equipment looked brand-new as if they had never been used, and the floor had been meticulously swept and mopped. Kane knelt beside the exercise bike, pulled on the body armour, and slid the rucksack back over his shoulders. He moved to the door and opened it softly, careful in case there was a creak in the hinges. It opened silently, and he moved down the corridor, treading carefully on the old floorboards.

Kane reached the bottom of the third-floor stairs and paused. Floorboards ahead of him creaked, and he caught the shifting shadow of a man ambling along the landing. Kane waited until the shadow vanished and then cleared the rooms on the first floor. Clearing rooms had its own science taught and practised by special forces teams across the world, and Kane lost count of how many rooms he had cleared on missions with the regiment. Doing it alone was a tricky business—far better to have a highly trained team behind you in constant communication, but Kane moved purposefully and efficiently.

He cleared the closest room first, a white-tiled bathroom with Victorian fittings, which again seemed barely used. Next was a spare room containing nothing but a double bed and a wardrobe. The third room on that floor had its pale-yellow door slightly ajar, and Kane eased himself inside where the rotund figure of Mr Antonov stared up at him from where he perched on the edge of the bed, a look of complete surprise on his face. He wore a white vest and boxer shorts, his shirt and suit trousers lying on the plush, beige carpet where he had discarded them.

Kane darted to him and clamped a hand around his mouth. Antonov bucked and shook his head until he felt the cold steel of Kane's knife at his throat. Kane pulled his prisoner to his feet and dragged Antonov to the ensuite bathroom, closing the door behind him and turning on the shower and its extractor fan to drown out any noise. Antonov's eyes were as wide as dinner plates and sweat beaded on his brow. Kane removed his hand and showed the knife to Antonov, and the Glock at his waist to make sure the Russian businessman understood exactly the situation he was in. Kane took off his backpack and removed the roll of grey gaffer tape. He secured Antonov's wrists and ankles and sat him down on the white toilet seat.

"You are making a huge mistake," Antonov said, setting his jaw and finding a sliver of courage.

"Call for help and you die," Kane whispered, just loud enough to be heard above the water cascading into the shower tray and the tumble of the fan. "Keep your voice down. You made the mistake when you burned down the training ground and sent your soldiers to the stadium."

"Are the Moores going to sell or not?"

"Not to you. Phoenix or Valknut."

Antonov smiled. "You have done your homework, but so have we, Mr Kane. Why are you helping Andrew Moore? Just walk away. We will pay you a million US dollars just to leave this alone. Let the deal complete. What difference does it make to you?"

"What do I have to do to convince you that the Moores won't sell? Ever. Back off and look for another club to buy."

"We want Wessex Celtic. The location is excellent, close to London, the price is good, the prospects are perfect. We want Wessex Celtic, and we will get it. There is nothing you can do about it."

"Who do you report to?"

"Nobody, I am the CEO of Phoenix Telecoms in London."

"Don't piss me about. Who in the Phoenix Group do you report to?"

"Fuck off, English pig. Let me go. I've had

enough of your bullshit."

Kane smashed the knife's rounded pommel into Antonov's cheekbone, and the fat man grunted in pain. "Who do you report to?"

"Mr Sidorov," said Antonov, blood dripping from the gash beneath his eye. "Do you know what that means?"

"I know what it means. Tell Sidorov to find a new club… I don't care how. Make something up. Tell him you have identified a better team, one more open to the sale. Do it today, or I'll come back and kill you, Mr Antonov."

Antonov laughed, his belly jiggling beneath his vest. "You think you frighten me? Have you any idea what would happen to me if I betrayed Mr Sidorov? You are like a fluffy kitten compared to Sidorov, not to mention Balakin."

"I'm warning you for the last time. Stop the sale. Check your bank accounts and you'll find yourself a bit strapped for cash. Let's see how you explain that one away. I want confirmation that Phoenix's pursuit of Wessex Celtic is over, or I'll kill you Antonov, I swear it."

"You have stolen from Mr Sidorov?" Antonov laughed again, shaking his head as though he pitied Kane. "You are about to enter a new world of fear and suffering, like nothing you could possibly imagine. First, we pay a visit to your girlfriend, Jess Moore. See how she likes Russian men. She is very attractive."

"If you touch one hair on her head, I'll—"

"Lots of threats, Mr Kane. Threats don't frighten me. Did you think we weren't watching her house, that we had not seen you going in late at night? You are here in my house, and we shall have men in her house this evening. They will sell the football club. There is nothing you can do to stop it."

Rage flared in Kane's mind, imagining Antonov's men breaking into Jess's home and harming her. He punched Antonov again with the knife's butt.

"The deal is off. What's it going to take for you to understand that?"

"Nothing is off. The club will belong to us, and now you must die, and the Moores must suffer until they do what must be done."

Antonov sprang forward, roaring like an animal. He drove himself from the toilet headfirst, crashing into Kane's midriff and forcing him backwards.

"Help!" Antonov shouted and continued shouting in Russian. Kane smashed the knife pommel into Antonov's head, and the fat man fell to the floor tiles where he rolled and bucked like a landed fish, his tied wrists and ankles making it impossible for him to stand.

Voices erupted from inside the house, shouting in response to Antonov's cries. Kane had to run. He must get out of there before Antonov's guards trapped him in the bathroom where he would surely die. Kane jumped over Antonov, but he jerked onto his side and caught Kane's leg. Kane slid on the tiles but grabbed the door handle, just managing to stay on his feet. He wrenched the door open, but Antonov kicked it closed with his tied feet. Kane pulled again, but Antonov had his feet wedged against the door, so that every time Kane yanked it open, it slammed closed again.

There were footsteps in the hallway, hammering on the floorboards. They were coming. Men were on the way to hurt Jess, the only woman he had been close to since Sally's death. Kane reversed his grip on the knife and knelt, thudding the long blade into Antonov's meaty thigh. The Russian roared in pain and his legs moved from the door as dark blood leaked onto the white floor tiles. Kane stabbed him once more in the belly, ripped open the door, and ran into the bedroom.

A thin man with blonde hair, wearing a black roll-neck sweater, stood in the bedroom, a gun in his hand and a look of surprise on his angled face. The gun rose and Kane instinctively threw the knife underhand. It turned through the air and the man flinched before it bounced end first off his shoulder. In those few heartbeats, Kane whipped the Glock free from its holster and fired from the hip. The sound shook the room like a monstrous war drum and the blonde-haired man fell backwards as a bullet tore through his face.

"Jack," Craven's voice crackled in Kane's ear. "The guards out front have gone inside. They look panicked."

Kane ground his teeth and set off through the door, the sounds of onrushing enemies beating on the stairs and landing floorboards. Kane dropped and rolled into the long landing outside the bedroom and a silenced gunshot fizzed over his head. As Kane came up from his roll, he shot the attacker in the calf and then again in the forehead as he clattered to the floor. Kane ran and bounded up the stairs, but just as he reached the top floor, all hell broke loose behind him.

THIRTY-FIVE

Gunfire thundered into the wall panels, showering Kane's head and shoulders with splinters. He ducked and jumped over the top stairs, and landed heavily on the gymnasium floor. Enemies pounded up the stairs behind him, bellowing orders to each other, baying like a pack of wolves. Kane glanced at the window, longing to run and climb through it to safety, but the enemy was too close. They would shoot him in the back before he had taken four steps. He rose and used his momentum to duck behind the exercise bike, pointing the Glock at the open space leading up from the stairs.

A scar-faced man with a thick neck popped his head up above the stairwell into the door space. Kane fired, but the head jerked away before the bullet could strike home and it thunked into the plasterboard on the room's rear wall. He kept his weapon trained on the space, heart hammering in his chest, and then a smoke grenade arced from the stairs, through the door, and clattered upon the wooden floor. It skittered and came to a stop too far away from Kane for him to kick it back down the stairs. Kane curled himself up and closed his eyes tight shut as the grenade whistled and began to emit a thick, chemical-smelling fog that filled the gym with heavy, cloying smoke.

Kane coughed and kept his face shielded as best he could. It wasn't poison smoke, or a flash bang designed to stun an enemy with loud noises and bright flashes, just a smoke grenade to provide cover. Footsteps sounded and whispered voices drifted through the smoke like ghosts. Kane opened his eyes. Figures shifted through the clouds, illuminated by light from the dormer window so that they shifted like ghosts. Kane slid the Glock back into its holster. The Phoenix and Valknut men believed the smoke provided them with cover so they could sneak into the gymnasium unseen and kill Kane. But it gave Kane the same cloak of protection.

Keeping low, Kane moved from behind the exercise bike, following the movements of the first shadow as it crept through the smoke still billowing from the grenade. He flanked the shape, moving swiftly around a weights bench, and then rising behind the shape like a predator, lithe, deadly and unseen. Kane grabbed the figure around the neck with both hands—one around each side of his head—but just before he wrenched his hands in a circle to snap the neck, the enemy fought back.

An elbow smashed into Kane's ribs, doubling him over, and then the other elbow cracked off his forehead. Kane stumbled backwards, and the figure emerged from the smoke and kneed him hard on the side of the head. Kane stumbled backwards and toppled over the bench to land heavily on the wooden floor.

"Over here!" the man shouted in Russian, which Kane had learned whilst employed with MI6.

Kane scrambled to his feet, glancing up at the tall, broad-shouldered man. Another, shorter, enemy with long hair tied back in a ponytail, came running through the smoke and Kane kicked the weights bench, driving it into both men's shins. They howled and stumbled in pain. Kane kicked one in the face, grabbed the second man's long hair and dragged him over the bench towards him. Kane reached behind him to a stack of heavy circular iron weights. Each stack held a different-sized circular weight with a hole in the middle. He grabbed a two-point-five-kilogram weight, whipped it around and crashed it into the ponytailed man's temple. He sagged just as the taller man leapt over the bench, and Kane punched the weight into his solar plexus. The man paused, gurning, and clutching at his chest, and Kane slammed the weight into his mouth, smashing teeth with an audible crunch.

The smoke started to clear, and Kane ducked into the thickest part as three more enemies swirled in the misting fog. Kane circled the gym, moving away from the window, knowing that was where they expected him to be. He came up behind a third enemy and cracked the weight off the back of his skull, dropping him instantly. Only two left, and Kane had the drop on them. He drew his Glock and trained it on a V-shaped back, but a foot cannoned into his wrist and sent the pistol spinning.

Kane twisted at the hip and threw a punch at the new attacker, but he blocked it easily with a raised forearm. Through the clearing fog, Kane recognised the man with glasses from the stadium. Ivanov. The Spetsnaz GRU special operator. Kane drove a knee at him and tried to stab at his eyes with outstretched fingers, but the Russian grabbed his arm and threw Kane over his hip, falling on him, swiftly trying to shift Kane into a jiu-jitsu hold. Kane held his breath and lifted his hips, twisting to stop his enemy from pinning him and mounting his chest. They rolled together on the hard floor. Kane pulled the man close and tried to butt him, but the Russian saw it coming and twisted his head away. A boot slammed into the floor an inch from Kane's head and panic welled inside him like a fire.

He was trapped in an enclosed space with three enemies, one of which was every bit his match. Kane had to act quickly and get out of the gym before they beat him to a pulp and ended his life. Kane turned his head around frantically, looking for something he could grab and use as a weapon. The blood-smeared weight rested on the floor two metres away, and the Glock lay beneath a rowing machine, black and matte and too far away to reach.

Ivanov tried to haul Kane over and clamber onto his back, aiming to choke Kane to death. A shoe kicked him hard in the ribs and another glanced off the side of his head. Kane was going to die if he didn't break free. He bucked, roaring with desperate anger, clawing and biting the man holding him. Kane caught a thumb and wrenched it with all the strength he could muster. He felt gristle shed and ligaments tear, and Ivanov released his death grip for an instant and Kane was off. He surged free in kicking, punching, butting fury. Kane whirled, using all his skills to hammer blows into the three men surrounding him.

A punch connected with Kane's shoulder, and a kick stung his calf, but Kane fought furiously, landing blows with fists, elbow, and knee. He ducked beneath a wild overhand punch to grab a short metal bar with rubber handles on each end, and cracked it across an enemy's forehead, dropping him like a sack of cement. Ivanov tried to grab Kane's wrist again, and he let him this time, allowing the enemy to believe he was securing Kane in a position to toss him to the ground. But just as Ivanov leaned back to execute the move, Kane dragged him forward with lethal speed. He lowered his head and pulled his attacker into a savage headbutt.

Glasses smashed, and the grip on Kane's wrist fell away. Kane jumped over the weights bench and picked up his Glock. He spun, shot the third attacker in the throat, dropped to his knees, and fired through the dormer window. The gunshots reverberated around the gym like a volcano erupting, and tiny shards of glass dropped to the floor like hailstones. Kane pivoted again, seeking to get another shot off at Ivanov, but he dived away just in time and drew his own weapon.

Kane cursed and leapt for the window, jumping through the shattered pane and hauling himself through the space. A bullet ricocheted off the window frame, a hand's breadth away from his head, but it was too late. Kane was up and fired another shot behind to keep the man with the glasses at bay. He set off at a flat run, racing along the rooftops and away from Antonov's house, leaping over partition walls like a hurdler.

Minutes later, Kane was clambering down the

drainpipe. Halfway down, he let himself drop, landing in a practised crouch on the patio slab. He risked a glance upwards but saw no sign of anybody following him.

"Craven, do you read me, over?" Kane said into his microphone, his voice urgent with adrenaline.

"Craven here. Is it time to go?"

"It's time. Meet me on the corner. We need to move. Fast."

Kane ran at full tilt down the street behind Antonov's row and met Craven at the corner.

"What happened?"

"We need to get back to Ravenford. They're going after Jess."

THIRTY-SIX

Jess Moore couldn't believe her luck. She sat back, letting the soft cushions of her plush couch envelop her. Perhaps things were looking up. A fan and wealthy owner of a big South American company had donated a substantial amount of the money to Wessex Celtic with no desire to purchase any shares or become a board member. The donation was a gesture of love for the game and appreciation for the work Andrew Moore had done to bring Wessex Celtic back to the upper echelons of the English football league.

The donor sent a brief but appreciative email, and Jess immediately phoned her father with the good news. The relief in his voice was palpable. The club was teetering on the edge of bankruptcy, and the cash injection would allow them to pay the players at the end of the month and keep a few creditors at bay. It was the breathing space they needed, the lifeline Jess had been searching for. It was a weight lifted off her shoulders, a chink of light after weeks of fear and stress.

Andrew Moore had finally agreed to get away from the country until the trouble with Phoenix was resolved. At first, her dad railed against travelling abroad.

"I won't let gangsters drive me out of my own country!" Andrew had said. But the stress became too much, and when his blood pressure increased beyond safe levels and Andrew's doctor recommended rest, he relented and was currently in Portugal resting at a friend's villa.

Jess checked her phone; it was seven o'clock in the evening and she wondered if Jack would call over. He'd left early that morning whilst she was asleep, and with the lucky donation, she hoped Jack could round off a good day with news that the problems with Phoenix were over. For the first time in a long while, the financial spreadsheet had green cells instead of red, and Jess closed the laptop with a smile. She went to the kitchen and opened her silver American fridge to see what was there for dinner. Jess thought she might cook for Jack. She had pasta, chicken and some pesto somewhere. The only problem was that she did not know when he might turn up—that's if he came at all. There was no way of contacting him because Jack changed his phone after every phone call, which was both annoying and frustrating.

She supposed it came with the territory. Kane was secretive and reluctant to talk about his past. His body was a patchwork of scar tissue, with fresh, lurid wounds on his hip. All he would say was that he was once in the army, and then did some work for the government. That was it. He closed up whenever she tried to probe him further, so Jess left it alone, instead talking to him about her own history, which he listened to patiently and attentively. Maybe the mysterious allure was part of why she felt so attracted to him. It was a cliche, she knew, but Jess allowed herself to enjoy it.

Something brushed against her front door, the sound carrying through the quiet house. It sounded like something heavy, like a dog or another animal sitting against it. Jess paused, listening carefully, but the sound had been quick and followed only by silence. Perhaps she was mistaken. There were ten guards around her house, five in front and five patrolling the rear garden, so she wasn't in any danger. Jess walked to the patio windows in the kitchen and peered out into the late evening. It was still light, but the sun sank beyond a distant sell of hills, casting the meadow in a red hue.

A rapid movement to her right caught Jess' eye, and she turned, peering into the garden. She swore she could see a pair of legs lying flat on the grass, black boots above black combat trousers poking out from behind a yellow-green conifer. She froze, eyes darting from side to side whilst her head remained as still as a statue. There should be five men in that garden. They had been walking back and forth for days, looking bored and resentful at having to perform such a mundane task, but there, nonetheless. Now, there was nothing but a pair of boots.

Another sound, a cracking, breaking sound. Jess pressed a hand to her mouth to stifle a small, involuntary scream. She hurried away from the window, running towards the kitchen and her phone. A man appeared in the doorway between the kitchen and the hall, a tall man in a sharp suit. He came forward, limping on a stiff leg.

"Miss Moore?" he said in an upper-class voice.

Jess shook her head and ran for the other door which led to the utility room, but it crashed open to reveal a man in dark clothes holding a small machine gun. Now she screamed. Jess turned, her white trainers squeaking on the floor tiles. She grabbed a kitchen knife from the wooden sharpening block on the island and waved it towards the gunman. He came forward and Jess made for the patio door, but before she could get her hand on the silver handle, another man loomed up beyond the long panes of glass. A big man, also carrying a machine gun. Jess fell backwards in terror, managing to find her feet and turned in a circle, holding the knife out towards each of the three men.

"Now, now, Miss Moore," the man in the suit said in his posh drawl. "There's no need for any trouble, or for anybody to get hurt. But I'm afraid you are going to have to come with us."

"I have guards," said Jess, doing her best to keep the quiver from her voice.

"Yes, you did. The ten chaps we found outside? They won't be coming any time soon. You have been rather reckless, I'm afraid. You should have closed your business deal when you had the chance... now it's got a bit serious. Take her."

The man with the gun came at her, and Jess slashed at him with the knife. He stepped backwards, shaking his head. He had a black, glossy beard and hair in a perfect side parting. Another three men came through the door after him. Jess lunged forward desperately and slashed at the gunman again. Her knife scored his forearm. He cursed in a foreign language and backhanded Jess hard across the face. She gasped and fell to the floor tiles; her face was numb, and her heart racing. He kicked the knife out of her hand and grabbed a fistful of her hair, hauling Jess to her feet.

Another armed man punched Jess hard in the stomach, and air whooshed out of her like a burst balloon. Jess fell to the floor. The pain in her stomach felt as if someone had stabbed her. A rough hand grabbed her around the arm, hauling Jess to her feet and she stamped on the gunman's foot as hard as she could and ripped her arm free. Jess ran for it, and managed two long strides before the second gunman shoulder-barged her, all his weight behind the push. Jess lifted off her feet, travelling three feet through the air before landing with a crushing thud on her glass-topped coffee table. The table smashed into a thousand pieces, and shards of glass whipped at her face and arms like an eagle's claws.

Jess lay for a few seconds, dazed and pulsing with pain. Rough hands pulled her to her feet. She sagged in their arms as though dazed, but when the two gunmen lifted her body out of the coffee table's wreckage, she struck. Jess was in a fight for her life. These men had already killed her guards, and she was certain they would kill her, too. Jess ripped her right hand free and raked her fingernails down the closest gunman's face, tearing his flesh from his dark eyes down to his oiled beard. He snarled and let her go, and Jess made for the patio in a last-ditch bid for freedom.

The second gunman kept tight hold of her arm and pulled her towards him. Jess screamed and lashed out again with her nails, but this man leant away before she could reach his face. He shook her like a rag doll with fearsome strength, and then thrust Jess backwards, hard, so that the back of her head hit the patio window. Jess groaned, and he punched her full force in the face.

She doubled over and her scalp roared with pain, because the bearded gunman whose face she had scratched dragged Jess from her own kitchen by her hair. Where was Jack now when she needed him most?

THIRTY-SEVEN

Craven held on to the car door handle so tight his knuckles turned white. Kane raced the Range Rover out of London at speeds Craven had never experienced before, faster even than when driving to emergencies as a serious and organised crime squad detective. The vehicle wove in and out of traffic, its engine roaring, Kane staring straight ahead with a look of controlled fury etched upon his face.

"No answer?" Kane asked for the twentieth time since they had left Chelsea.

"None," replied Craven, the phone in his right-hand burring with a dial tone as he waited for Jess Moore to answer.

"Call Cameron, see if he can log into her security cameras. I want to know if she's OK."

Craven couldn't remember Cameron's number to punch into the burner phone, so he pulled a scrap of paper from his trouser pocket on which he had it scribbled down along with Barb's phone number. He typed the digits into the phone and Cameron answered. Craven passed on Kane's request, and Cameron asked Craven to call him back in five minutes.

"They might not have got to her yet. All the Russians we have seen so far were at Antonov's house," said Craven, closing his eyes as Kane came within a finger's breadth of crashing into a Transit van.

"Unless there are more. There could be an entirely new team in Ravenford as we speak. We are talking about an organisation with almost unlimited funds and military force to call upon as and when required."

Craven tapped the burner phone against his thigh, counting down the five minutes on the car's dashboard clock. He glanced over at Kane, driving at top speed, but his body seemed as relaxed as a man cruising along a country road at thirty miles per hour. Craven thought about asking Kane again how he was so sure that Phoenix would go after Jess, but the look in Kane's eyes put him off. That dead stare was the only sign of his anger, his focus, and his fear. Kane was usually so calm, so in control.

Jess Moore hadn't warmed to Kane when they had first met. Craven would even say she downright hated him. But now Craven realised that Kane and Jess had become close, perhaps closer than Kane had been to any woman since Sally's death. No wonder he was so determined to get back to Ravenford at light speed. Craven thought about what he would do if he suspected some nefarious bastards were going after Barb. There was nothing Craven wouldn't do to protect his wife, and Craven had seen Kane do a lot of things, things he hadn't known men were capable of. So, if Jess Moore was in trouble, then there was about to be a serious reckoning.

The five-minute mark passed by, and so Craven dialled Cameron again.

"Frank?"

"Yes, it's me, Cam. I'll put you on speakerphone so Kane can hear you. Did you find anything?"

"I'm afraid so. I accessed the cameras. The guards put on her house are all dead, taken out by a professional squad led by a tall man with a limp. Jess is alive, but they've taken her. They weren't gentle with her."

"A tall man with a limp?" asked Kane without taking his eyes off the road.

"Yeah, he was their leader. The rest looked like standard special operators, not up to the regiment's standard, but decent soldiers."

"It's Jacobs."

"How the fuck did he get out of prison

so quickly?" asked Craven. It hadn't even been twelve hours since his arrest.

"I'm watching the cameras on the house here at the moment," said Cameron. "And it looks like some sort of cover-up is underway."

"A fucking cover-up? What do you mean?" Craven wasn't a fan of conspiracy theories, but had seen his fair share of shady situations during his career.

"The authorities won't want the news of ten men being killed in sleepy Ravenford to get out. Most likely, MI5 have now taken over and will handle the bodies and the search for Jess Moore. Maybe it's time to get in touch with some old friends, Jack?"

"What do you mean, old friends?"

"I think we need help on this one. We are talking about serious forces at play here."

"No," said Kane. "I'll get her back."

"We still know some lads on active service. Billy and Scooby are still in the regiment. You know people in MI6, Jack. Reach out to them. Surely, they are tracking Phoenix and Valknut?"

"Try to keep tabs on their vehicles if you can. I want to know where they take her," Kane said, ignoring Cameron's suggestion.

"I think Cameron's right," said Craven once he hung up the phone. "We can't fight everyone,

Jack. You barely got out of that house in London alive. Phoenix, or some other bastards, have taken Jess. They burned down the Wessex Celtic training complex. How much more fucked up do things have to get before you realise it has gone beyond anything we can handle?"

Kane ignored him and kept the Range Rover speeding for Ravenford. Craven left him alone, but inside, he worried about Jess Moore, and about what Kane would do next. He had a sudden urge to call Barb in Seville, but kept that to himself. They needed a new plan, a different solution to this problem. Kane's plan had failed. Jacobs was out of prison, and the Russians were still in play. The threat to Wessex Celtic had worsened, beyond what either Craven or Kane had thought possible when they took the job. Craven stared out of the window at the streetlights as they blurred past, wondering how he had got himself into this mess and how they were going to get out of it.

THIRTY-EIGHT

Four men in suits and long dark coats stood guard outside Jess Moore's driveway. They were MI5 men; it was written all over their serious faces and the cut of their suits. Darkness enveloped the cul-de-sac, brightened only by the golden glow of streetlights and the torchlight of men patrolling Jess's property.

Kane watched them from the garden of a house fifty metres away, looking for a way to get in. He needed to look at the scene, to get a feel for what had happened. Jess's phone and laptop might still be inside and there could be a fragment of evidence there to help him get a location on Jacobs and where he had taken Jess.

MI5 had evacuated the occupants of each house in the cul-de-sac to get the scene under control and surrounded the entire street with yellow tape. Armed police patrolled the cordon, whilst a series of white tents dotted around Jess's property allowed the agents and the police to conduct their clean-up job away from prying smartphones and nosy neighbours. It was a complex task. Kane had always been at the sharp end of things during his career, but was aware of the complexity of the clean-up work that took place behind the scenes. Each one of the dead men was a person with family, friends, and loved ones who would want details on their whereabouts, how they had died, and obviously to take possession of the bodies for funeral arrangements.

Craven waited at the bed and breakfast in case a call came in from Andrew Moore. They wouldn't contact Andrew and notify him of the abduction until Kane could find more information. Andrew would panic, and there was little he could do to help the situation, other than agree to sell the club, which Kane thought he might just do when faced with this latest and most brutal attack upon his family. Kane doubted Phoenix would release Jess now, even if Andrew Moore agreed to sell. It was too messy and there were too many loose ends. Kane had to find Jess and get her back.

There was no way in through the front, so Kane made a long, circuitous walk to reach her back garden, avoiding the police cordon and climbing through a line of thick, green conifer trees. He cut through the gardens of houses on the same road, slipping over fences, shifting through the shadows. It was a risk, and MI5 would watch the place closely. But not too closely. It had already been the scene of ten murders and a kidnapping, so who would want to break in? It was unlikely that the perpetrators would return to the scene of the crime on the same day it was committed.

Kane had seen similar situations throughout his career. The people of Britain needed to be protected from some news. The country would descend into anarchy and chaos if people knew the full extent of what went on behind the veil of television news and newspaper reporting. Bloggers and YouTubers, who were the go-to sources of news, however fake, for the younger generation, had no access to this sort of highly complex crime. So, they would tidy up and play down the incident until Jess was found, and they would swear her to secrecy to make sure it remained that way—if they found her alive, that was.

Two MI5 agents talked together outside the house, a tall woman with a severe face, and a thin Asian man in a long coat. They talked about the bodies, and the skill level of the men who had taken them out.

"All clean shots," said the woman in a West Country accent. "Professional, two to the chest and one to the head."

"Serious shit," said the man. "The techies are looking into it all now. Why did the woman need so much protection? Who was after her and why go to such measures to get at her?"

"Well, she's gone now. Gregory said the victim is involved with a local football team."

"Gregory should hurry with the fucking coffees and keep his hypotheses to himself. The nerds will turn her life upside down. By sun-up, we'll know where she buys her lipstick, the names and addresses of her social media contacts, and all the people she called, messaged and texted in the last six months."

Kane eased past them, treading carefully so as not to make a sound. He reached the front door, pushed the handle, and slipped inside. Kane left the door slightly ajar so that it wouldn't make a sound. He could have tried to get around the back and find a way in that way, but sometimes, the most obvious entry points were least expected. Kane waited and listened for any sign of agents inside the house. Footsteps tramped across the upstairs landing, and he caught a flash of white overalls moving between the banisters.

Kane went to the kitchen, paused at the door, and scanned the room for any sign of agents. It was clear. The lights were on, and he knew guards would be in the back garden. He was still wearing his suit, and so Kane strolled into the kitchen like he belonged there. He would look more suspicious if they caught him crawling and snooping around, so he walked confidently, like he was one of them.

The kitchen island stools where he had drunk wine with Jess lay on the floor. Plants and furniture were askew and showed signs of the disturbance. He would have expected Jess to put up a fight and was proud that she had. Kane searched the granite worktops for her laptop and phone. But the agents must have already taken any devices in the house to search for clues. Something caught Kane's eye, a white business card left on top of a pile of Jess's letters on the worktop. The card contained a single phone number and an image of a hammer below it.

It was Jacobs. An innocuous card was left there amongst Jess Moore's electricity bills and a Tesco Clubcard circular. The hammer signified Mjolnir, the Norse God Thor's hammer, and the name of Kane's old MI6 counter-intelligence agency. Jacobs had once headed up Mjolnir under the code name Odin, and he was fixated on Norse mythology. Each agent had a Norse-related codename. Kane's had been Lothbrok. It was a message for Kane that only he would understand. Jacobs knew he would come looking.

Kane tucked the card into his jacket pocket

and marched out of the kitchen and towards the front door. He pushed it open, and the two MI5 agents turned to stare at him in surprise.

"Gregory's back there with the coffees," Kane said, walking past them both as though he were part of the team. "There's only one Americano and a flat white left. Best get in there before they all go. I'll watch here for a minute."

The MI5 agents glanced at each other for a moment, and the woman cast a suspicious glance at Kane but thought better of it and followed her partner inside the house. Kane's hands balled into fists as he left the house. He would call the number and play Jacobs' game. He had no choice.

THIRTY-NINE

Jess Moore ground her teeth so hard she thought they might shatter. She fought against the urge to shiver, cold and fear taking turns to wash over her body like the tide on a desolate beach. Her scalp throbbed where they had used her hair to drag Jess from her own house. A burning, stabbing sensation seared across her ribcage, making Jess want to curl up into a ball. Her face pulsed from the blows taken during the abduction, and dried blood crusted her nose and lips.

Rough, plastic rope held her hands tied behind the chair she sat upon, its hard back keeping her upright despite the protests from her hurting body. They had stuffed her into a jeep, covered her head with a black hood, and carried Jess away from Ravenford at high speed. She saw nothing on that terrifying journey, but tried to listen out for anything that might mark out where her abductors were taking her. She had counted bumps in the road and when the vehicle had turned, causing her body to lean left or right. But the journey had been too long. Jess had lost all sense of time within the dark hood, and all the bumps, twists, and turns all melded into a muddled mess in her mind.

Jess still wore the dark hood. She was cold, in some sort of large space where footsteps echoed, and she wanted to cry. She was afraid and alone. Rough men had beaten her and driven her in silence for what could have been one hour or four. The darkness under the hood seemed to have stolen her reason and ability to think. All Jess had left was her anger and her pride, and so she did not cry. She knew Phoenix was behind her abduction. Who else could it be? When her father found out she had been taken, it would wound him to the heart, and with her life being used as blackmail, it would only be a matter of time before he sold the football club and caved in to Phoenix's demands.

Footsteps emerged from the darkness, and Jess forced down the urge to whimper. She stiffened as they approached, pulling her wrists to test the rope's strength in case there was a chance to get away, but it was firm and tight, burning her skin as she twisted and pulled at the knots. The man whistled a jaunty, happy tune as he drew close, which unnerved Jess even more. He whipped the black hood away from her face, and Jess scrunched her eyes closed against the brightness of overhead lights.

"Good morning, Miss Moore," said the man in the sharp suit with the posh accent.

"What do you want with me?" Jess said. Slowly, she opened her eyes, squinting as they adjusted to the light after being in the dark for so long. She was in some sort of warehouse; she noticed a desk on her right with an old-fashioned PC and a monitor covered in dust. Behind the suited man, she could make out factory-type machinery, but she did not know what type of machines they were, except that they were large, oily, and appeared unused for some time.

"Isn't that obvious? Do we really have to play this tiresome game?"

"My father won't sell, no matter what you do to me."

"I rather think he will. You are the apple of his eye, the jam inside his doughnut. We, however, are not the people who want your precious football club. I am merely my client's weapon, and they will come to collect you later this morning. Once they send a video to your daddy of you looking so distressed, the deal will close quickly enough."

"You won't get away with this." She spoke half-heartedly, wanting to threaten the men who had hurt her.

"I already have. Or are you referring to your friend, Jack?"

"What?" His mention of Jack's name caught Jess off guard. But then she realised they must have been watching her, observing who came and went from her house, her movements and who she spoken to.

"Your friend Jack is also my friend Jack. Did you know that? Oh, yes. He and I were colleagues once, back in the good old days. I imagine you think him rather mysterious?"

"What are you talking about him for?"

"There is a chance here for me to kill two birds with one stone. Jack tried to kill me once. He took everything from me. My country cast me out into the wilderness. One day, I had access to a billion-pound counter-intelligence slush fund, and the next, I had nothing. Wounded, shot, without access to funds, home, or friends. Forgotten by a country to which I had devoted my life. But I clawed my way back, and now here I am. Fate has dealt me a fortunate hand, and this job presents not only the opportunity to be paid rather handsomely by a wealthy client, but also for revenge."

"He'll come for me," Jess said the words as a

threat, though she did not know how Jack would find her, and even if he did, what could he do against a band of ruthless killers armed with guns?

"I'm banking on it. Jack probably didn't tell you much about his past, did he?"

Jess shook her head.

"He's still a good boy. It's conditioned into him to follow orders and keep his secrets close. I am afraid that your boyfriend is a killer, a ruthless assassin, and a murderer. He's done things that would make your pretty eyes water. Despite what you might think, he is not a good man, and you most certainly cannot change him."

"Why are you telling me all of this? What do you want?"

He smiled and shrugged. "Nothing. My clients will be here soon to whisk you away to whatever fate they've got in store for you. I just thought we could have a little chat, kill the time. But so be it."

His smile dropped, and his face set into a mask of uncaring harshness. Dead eyes inside a stony face. He thrust the hood back over Jess Moore's head, and the fear came back like a tidal wave. Phoenix had already gone to extraordinary lengths to force the sale, so they would stop at nothing to drive fear into her father's heart. Jess allowed herself a shiver as she pictured the terrible things they might do to her, and she was powerless to stop them.

FORTY

Kane paced back and forth, clutching the white business card. Jacobs had left the number for him to find. It wasn't subtle, more like a sledgehammer of a message, a worm designed to wriggle into Kane's head and distort his reasoning, to cancel out his training and experience and play on his emotions. Rage clouded judgement, and Kane must ensure he acted with logical reason if he wanted to get Jess back alive.

Jacobs expected Kane to search the house, and Kane expected Jacobs to leave a breadcrumb for him to follow. There was too much bad blood between them for Jacobs and his team to disappear into the wind with Jess. Jacobs wanted Kane badly, and as he paced up and down the pavement, Kane tried to calm himself. Because he wanted to kill Jacobs—each had taken so much from the other. Jacobs had sent the team the day Sally died, and Kane had taken away Jacobs' life, his role as head of Mjolnir. There was visceral hate between them. Kane could use that to his advantage. If he could think clearly.

"Walking to and fro like that won't fix it," said Craven. He sat on a bench outside a petrol station off the dual carriageway, which led both in and out of Ravenford. "Just call the bastard."

"I could ask Cam to put a track on the number, but Jacobs will have thought of that. It's all too obvious. That worries me."

"Why does his plan have to be sneaky? He has Jess, and he wants you. He's going to tell you to meet him somewhere to exchange her life for yours. Simple as that. When you get there, he'll kill you. Or try to kill you, rather."

"Unless Phoenix gets there first."

"So, call him."

Kane stopped pacing and took out a burner mobile phone. He punched the numbers into the backlit keypad and waited as the phone processed the dial request. The tone rang three times.

"Jack?" said Jacobs cheerfully, down the phone. "Is that you?"

"Just tell me what you want."

"I want your blood, and I want you to suffer.

Like your girlfriend here is going to suffer when I hand her over to my clients. Russians can be ruthless, but I'm sure you remember that from the old days."

"You are working for Phoenix, then?"

"A man has to make a living. You took mine away."

"Why leave the number if you are going to hand her over to Phoenix, anyway?"

"To give you a sporting chance to win her back."

Jack sighed. "Give me the details."

"There's an old army base from the 1950s an hour outside London. I'll send the co-ordinates to this phone. I'll meet you there tomorrow with the girl. But that's also where I'll hand her over to my clients, and I will give you a little window to get her away before they arrive."

"What's the catch?"

"No catch. A simple exchange. Your life for hers. You stay with me, and she goes free. No tricks, though. You walk in and she walks out. Any messing around and she goes to our friend, Mr Ivanov."

"Send me the location and I'll be there."

"Midday. Sharp. Come alone. Keep this phone active so I can keep my eye on you, Jack."

Jacobs hung up and Kane dropped the phone into his jacket pocket. It was a trap, and Jacobs wasn't even pretending otherwise.

"Well?" asked Craven, standing up from the bench and rubbing a hand across his bald head.

"He wants to swap her life for mine. I hand myself in, and Jacobs will let Jess go."

"I wouldn't trust that bastard to wipe my arse, never mind release Jess Moore. He'll kill you and still hand her over to the Russians."

"But what choice do we have? We can't leave Jess there so Ivanov can torture her and send videos of her suffering to Andrew Moore until he capitulates."

"So, we go to the meeting?"

Kane nodded, but his stomach curdled at the thought of walking into Jacobs' hands. He cursed himself for getting too close to Jess Moore. He should have kept their relationship purely professional. His first responsibility was to Danny and Kim, and handing himself over to Jacobs all but guaranteed his death. Kane glanced at Craven, wondering if his friend would care for his children if he died. His offshore accounts had enough money to give them a comfortable life. Not for the first time, Kane wondered if his kids would be better off without him, anyway. He wasn't exactly father of the year.

"I will go to the meeting, Frank. You can come with me, but not into the actual base. We'll get you close in case I need to get out of there fast."

Craven smirked. "You aren't going to hand yourself in quietly, are you?"

"Not if there's even a remote chance I can get Jess out of there alive. No. Even now that I'm out of shape and middle-aged, I'm not an easy man to kill."

FORTY-ONE

McGovern hammered away at her keyboard, the monitors on her desk sparking and fizzing into life as she activated the trace on Jack Kane's phone. A satellite image of the United Kingdom flickered onto her screen and then zoomed in to pinpoint his exact location—a little blue dot in a car driving along a road in southwest England.

McGovern picked up her desk phone and dialled Mr Hermoth's number. It made flitting electronic sounds in her ear as the phone line bounced off various satellites and call-masking interfaces before ringing the actual line.

"Is it done?" asked Mr Hermoth.

"It's done. I have him pinned. I'll send you the link now."

"Good. Watch him. Use the location to zero in on his activity. If he uses any other phones, I want to know who he speaks to. If he visits any location en route to the meeting tomorrow, I want to know. Have the team send me regular updates on his location and activity."

"Yes, sir."

"We have him. Kane will come to me. By this time tomorrow, he will be a dead man. Call the Russians and set up the exchange. But tell them I want half the money now, and the rest when I hand over the woman."

"But that isn't the arrangement? They aren't exactly flexible. We exceeded their deadline for the operation and they are not happy." McGovern had dealt with Phoenix Group during the operation's latter phases and her contacts were impatient, rude, and demanding. The deal between Balder and Phoenix was to deliver Jess Moore in one piece, on time, and Phoenix would pay Balder's fee in uncut diamonds, to be delivered to a Balder agent on standby in Prague. Balder's role in the relationship was to capture Jess Moore, provide supplementary support to Phoenix and Valknut's agents on the ground in the UK, and provide various digital and spyware intelligence services, all of which came at a hefty price.

Before McGovern had joined Balder, the group had worked for Valknut, the military arm of the Phoenix Group, in various locations across the Middle East and Africa, but never in the UK.

McGovern's home, the country she had loved and worked to protect and serve her entire life. Until now.

Although she now lived in Dubai, a place which provided a host of social opportunities for one wishing to embed themselves in the expatriate culture, McGovern spent her nights alone, reading through files, familiarising herself with Balder's operational history. Its theatres of operations left a bad taste in her in mouth. But what choice did she have? Intelligence work was all she knew, and if McGovern returned to the UK, the investigation into her conduct would resume. She found herself trapped, with Balder being her only option to continue working.

McGovern picked up the phone again and took a deep breath to prepare herself for what was going to be an unpleasant call. Before she dialled, however, McGovern reflected on how the tables had turned. She had worked for the British Government for her entire career, and though some of her operational decisions might have blurred the lines between what was right and what was necessary, she had always acted in the interests of Britain's national security. Now, she was working with groups with more than questionable motives and operational directives. She was a gun for hire now, a mercenary rather than a soldier of the realm—albeit from behind a keyboard and in meeting rooms rather than battlefields.

McGovern dialled the number for the Phoenix Group in St Petersburg and tapped her fingers lightly on the desk as she waited for her opposite number to answer. The warmth of nervousness was unfamiliar and unwanted in her chest.

"Privet, kak ya mogu vam pomoch?" said the voice on the other end.

"Mr Berezov, please."

"Just one moment."

"Berezov," said a gruff, heavily accented voice after a few moments.

"I am calling from the Balder Agency. We have Jess Moore and are prepared for hand over."

"About time. We hire you people for results, not time wasting and failures. Give me the details."

"Before we go into that, we must make some changes to our initial agreement." McGovern paused, waiting for Berezov to shut her down immediately, but he said nothing. He exhaled loudly, likely smoking a cigarette, as he waited for her to finish the sentence. Berezov was a senior Phoenix executive and held a commander position inside Valknut. McGovern's research showed that he was a veteran of the Russian military, as well as an experienced businessman.

"We require fifty percent of our fee to be paid in advance of the exchange. The rest to be paid as per our original agreement."

"We already have an agreement. Why would we agree to this last-minute change?"

"Agreements change. The situation around the operation has changed. There is now a significant amount of risk attached to our activities in the UK and therefore a change to our remuneration structure is required."

"We hired you for specific tasks. Your men getting arrested delayed our plans. Now, someone has hacked into our UK facing bank accounts and stolen a significant amount of money. We hired you for a cyber security service, and yet someone robbed us?"

Another pause. "I shall need to look into that, Mr Berezov."

"So, you are not aware of the theft?"

McGovern's cheeks reddened, and she scowled at her door, vowing to drag her team across hot coals for not properly monitoring the cyber security framework for Phoenix's UK arm, Phoenix Telecoms. "I will come back to you with a report on the incident. Now, about the payment?"

"We pay you half now if you need it. But our overall bill reduces by thirty percent because of your mistake. If you fix it, and return the stolen funds to us, we pay you the rest."

"Our agreement states that…"

"Agreements change. Thirty percent less. We send courier to your man in Prague later today."

"We will return your stolen funds to you."

"See that you do, Miss McGovern. We hope you are enjoying your new life in Dubai."

The phone hung up and McGovern slowly replaced the receiver. *They know my real name.*

FORTY-TWO

Craven waited patiently in Andrew Moore's study. It was exactly the type of study Craven imagined the old man spending his evenings and weekends in, reclining on the plush leather sofa and smoking cigars as he closed important business deals. The desk was long and heavy, with a gold lamp in one corner and a large rectangular pad of blotting paper cornered with leather at its centre. The chair behind Andrew's desk and the couch across from it were of studded, creased brown leather. Bookcases lined the walls crammed with leather-backed tomes. Old copies of The Times newspaper and more recent copies of The Racing Post littered a low pine coffee table.

Muffled voices spoke in the next room, one of many rooms in Andrew Moore's sprawling home on the outskirts of Ravenford. Two women in dark-coloured pantsuits were busy briefing Andrew on MI5's investigation into his daughter's disappearance. Craven shuffled about the office, lifting an old globe and spinning it around, then examining an expensive-looking fountain pen on the desk. He glanced at gold-framed pictures on the wall of Andrew Moore with various business high-flyers, and Craven reminded himself that Moore wasn't simply an old man who ran a football club, he was an extremely wealthy, self-made millionaire.

The voices moved out into the hallway, and the front door closed heavily. Craven swallowed and brushed down the front of his jumper. The situation reminded him of breaking bad news to families back when he had been a copper on the beat, in what felt like a different life. Craven had often sat on small couches in suburban sitting rooms to impart the dreadful news of a deceased person to their relatives, and it never got easier, no matter how many times he had done it. There was always the apprehension about how to break the news, how they would take it, and the gut-wrenching look in their eyes as they realised that a son, daughter, husband or wife was gone forever.

In Craven's experience, the best way to deliver bad news was to come straight out with it. No bullshit or beating around the bush, and the same was true today. The brass office door handle turned, and Andrew Moore entered, his face looking paler and even more lined than ever.

"Mr Craven," Andrew Moore said and smiled sadly. "Did anybody offer you a drink?"

"They did, but I'm all right, thanks," Craven replied. Andrew Moore had a staff to run his sprawling mansion. There was a housekeeper, cleaners, an estate manager and an executive chef. Craven did not know what was executive about cooking a few omelettes and steaks for a wealthy old man, but this was the world of the rich, an entirely different existence to Craven's life.

"I flew back as soon as I heard the news."

"Your people told you?"

"Yes. I can't believe it has come to this. All this cloak and dagger stuff has made the situation worse... I need Jess to be OK. How did it come to this?" Andrew Moore sat down heavily on his couch, one elbow on the armrest so that he could massage the bridge of his nose.

"Phoenix has taken things to a different level. They've brought in their military people, and things have become much more dangerous."

"With all due respect, Mr Craven, that is why I brought you and Mr Kane in. To prevent this exact situation, or at the very least handle it so that no harm comes to me or my family."

"We are handling it; Jack has arranged to meet

with the abductors tomorrow and get Jess back safe."

"What? We should notify the authorities. I've spent the best part of an hour with MI5. They should take control of this meeting and ensure that it is done properly. We've gone beyond even the police now. MI5 is as serious as it gets. I'm not comfortable leaving my fate to you and Mr Kane. Forgive me, Mr Craven, but dire situations require plain speaking."

"That won't work. The abductors only want to deal with Jack. If anyone else turns up, or they get a sniff of anybody watching, we've got a problem."

"Why Jack Kane? What difference does he make to my decision to sell the club? That's what it boils down to, after all. They want the club and I have to sell, or they are going to hurt Jess. I can't have that… I can't. The club is nothing compared to Jess's wellbeing."

"If anybody can get your daughter back, it's Jack. Trust me on that, Mr Moore. Let him handle it."

"You've both made a pig's ear of it so far. I should have gone to the police earlier, or just sold the bloody football club. Then none of this need ever have happened."

"We'll make it right."

"And what if you don't? You can walk away into the sunset and leave me here to pick up the pieces. I don't know what to do."

"Give Jack tomorrow, and after that, we'll see. Hold fast, Mr Moore. Do nothing rash. You can't sell the club now after everything you have been through."

"I'll give you until tomorrow. You have until tomorrow to make it right, otherwise I'm going to MI5."

Craven shook Andrew Moore's hand and made for the door, eager to get away from the uncomfortable situation. There was steel in the old man's voice and the blaze of his eyes, evidence of the grit required to become a self-made millionaire.

"Mr Craven," said Moore as Craven was halfway out of the door. "If she dies, her blood is on your hands."

Craven nodded and left. Andrew Moore had spoken harshly. Craven and Kane weren't behind this terrible situation. They had received a request to come and help, and had responded to that call. But much of what Andrew Moore said was true. He and Kane had done little to improve the Moores' situation. Phoenix still wanted the club, and things had gone to new heights of pressure and fear. He and Kane simply had to get Jess back in one piece. If MI5 got involved in any sort of rescue attempt, then Jacobs, Phoenix and its Valknut soldiers would kill Jess, and still force Moore to sell his beloved club. Everything rested on tomorrow, and as Craven left the Moore mansion, he hoped to God that Kane could pull it off.

FORTY-THREE

Jacobs set the meeting at a disused military facility in a place called Elm Brook, south of London, between Tunbridge Wells and Eastbourne on England's southeast corner. Cameron pulled together an overview of the place with his usual attention to detail, and ability to pull detailed information from the internet. Elm Brook was once an RAF air base during the second world war, serving as a maintenance facility for US aircraft and servicemen stationed there. After the war, and during the Cold War, it became a storage facility for equipment held in reserve in case of another war in Europe. The equipment included medical supplies, mobile hospitals, protective clothing against biological and chemical weapons, rations for troops, and storage of thousands of vehicles from trucks to jeeps. When the cold war ended, the RAF and US forces phased out the site and eventually vacated it in the mid-1990s.

Cameron pulled some detailed satellite imagery including overhead pictures of Elm Brook's buildings so that Kane wasn't going into the place completely blind. It had a series of huge, disused warehouses and rows of prefabricated homes behind green plastic fencing; sprawling green fields once packed with US service jeeps sat empty. The abandoned base was now a ghost town with out-of-use housing, a bowling alley, swimming pool and basketball court.

Kane and Craven arrived at the old base with time to spare. The meeting was set for midday, but with no contact received from Jacobs since their last call, Kane wasn't sure where exactly inside the base they would hold the meeting.

"The place could be crawling with Jacobs' men," said Craven as they pulled into a lay-by half a mile from the base. Craven shifted uncomfortably in his car seat, grimacing at Kane.

"It will be," Kane replied. "Could also be full of Phoenix and Valknut men. Jacobs has arranged to meet me here and exchange my life for hers. He has Jess, so we must go through with it. Presumably, he also must hand her over to Phoenix at some point and collect his bounty, so he probably plans to kill me and then hand Jess over. But I'm still going in, no matter what the danger. Stick to the plan."

"What plan? You are going in there alone, strolling into a trap where you are certain to die, and I'm going to wait here in case you need me. That's literally our entire discussion. That isn't a plan. It's a Hail Mary at best."

"I will contact you through our earpiece radios when I need you, then you bring the car in. Don't stop, drive through the gate and follow my instructions. I've left you the Glock in case you run into any trouble. There are seven rounds left in the magazine, and you know how to use it."

"I know how to pull the trigger, and that's about it. If you suspect Jacobs intends to kill you, which is so obviously his fucking plan that he might as well come right out and say it, how are you going to get Jess out and save your own life?"

"I imagine that's exactly what he intends, Frank. But I can't leave her there. Once they get what they want, there's a high chance Phoenix and Valknut will kill Jess."

Craven shook his head, and rubbed and pressed his forefinger and thumb into his eyes. "There's fuck all the police can do about it, and MI5 are investigating. Ever thought that we should leave them to it?"

"It's gone too far for that now. Perhaps if it was only Phoenix and the Moores. But you know as well as I that this is personal with Jacobs. He wants me dead, so he and I are intertwined in this whole business."

"I assume you aren't going to saunter in there and let the bastard kill you?"

"No. We have no idea where they are holding her inside the base. Could be in one of the old residential buildings, or the basketball court. Could be the bowling alley, swimming pool, or a warehouse. When he spots me coming in via whatever surveillance he has in place, Jacobs will call and give me instructions. When I get to the location, his men will disarm me, and Jacobs will do his worst."

"Why can't you shoot your way in?"

"In case they hurt Jess. I need to see her. Once they take me to her, or I have an idea where she is, I must try to figure a way to get her out."

"Before they kill you."

"Yes."

"I'll be ready. You tell me to come, and I'll come like the fucking cavalry in a cowboy film."

"Keep in touch with Cameron. He's watching through satellite imagery. Brief me over the comms if anything out of the ordinary happens."

"Good luck, Jack."

Kane smiled at his friend with a confidence

he didn't feel. He got out of the car and started the walk towards the disused army base. Sycamore trees lined the approach road, with old rotting helicopter-blade seeds thick in the gutters, and the breeze shook the leafy boughs. Kane checked the Beretta in its hip holster. He had eleven rounds left, plus a spare magazine. He was marching into a bear-pit, a certain trap, but he had no choice. Kane straightened his suit jacket and adjusted the straps on the bullet-proof vest he wore beneath his shirt. He walked confidently towards the green wire fencing and paused before an old gate complex, complete with an empty guard hut and a barrier which, when the base was operational, the US Army guards would raise and lower to allow access to authorised vehicles. Now graffiti covered the hut, its windows left jagged and smashed by vandals.

Kane paused at the entrance and crossed his hands in front of him, waiting for the call. Sure enough, after less than thirty seconds, the burner phone rumbled in his pocket and played its jaunty digital ringtone.

"Jacobs?" Kane said into the handset.

"Jack!" Jacobs replied effusively. "So glad you could make it. We are waiting for you in the sports hall. I'll send a chap to pick you up."

Kane hung up the phone to deny Jacobs another of his glib remarks, stepped underneath the barrier, and waited for his ride. It was time.

FORTY-FOUR

A grey Mercedes jeep with blacked-out windows arrived at the guard hut five minutes later from inside the base. Its shining tyres screeched on the road as it turned quickly around the small roundabout beyond the entrance barrier. The jeep came to an abrupt stop, and a broad-shouldered man in dark combat trousers and a navy jumper hopped out of the passenger seat. The man had a long, serious face, and a mashed nose broken in some distant fight. He pointed a Glock fitted with a suppressor at Kane and gestured to the front passenger seat. Kane walked calmly around the barrier, got in, and long-face sat directly behind him in the rear passenger seat.

The driver was a heavy-set black man in similar clothes and dreadlocks tied back in a loose ponytail. He leant back comfortably in the driving seat, without his seatbelt fastened, and set off towards the meeting, speeding at fifty miles per hour along the base's narrow roads. They hadn't frisked Kane; he presumed that would happen outside of the meeting place. He could sense the Glock pointing at him from the back seat.

The driver took the manual gearstick through the motions as they turned a sharp bend, dropping it to second and shifting back up fifth, skipping fourth. A faded sign on the roadside directed Kane to the basketball court, located on the edge of the base's housing section. Kane closed his eyes and recalled the base's overhead layout. Kane was sure from their direction that the meeting would take place at the basketball court. There were no other significant buildings in that location. That, at least, was information Kane could work with.

The driver took another bend almost too fast, thrusting Kane against the passenger door window as the jeep made the turn. In his mind, he visualised stepping into a vast basketball court. His footsteps reverberated on the floor adorned with bright court lines. In front of him stood armed men, leaving him entirely vulnerable to Jacobs' mercy. What could he do in that situation but die? He had to get into the court with his gun and bring the fight to Jacobs.

The jeep sped around another bend and Kane set his jaw. Improvisation was the key to surviving desperate situations, or so he had learned during his time in the regiment and as an MI6 agent. Missions often went wrong, and the operators must improvise to stay alive and complete their mission. So, despite the risk to his own and to Jess Moore's life, Kane decided to take a chance.

The driver dropped the gearstick into second and leaned into the left turn. Just as he spun the wheel, Kane reached over and yanked on the handbrake. The driver shouted and wrestled with the steering to keep the jeep steady. The broken-nosed man behind Kane slid across the back seat and Kane grabbed the steering wheel and pulled hard towards him. Before the driver could right the vehicle, it toppled onto its side.

Metal scrunched and creaked on the tarmac. Kane, long face, and the driver all tumbled about in the vehicle's cabin like ice in a cocktail shaker. None wore seatbelts, and Kane himself only knew what he was about to do in the split second before he acted. Chaos birthed opportunity and fear, and it was time for Kane to bring some chaos. The vehicle half rolled again and came to rest with the passenger side lying directly on the road. The driver flailed about with his arms, his back resting in Kane's lap. Kane wrapped his hands quickly around the driver's skull and broke his neck with one savage twist and a sickening crunch.

Long face shouted something muffled from the back seat, and Kane turned to see the man desperately trying to push himself away from the door. The car's flip tangled his legs in the footwell, and his gun sat awkwardly, pressed against his own midriff. Kane clambered around the dead driver and stamped down hard on broken-nose's chest.

"You fucking bastard!" spat broken-nose, in a Cockney accent. Kane stamped on his face so hard that his skull cracked the window beneath him. Long face groaned, and Kane wrestled the Glock from his grip, shot him once in the guts and again in the face. The silencer muffled the gunshots so that they spat rather than boomed in the enclosed space. Neither man wore a radio, but Kane found a short knife strapped around the dead driver's ankle, so he took it and fitted it to his own leg.

Jacobs' men would know something was up within minutes, so Kane climbed out of the crashed jeep and ran along the cement pathway towards the basketball court. His neck and shoulders ached from the crash, but he carried the silenced Glock still in his hand, and he had a few moments to surprise Jacobs before all hell broke loose. Weeds and tufts of grass grew between the pavement slabs where US soldiers and their families had once lived their lives. Kane sprinted towards the basketball court until its whitewashed walls, now cracked and faded to grey, emerged above the lines of identical, pre-fabricated, empty houses.

Kane veered left, jumping over a waist-high garden fence, and then another so that he could come at the court building from the back. Jacobs expected Kane to come quietly, but he was in for a shock. Kane jumped over a border fence and pushed his way through a hedgerow, blocking its scraping, clawing twigs with his forearm. He emerged into a grass-filled gulley, running between the basketball court building and the neat rows of single-storey housing. Kane ran up the gulley's north side until he came up beside the court building then followed along its perimeter until he reached the front door.

Two men in combat trousers stood guard, both with handguns holstered at their hips and peering along the road in the direction from which they expected the jeep to arrive. Kane lifted the Glock and shot the closest man in the midriff, and he fell, groaning in pain. The second man instinctively ducked and rolled, which was the right thing to do, and the two shots Kane fired at him missed. Kane took three steps forward with the gun raised, staring down its sight towards the target. The second man dashed for the door and Kane fired another shot, this time taking the man between the shoulder blades. Kane turned and shot the first man again in the forehead.

Kane turned back to the second man just in time to meet a wild lunge for his gun. He wore body armour, so the bullet had not penetrated his flesh, and he grabbed Kane's gun with his right hand whilst trying to draw his own with his left. He was strong, and his blue eyes bore into Kane's with the desperation of a man fighting for his life. Kane kicked his shin, then hooked his foot around a standing leg and threw the man over his hip. He landed heavily and Kane shot him in the throat. Red blood spattered the pavement like a dropped a can of paint, oozing into the gaps between the flagstones as the dying man shuddered in his death throes.

The double-doors to the basketball court were unlocked and Kane slipped inside. Keeping his gun raised, he moved alongside a long desk and walls painted pale blue with old, faded posters of basketball stars like Michael Jordan and Charles Barkley. Heavy pine doors led to the basketball court itself, and through a narrow window slit in each door, Kane could make out the golden hardwood floors and brightly painted court markings. To his right, a staircase wound away from the entrance hall and Kane surmised it must lead to an overhead spectator gallery, so he ran towards the stairs and took them two at a time.

Moments later, Kane found himself in a

gallery of three rows of six plastic seats. He kept low, moving towards the edge, then peered over the gallery wall. Jess Moore sat on a chair in the centre of the court, her hands tied behind her back and her face a pale mask of fear. Jacobs stood close by in a finely tailored suit, talking to a burly man in the now familiar combat trousers and jumper. Another man guarded a rear exit. Jacobs checked his watch and shook his head, and nodded to the burly man who strode across the court towards the front doors. His shoes squeaked on the polished wood, and he beckoned to two more of Jacobs' operators from the court's side walls.

Just as they opened the doors into the sports hall's entranceway, Kane leapt over the viewing gallery and landed, rolling on the basketball court to break his fall. Jacobs stared at him open-mouthed, and Kane stood, pointing the silenced Glock at Jacobs' chest.

FORTY-FIVE

Craven pressed his finger onto the small radio receiver in his ear, fiddling with the unit until it sat more comfortably. Waiting for Kane to make contact was taking an eternity. He found it hard to get used to any of the contraptions and gadgets Kane constantly came up with. Back in Craven's day, he carried a proper police radio in his car—one you had to lift and click to talk. Everything was simpler back then. It worked. Why did people always want to make things smaller? Modern gadgets were OK for people with little, gentle fingers, but Craven was a big man with thick and clumsy fingers. Craven worried that if he ran, the radio might fall out of his ear, and he wouldn't notice until it was too late. He tutted and shook his head, needing something to distract him from the anxious wait, so he turned on the car radio and listened to two old footballers on Radio 5 Live talking about the big matches coming up over the weekend.

Barb would collect Danny and Kim again on Friday if Craven and Kane were still not home, and Craven worried about the kids and their relationship with their father. Kane took them for days out whenever possible, but he was hardly the stay-at-home dad type. He could be fun when he wanted to be, and Craven had seen Jack playing with Danny and Kim in the swimming pool, splashing and dunking one another. Kane played Monopoly and other games with his children, and they watched movies together. But Kane was away often, and it was tough for Danny and Kim to be in boarding school all week in a foreign country with no friends and no familiar face to talk to until Fridays. At least then Barb would collect and spoil them for the weekend.

Craven resolved to call Barbara that evening and see how she was, how her hospital appointments were going and how the kids had seemed over the last weekend. He missed her smiling face, the cup of tea and slices of toast Barb made for him each morning. He had always imagined his retirement as time spent reading, walking his dog, and relaxing with Barb. But here he was, dodging bullets and getting beat up when he should be watching re-runs of Sharpe on the telly in his living room. Craven drummed his fingers on the steering wheel and fiddled with his earpiece again. Kane had been gone for ten minutes, and Craven didn't want to miss the call when it came. He thought about turning the engine on to keep it running in case he had to hurry but decided against it.

The pundits on the radio were ranting about a player Craven had never heard of, their voices getting higher in pitch the angrier their discussion became, so he turned the radio off. Craven sighed and glanced up and down the road leading to the base.

"Fuck," Craven whispered. A line of ten men in black combat clothing and body armour ran across the road twenty-five metres ahead of him in a long line, like a column of ants. They wore balaclavas, and each carried a small machine gun strapped to his chest. They crossed the road, seeming not to notice him waiting in the car, and each man came to a stop with his back leaning against the base's green wire perimeter fence. A few moments passed, and then the men filtered through a circular hole they had cut in the fencing before disappearing inside the base at a flat run.

"Cameron," Craven said, touching his earpiece. "Did you see that? Looks like a bloody army squadron just entered the base."

"I saw it," Cameron replied. "They are jamming the satellite signal, so I've lost them now. It looks like MI5 or MI6 to me, Frank. Best get out of there quickly."

"How the fuck did they find this place?" Then it dawned on him. The MI5 agents at Andrew Moore's house. What if Moore had caved in out of fear of Jess's life and had told them everything? If so, then it was possible that the two MI5 women at Moore's house had placed a tracker upon Craven's car outside Andrew Moore's house whilst he was inside talking to the old man.

"It doesn't matter now; they are here, and I have lost all visuals. It's down to you and Jack now."

Then, as Craven's earpiece went quiet, a throbbing, vibrating sound replaced Cameron's voice. A repetitive whump-whump sound which grew louder and louder.

Craven craned his neck to look out of the car windows but could see no sign of anything making the noise, but its noise grew louder and closer. Craven opened the car door and stepped outside. The sound was shocking in the open air, and he took two steps away from the car and the surrounding sycamore trees to peer upwards. Craven shielded his eyes with his hands, gazing into the pastel blue, cloudless sky. The noise could only come from above. There wasn't much around the old base other than the road leading up to it from a nearby dual carriageway, so he would have seen anything approaching on the ground.

A sudden, but sustained gust of wind buffeted Craven, and then his head shrank into his neck as a helicopter thundered overhead, so close that it violently shook dozens of swirling sycamore seeds from the trees. Craven followed the helicopter's path, and cursed as the helicopter flew over the old army base, slowed and descended. He touched his earpiece and shouted to get Kane's attention, but then almost fell over as another helicopter whizzed over his head, lower this time, its sound brutally loud.

"Jack, Jack," Craven shouted, desperate to be heard over the roar of the helicopter's rotor blades.

Craven jumped into the car for a quieter space to get in touch with Kane. "Jack, it's Frank. Can you hear me? Over."

Craven paused. Nothing. He slammed his hands on the steering wheel. Two helicopters landing in the base meant trouble. More enemies had come to stop Jack from getting out of there with Jess.

"Jack, I don't know if you can read me, but there are two fucking helicopters landing inside the base right now. I can't see how many men are inside, but it can't be good. A team of MI5 soldiers has gone inside the gate. It's about to kick off like

World War Three. Get out of there, now. If I don't hear from you soon, I'm coming in."

Craven opened the glove box and pulled out the black gun. He looked it over, holding the grip. Even touching the thing made him uncomfortable. Kane was able to take a gun like that apart and rebuild it in minutes, but Craven didn't even know what type of gun it was, or how many bullets it could bloody fire. Craven sighed and placed the gun on the passenger seat. He forced himself to calm down, focusing on Kane's instructions. It was a Glock with seven bullets in the magazine. Only seven.

Guns and violence were Kane's thing, not his. Craven had received firearms training back when he was on the serious and organised crime squad, and he would shoot if he had to. But badly, and he didn't relish the thought. The men he and Kane faced were Valknut soldiers and MI5 agents, as familiar with guns as Craven was with investigation and interview techniques. Craven was a big man, and over the years, he'd developed his own way of dealing with criminal scum on the streets of Manchester and Liverpool. He could look after himself, or at least Craven believed so. Craven could hold his own fighting against normal people, but not the special forces types Kane was used to dealing with. That was a different kettle of fish altogether compared to a scraggly, tracksuit-wearing drug dealer in

Stockport.

The second helicopter turned slowly in mid-air and began its descent. Craven did not know how many men travelled in those helicopters, but whether it was three men or thirteen, they were more enemies to get in Kane's way. Too many, even for Kane to take on alone.

"Fuck it," said Craven. He gunned the accelerator and raced the car towards the old army base. His friend needed him, and Craven would not sit and wait whilst they shot Kane to pieces.

FORTY-SIX

"Drop your guns," said Kane, pointing the silenced Glock at Jacobs, and then at the short, stocky man guarding the rear entrance to the basketball court, who stared belligerently back at him with a curled lip and hard eyes.

"Don't be a fool, Jack," said Jacobs, in his best attempt at remaining unruffled despite the gun barrel pointing at his chest. "You don't stand a chance. Lower your gun and let's talk about this sensibly. Once Phoenix comes for her, there's no going back."

Kane shot the stocky man behind Jacobs in the solar plexus of his body armour. He fell to the polished wood floor, gasping for air and clutching at his chest. The sound of the silenced shot echoed around the court, and Jacobs jumped, surprised at the sudden escalation of serious violence.

"The next one goes in his head, and the one after that in your kneecap," said Kane.

Jacobs' patrician face slipped from its mask of relaxed calm. It twisted into a rictus of hate for a fleeting moment, but he mastered himself once again and forced a smile.

"Very well." Jacobs dropped his gun, and it clattered on the court floor. Kane rose and moved quickly towards Jess, who just stared at him with big, frightened eyes. "But you are making a big mistake. I have men returning any moment. You can't possibly have any hope of getting out of here in one piece. It didn't have to be like this, it was supposed to be a simple exchange, you for her. But you were always that little bit too keen to fight, weren't you, Jack? You always chose violence, even if there were other options. Your missions always ended in blood, and today is no different."

"You talk too much. Get your man there and stand over by the far wall." Kane gestured towards the beige-painted brick wall to his right. Jacobs held up his hands and shrugged. He strode over to the stocky man, who was still choking from the force of the bullet to his protected chest. Jacobs helped his man to his feet, and they stood, glowering at Kane.

Jacobs' words cut deep. Kane had never thought of himself as an overly violent man. He had known soldiers in the regiment who had loved to get their guns off, no matter the cost. Kane wasn't one of those men. The missions he had fought required lethal force. That was when he was called in, when all other methods of resolving a situation had failed. Or so he hoped. Briefings from decades ago suddenly whirred around his head, discussions on ways to enter or exit a particular target location, questioning himself whether he had sought hard enough for ways to not kill and still complete his objective. Had he always chosen violence? The truth was a hard one, something he had never considered before because it had been so normalised back then. Kane had chosen violence, sought it, enjoyed it, and became an expert at it. So, when things turned bad, when there was no other solution, they had sent Jack Kane in to fix it the only way he knew how.

Kane shook his head to clear out the soul-searching fog, the worm planted in his head by Jacobs. "It's going to be all right, Jess. I'm here now."

Jess looked away from him. Her bottom lip trembled, and she sobbed silently. Kane snapped open the cable ties at her wrists and helped her rise from the chair. He tucked one hand beneath her arm and helped Jess rise to her feet.

"I thought they were going to kill me," she said through wet sniffs. "Is my dad OK?"

"Andrew is fine. He's just worried about you, that's all. Come on, we must get out of here quickly."

He turned Jess around and led her towards the rear doors. There were two emergency exit doors closed by pressable bars across the middle with the words *Emergency Only* plastered in green above them.

"There's no way out, Jack," called Jacobs, the sound of his voice echoing off the high iron rafters of the basketball court roof. "You're going to get the girl killed."

"We have to hurry before his men come back," said Kane, leading Jess towards the double doors. He could have followed the men as they left the court and attacked them in the entranceway, but that way could easily bog him down in a gunfight, wasting precious time—better to get Jess out into the open. Outside, Kane would have a better chance at evasion. There were more hiding places amongst the many empty houses and buildings and Kane could work his way back towards the entrance of the base.

The doors on the opposite side of the basketball court crashed open, and Jacobs' three men came charging into the basketball court with their pistols raised and ready to shoot.

"Hold your fire!" Jacobs bellowed. "You might hit the girl."

"We have men down, sir," said the leading man in an American accent, keeping his eyes and his weapon firmly on Kane. "There's more, sir. The British Government is here, ten heavily armed operators. It's time to get out of here." The man stopped and turned as doors opened and slammed somewhere in the building behind him.

"Jack, Jack," came Craven's voice, shouting in Kane's earpiece.

The entrance doors opened a crack, and two flash bang grenades flew in and bounced on the basketball court surface. Everyone inside stared at them in shocked fear. Kane knelt, pulling Jess close to him, burying her head in his chest. He closed his eyes and covered his ears, just as the grenades exploded, filling the hall with an eye-searing, blinding light and a bang like the sounds of two trucks crashing at top speed.

The doors smashed open, and a line of men clad all in black entered, running in a low crouch with their weapons raised. Each followed the last with a hand on the shoulder of the man before him. Professionals come to recover Jess from her captors.

"Everybody on the fucking ground!" shouted a northern English voice. "Now! We are MI5, here by order of the British Government, and you are all under arrest."

Kane saw no way out of the situation. There were too many MI5 operators for him to evade. He remained on his knees, ready to lie down and let the MI5 force rescue Jess and take her to safety. It was for the best. The kidnapping would be over, and she would be back with her father before nightfall, safe and warm. Phoenix was a different question. He doubted they would give up so easily. Perhaps MI5 could warn them off or order the Football Association not to ratify the takeover, even if Phoenix forced the sale. But what would become of Jack Kane? He would fall into government hands, and he could not be sure they wouldn't hold him to account for all that had happened with Mjolnir. That was a dangerous game. Perhaps they would welcome his testimony about his former employers, or perhaps they would end him—sweep an inconvenient problem under the rug. All those possibilities raced through Kane's head as he prepared to surrender.

Kane dropped the Glock, and the weapon clattered onto the hardwood floor. The moment he was about to lie down and give himself up, a roar from above stopped him. He glanced around as the MI5 agents rounded up Jacobs and his men on the basketball court. Something was off. Something dangerous set the hair on the back of Kane's neck prickling and he picked up his gun.

Suddenly, the sound of a chopper thundered

overhead as though it came from nowhere. Kane glanced upwards, just in time to see the grime covered skylight shatter into a thousand pieces. Two thick, black ropes tumbled through the open space and the sound of helicopter blades thrumming was deafening. Jess screamed and Kane dashed to her, pulling her close to him. Two men in military gear rappelled down the black ropes, clad in black and with MP5 type weapons strapped to their chests. The MI5 agents looked at one another in confusion, roared orders at the rappelling soldiers, and then everything turned to chaos. One man on the rope opened fire, shooting the MI5 commander in the face in a spray of bright blood. More guns went off, and the basketball court echoed and shook with the carnage.

Kane stared at the military-trained soldiers who had burst through the skylight. It was the Russians coming to collect Jess. It had to be. Kane pulled Jess with him, ignoring the bullets flying across the basketball court like it was the D-Day landings, hammering into the concrete walls, filling the enclosed space with ear-shattering noise. He kicked open the emergency exit doors and pushed Jess into the bright sunlight beyond, and straight into the arms of the man with the glasses, Valery Ivanov. Ivanov looked surprised for a moment, then mildly amused as he grabbed Jess Moore and thrust her back towards a line of four men standing behind him. Kane reached out desperately for Jess, but she was beyond his reach and in the arms of their enemies. He surged forward, but Ivanov front kicked him hard in the chest, sending Kane flying back through the doors and into the furious gunfight inside the building.

Ivanov drew his weapon and opened fire on the MI5 operators, joining the men on the fast ropes and Jacobs' men, who now surrounded the British agents, hammering them with a barrage of brutal gunfire.

Kane landed heavily on his back inside the basketball court. Craven's voice rattled in his earpiece, but the roar of the helicopter overhead and the surrounding battle drowned the sound out. More armed men rappelled down the black ropes and Kane raised his gun. He must fight, or he would die where he lay. He shot the first man down the rope in the groin, sat up and shot at Ivanov, but the man in glasses was already moving with catlike speed away from the doorway. Kane spun and fired quickly at Jacobs and shot out the knee of one of Jacobs' men to give the MI5 men a fighting chance. Kane rolled and sprang to his feet and squeezed off another shot. Jacobs shielded himself with his arms and dived behind the stocky man next to him. Gunfire burst through the basketball court and a bullet fizzed across the hardwood floor, with more bullets thunking into the walls.

Valknut and MI5 had come to the meeting with military force, and Kane found himself caught in the crossfire. They had Jess, and to get her, Kane had to fight his way through a hail of bullets and half a dozen Valknut special forces soldiers. His mind raced and time slowed. The only way to survive was to attack, and so Kane did what he was trained to do, what he was born to do. He snarled and attacked his enemies with ruthless, brutal violence.

FORTY-SEVEN

Kane knelt, half-turned and fired three shots at a fire extinguisher on the western wall. The first two shots missed, hitting the cinder block and cement wall in a spray of debris. His third shot hit home, and the extinguisher popped from the wall as it pumped out a stream of thick cloud. The red cylinder spun as it hit the floor and Kane rolled backwards towards the centre of the court.

Bullets rattled around him, men shouted, and the deafening whir of helicopter blades came from above. Kane fired once at the retreating figure of Ivanov and the doors, and turned to empty the Glock's magazine into the soldiers who had rappelled from the black, fast ropes. The men retreated in a controlled manner, holding their MP5 weapons ready, but refrained from firing to avoid hitting Ivanov and his men on the fire escape. Two of them fell under fire from three MI5 agents left standing, and then the Valknut gunmen turned their firepower on the MI5 men, peppering them with a relentless volley of bullets.

Kane used that hesitation to his advantage. Due to the crossfire, only the men at the main entrance were able to shoot at him. Kane then positioned himself between the crossfire by shifting to his left. Jacobs had a clean shot, the only enemy who could fire without fear of hitting his own. However, he dropped his gun and Kane hoped to escape the chaos before Jacobs could retrieve it. Kane whipped the Glock free from its holster at his waist and fired three more rounds at the Phoenix men.

The black ropes dangled before him, and the black helicopter chassis became visible overhead through the shattered skylight. Kane wrapped his arm around one of the fast ropes and shot twice at the helicopter, hitting its underside with a metallic clang. The helicopter surged upwards and backwards as the pilot took evasive manoeuvres in the face of gunfire he clearly had not expected. The rope yanked Kane off his feet and as he rose, he coiled his left leg around the rope to keep himself secure. He shot up into the air—figures below him shouted and fought.

Smoke from the burst fire extinguisher swirled about the court, and Kane shot once at all four corners of the room as he hurtled towards the skylight. He held his breath, gripping the rope tightly, hoping that he hadn't rushed into a huge mistake. MI5 was outnumbered and outgunned, almost defeated as Kane surged up and out of the basketball court, desperately holding onto the rope. He felt for the fallen MI5 men; they were the good guys, and he could easily have been one of them in another life. None of them deserved to die, but all knew the risks whenever they picked up a firearm and went into battle.

Grabbing the rope was a ludicrous risk, but Kane had little choice unless he wanted to join the dead. The personnel in the chopper might easily unhook the ropes, or Kane could hit the roof on the way out and fall to his death. But as the furious fire of fear burned in his guts, Kane found himself lifted out of the basketball court and out into the crisp air above. The helicopter veered hard away from the sports hall and Kane let go of the rope, landing hard on a ridged, corrugated roof. He rolled and grunted as the impact bruised his ribs and shoulder. The still healing gunshot wound on his hip stretched and burned, but Kane ignored the pain.

Kane slid down the roof on his back, gun in hand, heading towards the fire exit side of the building. He peered over the edge, one foot braced against the guttering to stop himself from falling over the edge. He searched the street for any sign of Jess. Nothing to his left, but to his right, four men marched quickly away from the sports hall with Jess at their centre, heading towards the swimming pool. Below him, Ivanov and three more enemies stared and pointed at the roof and the helicopter with weapons drawn.

Smoke from the fire extinguisher billowed up out of the smashed skylight to be snatched away by the light breeze, and Kane shuffled along the old roof, heading for the eastern side of the basketball court. He had to get down and follow the men who had Jess, but avoid Ivanov and his Valknut soldiers. Kane was no good to Jess dead, but he was outnumbered and outgunned. He reached the eastern wall and peered over the edge in search of a way down. Kane shuffled further along the roof's edge then he lowered himself down until he hung from the gutter, shoes scraping against the wall as he sought purchase.

Kane found the window ledge with his left foot and braced himself with his feet. Carefully, he lowered himself down over the edge until he could grab the top of the window with his right hand. From there, Kane crouched into the sill and let himself drop onto the overgrown grass verge below. He landed with a grunt, rolled to absorb the impact and set off at a flat run, in pursuit of the men who had Jess.

"Jack?" shouted Craven in the earpiece. "What

the fuck is going in there?"

"Frank, it's time to make your entrance. Don't stop for the road barrier… just drive through it. I need you to meet me by the swimming pool."

"Where the fuck is that?"

"You'll find it."

Kane sprinted along the cracked pavement and alongside a row of abandoned houses. More shouting behind him, followed by the crackle of gunfire. He risked a look over his shoulder and Ivanov led the chase, followed by three of his men. Kane ran as hard as he could, desperate to get to Jess before they whisked her away to certain death.

FORTY-EIGHT

Craven stamped his foot down on the accelerator, and the car sped towards the air base. He gripped the steering wheel in two sweaty hands and kept the vehicle heading forwards. Kane needed him, and it was time for Craven to act. He glanced down at the gun on the passenger seat, its shiny frame and sleek grip menacing. Craven hoped he wouldn't have to fire it.

Sycamore trees whipped by in a blur as the engine roared at high speed. Craven turned a sharp bend, wrestling with the car's back-end as it spun around behind him. He broke hard, shifted from third gear into second, released the clutch, and stomped on the accelerator again. The entrance to the military base loomed up before him, an old guard hut complete with manual traffic barrier criss-crossed in faded red and black chevrons. Craven clenched his teeth and hoped he wasn't driving to his death. Barb needed him, and he needed her.

The car picked up speed and Craven shifted the gearstick into fifth, skipping fourth gear completely. The barrier seemed to grow larger as Craven approached. He checked the speedometer, and he was flying along at sixty miles an hour. The needle pushed upwards towards seventy and Craven ground his teeth, tensing his shoulders for impact.

"Bastards!" Craven shouted, more for courage than at his enemies, and the car smashed into the traffic barrier, sending woodchips and chunks bouncing off the windscreen and bonnet to fly over the car's roof. The impact barely even jolted the car, and Craven allowed himself a little laugh at his success before realising that a roundabout came hurtling towards him. He crushed his left foot into the brake pedal, turned the steering wheel and the car screeched around with its tyres smoking. The car bludgeoned its way over the roundabout, throwing Craven up and down like a rag doll, before crashing bumper first into the road again.

Craven laughed, half at the thrill, and half out of sheer surprise that he hadn't crashed yet. He sped along the deserted road, past rows of prefabricated, grey houses until he saw signs for the basketball court and the swimming pool in opposite directions. Craven turned the vehicle right, away from the basketball court and towards a long, low, bone- white building, which the signposts showed was the swimming pool. To his right, a helicopter landed noisily in a field two hundred yards away and its rotors shook the treetops as though they were a child's rattle.

"Jack, it's Craven, come in?" he shouted, touching his earpiece with his right hand and keeping his left on the steering wheel. Four people ran across the road in front of him, three men and one woman. It was Jess Moore, led by hard-looking men with guns. He slammed on the brakes, bringing the car to a sudden halt. One man with Jess flashed Craven a murderous look but continued on his way.

"Where are you?" Kane's voice crackled in Craven's ear.

"I'm inside the base, by the swimming pool. I can see Jess being led in there by three men."

"They are probably holding her there whilst they try to deal with me. You go in and get her, whilst I lead Jacobs and Ivanov away from her."

"Me? Get her?" Craven thought he was hearing incorrectly.

"It has to be you, Frank. There's too many for me to fight alone. I'll draw most of them off and you get Jess out of the swimming pool building. Don't wait for me. Get her and get out."

"For fuck's sakes," said Craven, and moved the car ahead at a crawl, turning into a small car park outside of the swimming pool building. The men bustled Jess inside through old, metallic doors and Craven stopped the car and picked up the gun. He wasn't ready for this, but he had no choice. Jess and Jack needed him. So, he stepped out of the car, tucked the gun into the waistband of his chinos and covered it with his jumper. Craven ran around the back of the car and took a wide route towards the swimming pool doors. He waited for two minutes, already out of breath and sweating hard. Craven checked behind the car in case any more of the enemy approached. Once satisfied that he only had to face the three men inside the building, Craven took four deep breaths and ran inside.

FORTY-NINE

Kane turned away from the swimming pool and paused in the road, staring along the faded painted lines and knots of grass poking through the cracks in the tarmac. Valery Ivanov came running around a bend flanked by four of his men and Kane waited until he was sure they saw him. Ivanov paused and fixed Kane with a cold, dead stare, which Kane returned. Two warriors facing off across an empty street. An understanding passed between them, and even from fifty paces, Kane noticed the smile playing at the corner of Ivanov's hard mouth.

Suddenly, Kane broke into a flat run away from them, and his enemies followed. It was the last throw of the dice to lure Ivanov in by plucking the strings of his soldier's pride. Ivanov was a warrior, and would find it hard, if not impossible, to refuse the chance and challenge to go up against Kane. They had scuffled before, like two stags in the forest, sizing one another up, each recognising the savagery in the other. If Kane could draw the dangerous Ivanov away from Jess, then he gave Craven a chance to get her away. So Kane ran across a verge so overgrown with grass that it had become like a meadow, heavy with thick grass and wildflowers.

A gunshot thundered behind him, and Kane zigzagged his run until he reached the glass-.fronted entrance to the base's bowling alley. The doors were locked shut, so Kane broke the glass panel with the butt of his gun and climbed through the shattered pane. He turned and fired twice at his pursuers, scattering them across the alley car park. Kane ran into the bowling alley, past a plastic-topped desk and small wooden box squares behind it filled with dusty red and blue bowling shoes. He came to the alleys themselves, eight lanes of long hardwood-panelled flooring with couches at the front end, and the pin-stacking mechanisms at the other.

Russian voices barked at the doorway in hurried tones. Kane jumped over the desk and slipped into the backroom area comprising a small kitchen, an office, and an electrical panel. He flipped open the green electrical fuse-board cover, revealing small white fuse levers with names written beside each one on labels in faded blue biro. Kane clicked one that read *lights*, the second which read *kitchen*, and then each one in order. Lights flickered on in the alley and a song by Vanilla Ice played over the tannoy, evoking the atmosphere of a Friday night twenty years ago when the base was at its prime.

Kane edged his way out of the control room, keeping low with his gun drawn. He checked the magazine, and he had four bullets plus one in the chamber. Kane peered around the side of the front desk and spied Ivanov creeping towards the bowling lanes with a silenced pistol in his hand. Another two men fanned out to Ivanov's right, and they spread out to clear the building. A man sniffed to clear his nose, so close that he was almost on top of Kane. Kane silently shifted backwards and passed the gun from his right to his left hand, and drew the knife strapped to his ankle with his right hand.

A combat boot stepped carefully past the desk, followed by a leg, and then a bulky man appeared, sweeping the space with his gun in front of his face. He moved professionally, like a tiger stalking its prey, but made one fatal mistake. He didn't look down.

Kane launched himself upwards, driving the knife into the enemy's throat and ripping the blade sideways to tear out his gullet. The wounded man shook, and his eyes popped wide with terror. Kane caught the weight of his body as he fell and lowered it carefully to the dusty carpet. He stared at Kane, body twitching and shaking his head as his life-blood pulsed from the terrible wound. Kane waited with him, watching the light go out from his enemy's eyes. A man who would have killed him without a second thought. The dying man's hands fell away from his throat caked in dark blood, and Kane noticed the Valknut skull symbol tattooed on his wrist. He took the man's weapon and crawled around the desk, hunting the rest of Ivanov's men.

The bowling alley's light cast the place in a blue hue, whilst the lanes themselves were old-fashioned—wood for the lanes and leather for the couches. No fancy lighting or frills, just the bare minimum to make the place authentic and comfortable. In front of each lane, there were racks of heavy bowling balls that brought back memories of Kane taking Danny and Kim bowling with Sally on weekends in what felt like a different life. Kane trained his gun on the closest of Ivanov's men, when he realised one was missing. He turned just in time to stare down the barrel of a gun ten yards away from him. Kane cursed and rolled away, and the chipboard desk exploded beside his head as a bullet ripped through it.

A shouted warning, followed by more gunfire. Kane sat with his back against the desk, trapped by Ivanov and his Valknut soldiers. Battering gunfire hammered into the desk, and the enemy closed in around him. There was no way out, no windows or back entrances. This was it. Kane found himself outnumbered and trapped.

FIFTY

The swimming pool stank of chlorine, even though it had been out of use for years. Craven crept through the corridor of changing rooms, little more than thick plastic curtains shielding single-benched cubicles large enough for one person to get changed in private. His breath came in ragged, shallow gasps, and Craven paused, leaning on his knees, still winded from his dash across the car park. Craven checked the gun for the tenth time. It had no safety catch and so would fire when he pulled the trigger. So, he kept his finger off the slender trigger out of fear of firing the damned thing and alerting them before he had even found the enemy. He held the weapon awkwardly, like it was red hot. The frigid grip of the deadly firearm made him uncomfortable, but he kept a tight hold.

A muffled scream echoed around the old building and its green-stained iron ceiling rafters. Craven paused and flattened his back against a changing room post. He peered downwards, below the stone poolside edging where once water glistened and shifted in small waves, but now the tips of three men's heads bobbed and turned in the empty swimming pool. The space, once filled with children's laughter and swimming joy, was now a vast hole covered in discoloured tiles and brown concrete slabs.

Craven chewed his bottom lip, unsure how to get Jess away from the three men. He swallowed at the lump of fear in his throat. These men weren't the drug dealers or thugs Craven dealt with on the streets of Manchester and Liverpool. They were Valknut soldiers, trained and deadly. The Valknut men spoke in Russian and two of them laughed at a comment from the third. They split up, two heads bobbing in the empty pool as they made their way away from its centre. One stayed put, and Craven assumed Jess was there, too, but below his line of vision. With his back pressed against the changing room, Craven could only see a yard into the pool.

The two heads moved away from each other towards the pool's opposite edges. They hadn't spotted Craven or heard him enter, otherwise, he would be dead, and he thanked God for his soft-soled, comfortable loafers. The two men left to sweep the building, Craven thought, to secure the exits or whatever it was soldiers did in this type of situation. He shuffled further back into the changing room, keeping his eyes on the moving heads, shifting his sweaty palm on the gun's grip. The two men stopped suddenly, turned and looked at each other. Craven cocked his head to listen carefully and heard a door banging somewhere in the pool complex.

Craven swallowed the lump of fear in his throat. If it was more Phoenix men, then he was dead. Even one against one, he didn't fancy his chances, but any over three would make it impossible for him and Jess to get out of there alive. The two heads set off at a flat run, sprinting towards the end of the empty pool and vaulting over the sides like athletes. Without breaking stride, they dashed out of the doors and left them swinging on old, creaking hinges, the noise echoing around the rusting rafters.

Kane must have drawn them off, but Craven did not want to speak into his communication gear to check for fear that the last guard would hear him. So, he waited, watching the last head walk around in a circle inside the empty pool. Only one man stood between Craven and Jess. However, Craven, a retired copper with limited experience in firing weapons outside of basic training with the serious and organised crime squad, was up against a trained soldier. He took quick breaths and rested his head against the cubicle's rear wall, trying to find the courage to do what must be done.

The remaining enemy laughed, and Jess Moore whimpered, hidden from view in the depths of the empty pool. Craven ground his teeth. He had to act. He stepped forward slowly, standing on his tiptoes to get a better look at the man in the swimming pool and hoping to see where exactly Jess was. The enemy leant forward and held Jess Moore's chin in his hand as she knelt on the pool tiles. He was making ridiculous kissing sounds, and Jess did her best to flinch away in revulsion. Craven glanced at the entrance doors, which had settled back into a closed position, and the other two enemies were nowhere to be seen.

Craven swapped the gun to his left hand and wiped his sweaty right hand on his trousers. He passed the gun back into his right hand and raised it, doing his best to keep the weapon level and pointed at the enemy. Jess turned away as her captor tried to lick her face, and her eyes opened wide as she spotted Craven over her captor's shoulder. He noticed the gesture and turned, staring in shock at Craven and his gun.

"Move away from her," Craven said in his best tough guy voice.

The man mumbled something in Russian and sneered dismissively at Craven. He was a tall man, rangy, with long limbs and an angled face below a shaved head.

"Get away from her now, or I'll shoot." Craven raised his left hand to steady the gun in his right.

The smirk fell from the Valknut man's face, and he reached behind him, moving as quick as a snake. He was going for his gun, and in two seconds, Craven would be dead. Craven squeezed his finger on the trigger, and nothing happened, so he squeezed it harder, and the gun fired. The sound of the gunshot boomed, and the recoil surprised Craven, forcing him to take two steps back. He realised his eyes were closed, so Craven forced them open. He had missed, and the man now had his own weapon drawn and a snarl twisting his flat features.

The enemy fired a shot of his own. A bullet ricocheted off the changing room somewhere behind Craven, and he flinched, but was relieved to find himself unharmed. The enemy cursed in Russian and took two steps towards Craven with his gun raised. Craven thought about shooting again but realised he had no chance of firing an accurate shot with his hands sweating and shaking. He took two deep breaths and clenched his jaw.

"Bastard!" Craven roared and charged at the man in the empty pool.

The Russian fired again, but Craven was moving too fast. He hurtled towards the pool's edge, all his bulk travelling with every ounce of speed Craven could muster. He launched himself over the edge, flew for a heartbeat, and then crashed into the Russian, his considerable bulk driving the surprised enemy down to the cold tiled floor.

Jess Moore screamed, and the man beneath Craven groaned and flailed with his arms. Craven let go of his gun and grabbed the man around the throat. Craven was taller and broader than most men, and his large hands curled around the Russian's throat like a vice. He squeezed, shifting his bulk so that his belly kept the writhing man pinned to the pool floor. Jess Moore darted towards him, and Craven twisted his head as she jumped on the Phoenix man's gun hand. Jess roared incoherently, stamping on the man's wrist until he let go of the gun.

A hand clawed at Craven's face, scratching his cheek and trying to hook fingers into his mouth. He snapped his teeth at the fingers and the man twisted beneath him, fighting desperately as Frank Craven squeezed the life out of him.

"Don't shoot," Craven said to Jess through gritted teeth. She stood beside him, holding the Valknut man's gun in two trembling hands. The barrel pointed at her choking captor, but in her panicked state, she posed a threat to both Craven and the enemy. The man shifted again, wrapping his legs around Craven's and twisting his pelvis. He was trying to pull some sort of martial arts move to get Craven off him, and so Craven grabbed his throat tighter, squeezing with all his strength until the Russia's face turned puce. His eyes goggled and a strange gurgling sound came from deep within him. Resistance slowed, the strength in the man beneath Craven faded away until he went floppy and still.

Craven kept tight hold of the man's throat for another minute. He stared into the open, glassy blue eyes of the man he had choked to death and Craven felt sick. He stood shakily, retched, and vomited on the white pool tiles. Craven had throttled the younger man to death, and the horrified look in those eyes would stay with him for the rest of his life. He wiped the vomit from his chin and stood, stumbling towards Jess, who still had her gun trained on the dead man.

"It's all right," Craven said. "He can't hurt you any more. Come on, let's go."

She nodded and let Craven peel the gun out of her hands. He led her to the end of the pool, climbed up a silver-coloured ladder and then pulled Jess up behind him. He walked with an arm about her waist, keeping Jess propped up as they barged through the double doors and towards the swimming pool exit. Craven had a gun in his right hand and Jess Moore in his left. Whatever Kane had done to draw off the other two men had worked, and all Craven had to do now was get Jess into the car and out of there.

Unless there were more enemy soldiers outside coming to kill him with their ruthless training and booming gunfire. Craven swallowed and steeled himself for the task ahead. Meanwhile, Jess Moore sobbed as they both stepped out into the open air and bright sunlight. Craven hoped desperately that they wouldn't be faced with more death and destruction.

FIFTY-ONE

Bullets rattled into the desk, each impact reverberating through the wood shaking Kane as he leant against it. He checked his gun and closed his eyes. This was it. He was going to die in a bowling alley. There was no way out, and Kane hoped Craven had got Jess Moore to safety. Kane thought of Danny and Kim, and in a moment of calm, knew they would be OK with Barb and Craven. With what Kane had taken from Phoenix Telecoms, there was more than enough money stashed away to last them for life.

If Kane was going to die, he was going to die fighting. He rolled away from the desk and launched himself to his feet. He rose, gun pointed and ready to kill Ivanov and as many of his men as possible before they filled him full of bullets. But the guns weren't pointing at Kane any more. Two lines of MI5 men entered the alley from the front and rear, throwing flash bangs and opening fire on the Valknut men. Ivanov dropped to his knees and shot an MI5 man in the chest, just as one of his own men sprawled dead on the alley floor.

The flash bangs exploded and Kane ducked again, the noise ringing in his ears like drums. Gunfire crackled, and he forced himself to stand again. Ivanov and his men moved through the bowling alley, firing at the MI5 agents with skill and precision. Another of Ivanov's men went down, but two more MI5 men fell. Kane raised his gun and aimed at Ivanov, but he moved too fast, running at the closest line of MI5 men and engaging them in close combat. Ivanov moved with ruthless efficiency, throwing them, and shooting at close quarters. In twenty seconds, four men were down.

Kane didn't wait to see how the battle unfolded. He leapt over the counter and made for the doors. He ran around two men writhing injured on the carpet and burst through the entrance doors and out into the car park. Gunfire and shouting reverberated behind him, and then Craven hurtled towards him, driving their car at top speed into the car park before bringing the vehicle to a tyre-screeching stop.

"Get in, for fuck's sake," Craven shouted at him through the open window. Kane slid over the bonnet and jumped into the passenger seat. Jess sat in the back, her hands clutched to her face, rocking, shuddering in terror.

"Get us out of here, Frank," said Kane.

Craven nodded and sped the car away, leaving the savage gun battle between Valknut and MI5 behind him. The car leant into the bends, Craven pushing the vehicle to its limits in his desperation to get out of the base as quickly as possible. A helicopter circled overhead, and the other remained landed in a field beyond the rows of empty houses.

"Jesus Christ, but that didn't go as we thought it would."

"Things are going to get worse. MI5 knows that a foreign military organisation is active on British soil, so this is only the beginning."

"Which is good, right?"

"Not if they can't piece together who Valknut and Phoenix are, and what they want. Who would believe that story unless there is hard evidence?"

Craven turned the car around the last bend and the entrance gate came within sight, debris from the smashed barrier littering the road and pavement. Craven slowed the car to turn around the final roundabout and suddenly slammed on the brakes. Jacobs and three of his men barred the road holding Remington Model 870 shotguns.

"Bastards were hiding behind the guard hut," Craven hissed, stopping the car and raising his hands.

Jacobs limped around the car, keeping his shotgun trained on Kane's face. Anger flared inside Kane, an impotent rage because Jacobs was about to win and he could do nothing about it. Jacobs opened the rear passenger door and pulled Jess Moore out slowly. She followed him, staring at Kane through terrified eyes, her face streaked with tears.

"Unlucky, Jack," Jacobs grinned. "I get the girl, and I get paid. And you get to go to hell."

"I'll see you there, Jacobs," Kane snarled.

Jacobs raised his shotgun to shoot, but then suddenly raised the weapon and ran away, dragging Jess with him. He limped quickly to a van and bundled Jess inside. One of Jacobs' men fired at Kane but missed, shattering the windscreen. He fired again over his shoulder and the wild shot blew out their front driver's-side tyre.

"Bastards," said Craven. They both jumped out of the car as the van sped away. Behind them, men came up the roadway brandishing machine guns, which was why Jacobs had stopped short of killing Kane in his panic to escape.

"Run," said Kane, and he and Craven fled away from the scene. Jess was gone again, and the whole fight had been for nothing. Kane had to get her back, no matter what it took, no matter what the cost. He must save Jess, and Jacobs must die.

FIFTY-TWO

Craven sipped steaming hot coffee from a large mug, his fingers wrapped around the ceramic oval, letting the heat seep into his hands and flow into his body. The remnants of a bacon and egg sandwich sat on a white plate on a table covered with a shiny plastic tablecloth. Kane sat opposite him, sipping a cup of tea poured from a silver teapot, the kind that always leaks when poured. Kane's sandwich sat uneaten, and Craven might eat it himself if Jack wasn't hungry. It was a shame to waste food, after all.

"Are you going to eat that?" he asked. Kane shook his head and Craven leaned forward, grimacing at the aches and pains in his ribs and back from the fighting at the disused army base. He grabbed the sandwich and took a bite, the salty bacon still warm and the white bread soft and delicious.

They had spent the night following the battle

at the army base in a cheap roadside hotel close to Salisbury and paid cash. Kane had stolen an Isuzu pick-up truck a mile from the base, and the two men had driven away from the carnage as fast as possible. Nobody had followed them, even though Craven could barely run. He had been sure that, as they fled the shot-up car at the base's entrance, their enemies would catch them.

"We need to talk to Andrew Moore," said Kane, staring out of the greasy spoon café with a thoughtful look on his face. "He put MI5 onto us, and it's turned this whole thing on its head."

"If he's gone to the authorities, he won't want to talk to us any more." Craven spoke through the side of his mouth, the other filled with bacon and bread.

"It's time he accepted Phoenix's offer to buy the football club."

"What? Give in to the bastards?"

"They've already won, Frank. They had helicopters and heavily armed soldiers operating inside Britain. We underestimated Phoenix and Valknut. They are going to get Wessex Celtic if that's what they want. Better he just let it go now."

"What about Jess?"

Kane took another sip of his tea and fiddled with a sachet of white sugar. "Jacobs took her.

Perhaps to get to me, but we haven't heard from him. He was working for the Russians, so I don't understand why he took her away from the base. Unless it was to hand her over safely, away from the threat of MI5."

"Do you suppose Jacobs has fallen out with the Russians? Turned against them?"

"He's not a stupid man, and to do that would sign his own death warrant."

"So, we wait to hear from Jacobs?"

"There isn't much else we can do. One thing bothers me, though."

"What?"

"Perhaps Cameron was right. Maybe it's time to contact some of my old colleagues. See if MI6 has any appetite to get involved in the situation."

"I thought they wanted you dead?" Craven finished his sandwich and stared at his friend. The relationship between Jacobs and Phoenix itself wasn't very clear to begin with, but now Kane was muddying the waters even further.

"Mjolnir wanted me dead. Because of what I knew, and it was all part of Jacobs' convoluted plan to gain more power for himself and his agency. There's no doubt MI6 is watching Valknut. MI5 handles intelligence and security at home in the UK, and MI6 looks after intelligence and counter-terrorism abroad. They will have eyes on such an existential threat to stability between the world's governments. Valknut clearly plays a part in the troubles in the Middle East and Africa, which we are assuming is why they want to buy Wessex Celtic. The club gives them a vessel to wash their ill-gotten gains, their diamonds and other wealth in the shiny blanket of popular sport. It gives Phoenix a friendly face, YouTube videos of famous footballers wearing their logo. That's what this is all about… Phoenix funnelling the millions, if not billions of dollars earned by Valknut into the mainstream."

"How are you going to contact MI6? Are you sure they won't try to kill you?"

"I'll ask Cameron to set something up. I still have a couple of old friends I can trust."

"And you believe they'll help us get Jess back?"

"I think if Moore agrees to sell, and the wheels of the deal start moving, things will cool down. They'll keep Jess alive until the deal closes. If they kill her before it's done, what incentive is there for Andrew Moore not to call the whole thing off? So, we have the time it will take Phoenix and Moore to close their deal to find and free Jess."

"But we don't know where she is, why Jacobs has taken her, or the situation between him and Phoenix."

"No. But we are going to find out."

"Jack, when this is over, we need to take some time off. This operation has gone off the deep end. It's way too heavy for me. When we got started in this line of work, I thought we would help people struggling with local gangster stuff we could deal with. This is something else. That was like a fucking war zone yesterday. We can't carry on like this." Craven had spent most of last night awake, reliving the events of the battle. Every time Craven had closed his eyes to sleep, the dead man's pale blue eyes stared back at him.

"I know. I didn't expect this to get as serious as it has. We'll take some time off. I'll take Danny and Kim on a holiday, give you and Barb some quality time together."

"Have you called them?"

"No. But I will. Have you spoken to Barb?"

"I have. As often as possible. They're fine. She is worried about Danny, though. He needs his father, Jack."

"I'll be there for him when we get back. But I can't leave Jess to die. We can't finish this alone, Frank, so let's talk to Andrew Moore and Cameron and get some help."

FIFTY-THREE

The mood in the office was tense. McGovern sensed it walking amongst the desks outside of her office, the strained faces talking into webcams as their fingers hammered into keyboards. The Balder organisation shifted into full tilt, working to find a way for Mr Hermoth and his team to get out of the UK. The debacle at the disused army base moved the entire country to lockdown. UK security services were heavily monitoring all private flights, so to charter a plane out of the region was a no-go. Unless McGovern's tech team figured out a way to mask flight records, or find a small airport somewhere in England, Scotland or Wales where the systems were lax, and they could hack in and alter the records.

Balder possessed plenty of funds, along with two jets used to fly teams around the world. But neither jet currently sat on British soil. It was

McGovern's job to coordinate an exit, and her team had worked throughout the night to find an out.

There was a knock at her door, and a young Asian girl in shorts and flip-flops shuffled in and placed a file on McGovern's desk without making eye contact. McGovern sighed. The world had changed. Her people were the best and brightest Balder could recruit, but they possessed the social skills of carrots.

She flipped open the file. It was a report on security systems at Sumburgh Airport in Scotland—a remote and small strip servicing the Shetland Islands. It might work, but then McGovern needed to figure out how to get Mr Hermoth and his team from southeast England to the northern tip of Scotland, which in itself was a logistical nightmare.

McGovern sighed and stared out into the Dubai morning haze, wondering where her life had gone wrong. She tried to pinpoint the moment that she had taken the first step down the wrong path, the error-stricken road of ill-judgment that had led her to this job, working for a man who had captured a woman they were supposed to secure for their biggest client. A dangerous client. Her phone rang. It was him. McGovern settled herself and swiped to answer.

"Mr Hermoth?"

"Have you found us an out, yet?" he barked down the phone at her.

"No, sir, but we are working hard to find a solution. We will have something for you before the end of the day."

"I could be dead by the end of the day! Get me a solution within two hours." The usual calm, upper-class drawl fell away as Mr Hermoth shouted down the line. He was all anger and desperation, short of breath and anxious.

"We will do our best, sir."

"Your best? I don't think you understand, Miss McGovern. If I die, this whole thing comes tumbling down. I plucked you out from under the British Government's falling scythe. Or have you forgotten? They were about to send you to prison for a long time, and if Balder falls, you might just find yourself back in that shitstorm. If we survive this current shitstorm."

McGovern stood, pacing her office. Hermoth's tone rankled her. She didn't respond well to threats. "I understand the difficulty of your situation, sir, but these things take time to do properly. We have worked through the night. By taking the client's target from the exchange point, you have brought down thunder from not only our client's immense intelligence and private military network, but now also the power and breadth of MI5 in their own backyard.

I can get you out of the UK now, at this very moment, but you wouldn't get very far before either of MI5 or our clients pick you up. To do this properly, and without risk, will take time."

"Do not get above your station. Do as I command and do it well." Mr Hermoth's voice became chill, anger replaced with cold malice, sending a shiver down McGovern's spine. "The girl is my only method of drawing Kane out. You and I both know what he is capable of, and he has burned us both. My purpose in life is to be avenged on Jack Kane. I must have revenge on Jack Kane, He will pay with his life for what he took from me. So, get me an out whilst I focus on terminating the cancer that is Jack Kane."

The phone went dead. McGovern placed the handset on her desk, hand trembling despite her best efforts to remain calm. Mr Hermoth's hatred was all-consuming. She realised at that moment that it was all that mattered to him. He didn't care about her, or the people who worked for the Balder Agency. Hermoth would gladly go down in bloody flames for Jack Kane's death. She hated Kane, but not enough to sacrifice her own life, or at least what remained of it. What would she have left if Balder dissolved? McGovern doubted she could ever safely go back to the UK without being arrested.

McGovern sat heavily in her chair. Her mind returning to search for the moment she had gone wrong, when she had sacrificed everything in life for her career. Love, children, friends, even her family had all fallen by the wayside. There was no exact moment, no footprint in her past. It was a slow process of her young self dying and morphing into her current cold, lifeless self. Now, all she had was Balder, and what future was there in a secret intelligence agency where the CEO was completely obsessed with the death of one man? Where should she go from here? Alone in Dubai, exiled from her country, isolated from everyone who had ever loved her?

McGovern picked up her phone and stared at the blank screen. For the first time in years, she wanted to call her mother. Perhaps a chance at reconciliation remained, an opportunity to meet up and pick up where they had left off? There had been no arguments, no bad blood between them, just a loss of touch as McGovern sank deeper into her career. The phone rang, surprising McGovern so that she almost dropped the handset.

"Hello?" she said, answering the private number.

"This is Berezov," said a deep voice in a Russian accent, cracked and gravelly like the bottom of an icy river. McGovern froze; all the moisture evaporated from her mouth, and she gaped like a landed fish. She still reeled from the call with Mr Hermoth, and this call couldn't have come at a worse time.

"Mr Berezov, how can I help you?" she said, the words fumbling out of her mouth. McGovern winced as she spoke. She knew full well why Berezov had called. He wanted to know why the company he paid to capture an asset had stolen that important asset from under his nose.

"You have six hours to return the target to us. Or face the consequences."

"There were complications, as you know. The security services turned up at the meet and…"

"No more bullshit. Call me back with a location for hand over before the deadline passes. Six hours."

"Yes, sir."

"We will pay no fee to the Balder Agency for this operation. We employed you to complete an important task, to act in a country where we must stay below the government's line of sight. However, we had no choice but to act anyway, and we lost good men. Agreements change, as you once said, and ours is terminated. I will await your call."

The phone clicked off before McGovern could respond. She covered her mouth with her hand and stifled a frustrated, angry scream. Her boss had gone rogue with a dangerous client's target, and that client was looking to her for a solution she didn't have. McGovern thought about calling Mr Hermoth to let him know, but what was the point? All he wanted was Kane, and he wouldn't listen to her advice. That advice would be to hand Jess Moore over to Phoenix and be done with the whole thing. Kane could wait for another day. McGovern knew all too well how ruthless Phoenix could be, of the resources they could access via Valknut, their military arm.

McGovern glanced out of the frosted glass that separated her room from the team in the office. She wondered if they were in danger. Would Valknut come for them if they failed to deliver Jess Moore on time? Back in the UK, McGovern worked within the safety blanket of the UK security forces. She had never felt afraid for her own safety within the walls of Vauxhall House, but now, suddenly, she felt vulnerable. She realised, in a horrifying moment, that she had become just like a person in the files she had spent so much of her life reading about. The soulless people with grainy photographs snapped using satellite imagery, assets to be used and disposed of as and when necessary.

She closed her laptop and turned off her phone. McGovern had some serious thinking to do. She was alone in Dubai, a stone's throw from theatres of war where Valknut active units deployed in war zones like Syria, Afghanistan and Yemen, and then the never-ending wars in central Africa. McGovern looked out at the wealthy trappings in Dubai harbour, at the high-rise apartment blocks and the shimmering water of the bay. Was she safe here? Who would protect her if Valknut came looking for retribution? McGovern's stomach turned over, hollow and churned by fear. Her life balanced on a knife's edge. Mr Hermoth wanted his out, and Phoenix wanted Jess Moore. McGovern must decide which course of action might result in her staying alive.

FIFTY-FOUR

Construction workers in yellow hardhats and dusty work boots rested against their Caterpillar excavator, talking and laughing but not working. The ruins of the Wessex Celtic training complex were almost demolished now. A skeleton of fire-blackened iron posts and jagged strips of plasterboard were all that remained of Andrew Moore's dream. Beyond the ruins and rubble, the astro-turf training pitch was already sparking into life at nine thirty in the morning. Coaches in tracksuits with whistles around their necks carried handfuls of brightly-coloured cones, laying them out in regular patterns to set up training drills for the squad.

Expensive sports cars and jeeps filled the car park, and the players walked slowly towards the astro-turf pitch, already dressed in their shorts and training tops, ready to begin their day's work.

"Life goes on," said a tired voice, and Kane smiled wanly at Andrew Moore, who approached him slowly from a Jaguar car. Two of his security team stood by the vehicle, staring at Kane with barely concealed anger. They blamed him for Anrew Moore's dire situation, and whilst Kane was not responsible for the old man's predicament, he had certainly not effectively resolved it.

"For the club at least," Kane replied. "How are you holding up?"

"The players are on their way in," he said, avoiding the question. "Before the fire, they would arrive in their normal clothes, overpriced jeans and gold chains, and head into the building for breakfast cooked by the club chef. Their breakfast was prepared to exact specifications, with just the right amount of protein and carbohydrate to allow them to train at optimum levels. Then, they would get changed into the club training gear, prepared and laid out by the kit man. They might head for a quick massage, or warm up in the indoor gym before heading out for their morning's training."

"I'm sure they'll survive."

"That was the point of the building the bloody place, to put us on a par with the big boys, to make the place feel like a Premier League club, not a small club. Facilities and ambition attract players, Mr Kane, and we wanted the best."

Andrew Moore spoke of Wessex Celtic in the past tense, Kane noticed. "You put MI5 on our trail?"

He nodded, lips curling in on themselves. "I had no choice. Things had gone too far. Beyond anything you or Mr Craven could fix. MI5 put a tracker on Mr Craven's car that night he came to visit me. I had already told them everything. They said they could get Jess back and make everything better."

"They made things worse. Jess is in the wind now. I don't know where she is, but I'll do my best to find her."

"Do you know what, Mr Kane? Looking into your eyes now, I believe you will. You understand the dilemma I faced, don't you?"

"We want the same thing. For Jess to come home safe. But before that can happen, it might be time for you to make a tough decision, Mr Moore."

Andrew Moore sighed and stuffed his hands into the pockets of the heavy jacket he wore over a grey suit and blue shirt. "I know it. They've won, haven't they?"

"Phoenix won't stop until they get your football club. For us to have any chance of getting Jess back, you must make that hard decision."

"When I bought the club, I was already a wealthy man." Andrew Moore sniffed, speaking wistfully as he surveyed the ruins of his dreams. "I started out with one betting shop. To get that little place, I scraped together whatever money I could get my hands on and re-mortgaged my house. I put all my blood, sweat and tears into that shop, and do you know what? It worked. I opened another, and then another, then came franchising. The big boys came sniffing around, making big offers, sometimes making threats as well. Then came online gambling, and I got into that early. Did well before it became saturated. I played a bit of football when I was a lad and I'd always dreamed of being involved in a football team. I've had horses. Racing is my bread and butter, but there's nothing like the thrill of match day, or when your team scores a goal. Those things are the fabric of life, Mr Kane, the smile on a child's face, or the happiness the game can bring to a working man who spends his hard-earned wages on a season ticket. Life isn't about money, Mr Kane, it's about feelings and joy."

"How long will it take for the transaction to go through?"

"It's complicated. The first phase of initial due diligence and deposit payment might take three or four days. Then, it goes into full due diligence and lawyers look through contract clauses and such. Then, it has to go to the Football

Association to be ratified. The whole thing could take six months, but the initial phase is less than a week. Jess was wild when she was young. She had no interest in sport or school. Jess just wanted to have a good time, to enjoy herself. She used to be so sweet, the apple of my eye, until her mother died. Then she went her own way. It was only in her late twenties, when she came home, that she and I grew close. I persuaded her to get involved in the business, and she thrived. She has a natural talent for it. Shame, really, that it was the business that got her into this infernal mess."

"You've already made your decision?"

Andrew Moore placed a hand on Kane's arm and smiled sadly. "What choice do I have? The club or my daughter's life is no choice at all."

Kane placed his hand over Andrew Moore's, the veins in the old man's hands as thick as ropes and his skin cold to the touch. "You probably won't hear from me again, Mr Moore. I'll do everything I can to get Jess back to you before the sale goes through. They'll keep her alive as leverage to stop you from backing out of the deal."

"Why can't the authorities stop them? I've been to MI5 and the police. Nobody seems to do anything."

"MI5 tried, but were outgunned. For the police to act, there must be a crime first.

The Phoenix business deal is one thing, and that's not a crime. Valknut is Phoenix's military arm, and they were certainly involved in this fire and the gunfight at Elm Brook military base, but how tenuous is the link between Phoenix and Valknut? Intelligence contractors abducted Jess, nothing to do with Phoenix, but undoubtedly contracted by them. There was serious trouble this week, extreme violence. But whether MI5 can pin that on Phoenix remains to be seen. Phoenix is a powerful organisation, Mr Moore. The government must tread carefully around Phoenix. Their heavy link to the Russian Government makes things even more precarious. To anger them or accuse them without absolute proof could trigger an international incident. It's complicated."

Andrew Moore waved to a coach on the astroturf pitch, and he returned the gesture effusively. "Can you get my Jess back?"

"I'll do my best. If there's a chance, no matter where she is in the world, I'll find her and bring her home. Or die trying."

"I'll get the wheels in motion for the sale, then." Andrew Moore left to walk back to his car but stopped and turned back to Kane. "Thank you, Mr Kane, and good luck."

Kane smiled and left the training ground. Craven waited for him a five-minute walk away, ready to drive Kane to his second difficult meeting of the day. This one was riskier, posing a direct and dangerous threat to his life. Cameron had set up the meeting with some contacts in MI6, and Kane needed their help, but couldn't know for sure if they would kill him, arrest him, or help him.

FIFTY-FIVE

"So, you know these guys?" asked Craven. He sat behind the steering wheel of a Ford Mondeo, rented using a new credit card and passport identity. Thankfully, not in the name of Shufflebottom.

"Once upon a time, yeah," Kane replied without taking his eyes off the kit in his lap. "I served with Scooby in the regiment, and Cameron says he's now with MI6 and I've met the other bloke before. Kieran Jameson is his name, an MI6 agent. We ran a couple of operations together in Africa a long time ago. He's a good man, or he was in those days, anyway."

"Scooby?"

"Yeah, a lot of the lads back in the regiment had nicknames. He looks like Scooby-Doo. That's where the name comes from."

"Seriously?"

"It was a name to wind him up, but it stuck. Better than some I've heard. There was a guy in another troop called No-Arse, and another called Camel, because he had skinny legs and a big torso, like a camel."

"Did they have any funny names for you?"

"Not really, just Jack."

"Can we trust Scooby and Jameson?"

"No. They still work for MI6 and will follow orders, no matter how friendly we used to be. Hence the precautions."

"We should be there soon." Craven drove towards a motorway service station between Ravenford and London. Kane selected it as the meeting point because it would always be busy with motorists stopping to fuel their cars, buy coffee or a sandwich. The location also had easy getaway exits running east and west onto fast roads. "What's in the bag of tricks?"

"This bag was in the rucksack we found in Jacobs' Range Rover. It's called a Faraday bag. If you put your phone in it, it completely hides your location. This other little device is a signal jammer. Cameron picked it out, and I bought it at the gadget shop earlier. It will pick up the Wi-Fi signal in whatever location I am in when I turn it on, and can track any devices within the same network frequency. Cameron will use the jammer to scrape those phones and see who is watching. I am still using the phone Jacobs gave me, so we should assume he is keeping tabs on me through that. When I meet Scooby and Jameson, we should also assume that they will keep tabs on me from that point on. But with the jammer device, I can also keep tabs on them."

"None of that makes any fucking sense at all. The world's gone bloody mad with gadgets and Wi-Fi and fucking Facebook, TikTok and all that bollocks."

Kane laughed. "When we get there, do three loops of the car park so that we see if anybody is following us. You wait in the car. I don't want Scooby or Jameson to see your face. They could wear photographic lenses in their eyes, and once they have your face, they can find you anywhere where there's a camera, CCTV, or any pictures of you online. When I come back to the car, do the same thing. Three loops of the car park, go through the petrol station and out on the motorway heading for London, get off at the next exit and double back."

"So you don't trust these fuckers at all?"

"Better to be safe than sorry."

Craven slowed the Ford and indicated to pull into the exit lane towards the service station. Food outlet signs glowed above the exit, McDonalds, Starbucks, Chopped, and a Happy Eater. His stomach growled, and he wondered if there would be time to grab something to eat before Kane's clandestine meeting.

Craven did as Kane suggested, entering the car park up the slip road, and performing three circuits of the car park before parking twenty metres away from the McDonald's drive-thru in a corner of the car park, which was empty of vehicles. As they made the circuits, Kane looked over each shoulder repeatedly, searching for any vehicles doing anything out of the ordinary.

"There," he said, and nodded to a Volvo XC90 jeep, which pulled up closer to the main building, inside which were the restrooms, other restaurants, and a convenience shop. "That car followed us around twice."

"Forgive me for being a wooden head, Jack, but you are meeting them, for fuck's sakes, so what difference does it make?"

"I want to know where they are, that's all. In case we need to make a quick getaway. I won't bother with the earpiece or any of our other communications equipment. They'll be listening in to all frequencies so we can't talk privately. If I'm not out of there in thirty minutes, get a flight back to Barb. If you see me coming out of there running, start the car up and get into the passenger seat."

"You will come out, though, right?" They had spoken before about the chance of death, or of their operations going pear-shaped, but they had always discussed it in a detached manner, as if it were something they should talk about but was ultimately highly unlikely to occur. But now, Jack spoke seriously, and Craven could tell from the look in his eye that he meant every word.

"I don't know, Frank. But listen, you've been a good friend to me and kids. They love you and Barbara like you are their grandparents. If something happens to me, you have the passwords to access the bank accounts. I have made you a co-signatory on everything I have offshore, and there's more in the kids' names held in trust for when they grow up. Take care of them, Frank."

"You don't need to bloody ask," Craven growled, swallowing a lump in his throat. "Go in there, you daft bastard, and come out in one piece. When this bloody thing is over with, like I said before, we need a break for a while. Time to rest."

"We will. Thanks for everything, Frank."

Kane got out of the car with his backpack slung over one shoulder. The handguns were in the glove compartment, though each one only had a handful of bullets left. Craven watched him go, hoping Kane could find a solution—one that would help Jess Moore, but would also keep them both alive.

FIFTY-SIX

Kane marched past the Volvo and resisted the urge to peer into the windscreen. He could feel their eyes on him, almost sense their scanners and electronic equipment digitally swarming over him. Kane sidestepped the automatic doors leading into the service station to let a woman and her daughter exit first. She smiled at him, and Kane winked at the little girl.

Behind him, the motorway roared beyond a covering of trees as lorries and cars sped along the three-lane motorway. Inside the service station, however, all was calm. Maroon 5 played over the speaker system at a low volume, and the open space was busy with people strolling between the shop, coffee shop, and restaurant, stretching their legs before resuming whatever journey they were in the middle of.

Kane walked calmly, as though he were one of the many folks who had stopped to take a motoring break. His head, however, swam with concern for Jess Moore. He worried about what Jacobs was capable of, if he was mistreating Jess, what conditions they held her in, if she was hurt. He imagined her crying and tied up in a dingy room somewhere, and forced the memory out of his consciousness. Jacobs had her, Valknut wanted her, and Kane needed to get Jess back. To do that, he must remain calm and think clearly.

The service station building was a bright atrium topped with a glass roof, all held together with large steel cylinders stretching from the tiled floor at jaunty angles to give the place a bit of quirky style. Food outlets, toilets and a shop were tacked onto the central atrium like square boxes, designed to give motorists the greatest opportunity to spend their money on bad food and snacks. Kane made a loop of the place, noticing that the coffee shop had emergency doors leading out into a space beyond the car park. That space was most likely a refuse collection zone or a staff entrance pathway and yard for smoking. He saw a couple sitting together outside the station's buffet restaurant, sipping from takeaway coffee cups, and assumed they were MI6 agents watching him. Kane dipped a hand into his bag, switched on the Wi-Fi hacking unit, and threw the bag over his shoulder.

Cameras stared down at Kane from above,

and he didn't bother wearing a cap or hood to hide his face. He was risking everything to show himself out in the open, so he stood in the middle of the atrium and waited. People flowed around him like he wasn't there. A truck driver walked past with two newspapers under his arm and a share-size packet of Cheetos in one hand. An overweight, middle-aged couple grumbled about the price of the all-day breakfast, and a businessman talked loudly on his mobile phone. A normal day at the motorway services.

Two men sauntered in through the main entrance. One was tall and slim, wearing a black suit and sunglasses, and the second was shorter and stocky. The second man wore a tight t-shirt over bulging muscles and a sleeve of tattoos ran down his right arm. He had dark hair shaved short, and a trimmed beard around strangely heavy jowls for a man in such good shape. Jameson and Scooby.

Scooby smiled when he saw Kane, white teeth shining behind his neatly trimmed beard. Jameson took off his sunglasses and fixed Kane with an impassive stare.

"Fucking hell," said Scooby in his broad Cockney accent, looking Kane up and down. "I heard you were dead, mate. Nice suit."

"Scooby. Shame you've given up the gym," Kane replied with a grin.

"Fuck off, mate. You've always had arms like Mr Tickle. I'm as ripped now as I was back in the day."

"And you still stand out like a sore thumb. The enemy could see those teeth from space."

"At least mine aren't all covered in moss."

The two men stepped towards each other and clasped hands. Scooby pulled Kane in, and they slapped each other's backs. Kane felt warmth flow through him. The familiarity of an old comrade, a brother of war, their bond created on the battlefield which could never break. Kane's mind suddenly became busy with memories of hard fights in distant lands, of drinking late into the night to celebrate a victory or toast to a fallen brother.

"Good to see you," said Kane.

"Same, mate. Can't remember the last time we served together. Might have been when that Chinook went down?"

"Could be."

"Maybe save the back slapping for another time, fellas," said Jameson. He spoke with a nondescript, clipped English accent. Kane thought he was from somewhere on the southeast coast but couldn't remember. Anything Jameson had ever told him was probably a lie, anyway. A cover story built around his MI6 persona. His real name was also highly unlikely to be Jameson.

"Jameson," said Kane in greeting.

"It's Stead, now. Kieran Stead. You picked a nice place to meet."

"Didn't want you boys getting the drop on me."

Scooby laughed, and Jameson, or Stead as he now called himself, frowned down at him.

"So, you reached out to us, Jack. What's going on?" Stead rolled his shoulders and stared Kane straight in the eyes. "To cut to the chase, we obviously know about the bullshit with Mjolnir and all that craziness in Manchester a few years back. We know you entered some sort of black hat witness protection programme, and that Mjolnir is up shit street with all its agents dead and its leader AWOL."

"Since the whole Mjolnir issue, I've been working privately. Helping people who need solutions beyond what the police can provide. One of those clients has got into a very bad situation. It involves the Phoenix Group, and Valknut."

Stead and Scooby exchanged a quick glance. "Phoenix and Valknut are obviously on our radar, as you well know," said Stead.

"Phoenix is looking to buy an English football club and has taken one of its owners as a hostage.

Or at least they have paid a third party contractor to capture her. Phoenix plans to use her as leverage to force the sale."

"Sounds a bit far fetched?" said Scooby, running a stubby hand over his beard.

"Sports-washing," said Stead.

Kane nodded. "I'm going after her. Valknut is operating on British soil. If you check with MI5, they will have a record of Jess Moore's abduction, and details of a shit storm of a gunfight at an old US army base this week."

"So?"

"So, we might have a mutual interest here. Presuming that you guys would take any opportunity to hurt Valknut, and other suspect private military organisations, where it hurts."

"We should take you in, Kane," said Scooby, narrowing his brown eyes. "You grassed on your old comrades. You're a wanted man. People have died. You're a murderer."

"All three of us are murderers. It's just that the government used to pay me to do it, so it was OK then. When I worked for MI6, for Mjolnir, I followed orders. Those orders became blurred. We did things we shouldn't have. But I didn't give the orders, I followed them. Just like you. Who are we to question where the jobs come from? An opportunity to get out and protect my family came up, and I took it. Some of the stuff Mjolnir was up to just didn't sit right. I wasn't sure we were the good guys any more."

"So why shouldn't we just bundle you in the back of van and toddle you off for some robust questioning?" asked Scooby, but Kane noticed a playful look in the creases at the corners of his old friend's eyes.

"You can try if you like. Those t-shirt muscles might help you get it done."

"I remember you, Jack, it would take more than the two of us to stuff you into the back of a van."

"Do you want to join forces on this one or not?"

"What exactly are you asking for? What's in it for us?"

"I'm going to find Jess Moore and free her. Phoenix and Valknut will try to get her out of the country, so this could end up as a job on foreign soil. It gives you a chance to help MI5 and thwart Phoenix from getting a financial and PR foothold in the UK through the football club and gives you a chance to get one over on Valknut. Valknut and Phoenix are an enemy of the UK, and all the western powers, that's as clear as day. The theatres of war they operate in are surely contrary to the interests of our government. They are growing ever more dangerous, amassing huge amounts of wealth in diamonds and other valuable natural resources. If it turns out they take her to one of their facilities abroad, there might also be a chance for an intelligence grab."

"You've missed your calling, Jack," grinned Scooby. "You should have been a salesman. MI6 doesn't work with criminals like you, though. We have our own teams for this type of work."

"You have my number, and I'll keep this phone active for two days. Call me if you want to work together."

"You're assuming we are going to let you go?" said Stead, who was once Jameson, and Kane's blood froze for a heartbeat. "But we are. For now. We'll be in touch."

Jack shook each man's hand and then walked towards the restaurant. He strolled inside, browsed the buffet bar, and then left. Scooby and Stead were gone, but the couple sipping takeaway coffee in the atrium remained. Kane went into the coffee shop and grabbed Craven an Americano before slipping discreetly out of the fire escape. Kane ran along a pathway beside a rack of bikes and a Perspex smoking shelter, inside which a young woman with pink hair stared at him nonchalantly.

Kane dashed to the car but indicated for Craven to stay calm, and Craven started the engine as soon as he saw Kane coming.

"Thanks," said Craven when Kane handed him the coffee, which he nestled carefully in the cupholder beside the gearstick. "Well?"

"They didn't kill me," Kane replied with a smile. "So, I think we're on. Do you remember the drill?"

Craven nodded and reversed the car to bring it through the circuit Kane had outlined earlier. Kane took out his burner phone with the number Cameron had already given to Stead, the same phone and number Jacobs used to contact Kane for Jess's exchange. He slipped it into the Faraday bag and secured it, so that he and Craven could get away cleanly to a place where neither Jacobs nor MI6 could find him.

They drove for forty-five minutes, making loops and so that Kane could search for any sign of a trailing vehicle, but all was clear. They pulled over to a side road, and Kane took the burner phone from the Faraday bag. The screen lit up with a text message notification.

"Who is it?" asked Craven, opening his coffee and grimacing because the drink had gone cold.

"Jacobs. He wants to meet again. On a high street in Swindon. Two hours from now."

"Do you think he still wants to swap Jess for you?"

"No. It's the same as before. He's using Jess to lure me in so that he can kill me, and then he will hand her over to Phoenix for his payday."

"So, what are we going to do?"

Kane shrugged. "Go to the meeting and try to get her back." It was an obvious trap, but Jacobs wouldn't care. He knew Kane had no choice. There would be a sniper somewhere or men waiting to bundle Kane into a vehicle and whisk him away to his death. Either way, the idea was to trap and kill him. Kane hoped to hear from Scooby and Stead before then—having them on board would make everything easier. With the might and resources of MI6, he would have a fighting chance of getting Jess back. But to get an operation approved by MI6 command would take time, certainly longer than two hours. Without them, he wasn't so sure he could save Jess and survive.

FIFTY-SEVEN

Jess Moore sat outside a café on a small round cushion on a white metal chair. It was not her first time in Swindon. It wasn't far from Ravenford and when Jess was younger, it had been a popular destination for a night out drinking with the girls. She pressed her knees together to stop them from shaking and wrung her hands beneath the table. Her captor sat across from her, leaning back in his chair with one leg crossed over the other as though he didn't have a care in the world.

Jess spent the time since the awful chaos at the army base in the back of cars, being driven to different locations before eventually coming to an empty house. There, Jess spent another sleepless night under guard in a cold, damp room. Mr Hermoth, as he called himself, had three men and one woman in his service. None of them spoke to her, not even the woman. She was tall and toned, like a sprinter or long jumper from the Olympic Games, with long limbs and the gait of someone who could explode into high speed at any time.

They kept her hydrated with bottles of water and fed her sandwiches and salads from packets bought at garages or service stations. Jess flicked a strand of greasy hair away from her face. She couldn't ever a remember a time when she had gone so long without a shower. Fear was her constant companion, along with silence and a complete unknowing of what her situation was, and if there was even a chance that she might get out this alive.

A waitress came outside with a black tray stacked with two large cups of coffee and two scones. Mr Hermoth thanked her in his annoyingly upper-class accent and paid her in cash.

"Eat up," Mr Hermoth said, pushing over a small white plate with a large fruit scone, a pat of butter and one of jam. "Jack should be here soon. Best to keep your strength up."

Jess didn't even bother to scowl at him. She was all snarled, scowled, cursed and cried out. So, she just ignored him the way they ignored her. Hermoth and his team didn't even bother to hide their plans from her. They talked openly about how they planned to wait until Jack Kane walked towards Hermoth on Swindon high street. The tall woman was already inside the coffee shop, poised and ready to strike like a leopard. Two men waited across the road in a pub, watching and armed to the teeth with shiny black guns. Then, a last man was driving around Swindon in a jeep. When Jack appeared, they would grab him, force him into the van and take him to his fate.

There still wasn't much sense in how this was suddenly about Jack when her disastrous interaction with Phoenix began as a strong-arm tactic to force her dad to sell the football club. The brutes had started out as Russians, but became a mix of English, American, and other accents she could not place. But Jess was beyond trying to figure it all out. It didn't matter. She just wanted to go home. Her dad should just sell the club so that they could live in peace, get this entire bloody mess over with and behind them.

It was a balmy day, and Jess blinked as the sun warmed her face. This part of Swindon high street held wide pedestrian pathways, and a small, winding road snaked its way through the bustling shop fronts. She squinted through the sunlight at the mixture of modern storefronts and historic buildings, and the smell of freshly brewed coffee and pastries masked the petrol fumes from the line of traffic on the road. A man in a white van honked his horn as a younger man in a red Citroen boy racer car stopped to shout a greeting to some friends on the pavement. Their conversation mixed with the chatter of passers-by and the rumble of a busy town centre.

The passers-by did not see her suffering, her life completely turned upside down by ruthless bastards who wanted to take her father's dreams away. It was all like a horror movie, something bad that was happening to someone else. Like a news story you watch on the television for thirty seconds and feel glad it's not you before you switch the channel.

No matter how much Jess had suffered, how tired she was, how traumatised and desperate to go home, she hoped Jack would not turn up. In her own way, she had grown close to him in those last few days. He was gentle and warm, despite his darker, violent side. If her getting freed meant Jack being taken or hurt, then Jess would stay with Hermoth and his gang of serious-faced bastards—better that than being released in a swap of her life for Jack's.

Jess let her knees tremble, tired of hiding it, and stared along the street, hoping that Jack wouldn't come. But the secret part of her, the dark corner of her soul which all people possess but rarely give voice to, that part hoped Jack came. That he came with his violence and his cold, dangerous eyes and killed them all.

FIFTY-EIGHT

"Are they close?" Kane asked, speaking loudly so that Cameron could hear him through the speakerphone setting on the mobile phone Craven held out before them both.

"Still in London," Cameron replied. "Both of them."

Kane cursed under his breath. The Wi-Fi jammer hacking unit had picked up both Scooby and Stead's mobile phone devices when they entered the motorway service station. The invitation to join the station's Wi-Fi allowed Cameron to access their phone's security, and he now had a trace on both men.

"Looks like we're fucked," said Craven in his usual laconic way.

"There hasn't been enough time," said Kane, which was true. There was no way Scooby and Stead could organise sign-off on a national security threat mission in two hours. That was how long Jacobs gave Kane to reach Swindon, and he and Craven made the journey with thirty minutes to spare. Even if Stead and Scooby wanted to help, they would need to write a report, brief their superiors, liaise with MI5 on the army base battle, outline their operational requirements, get approval and put the operation together.

MI6 could, of course, work fast when required. But there were too many shadows, too many moving parts in the Phoenix and Wessex Celtic affair. The only crimes so far were the kidnap of Jess Moore, which MI5 was investigating, and the wild gunfight at the army base.

"Did they seem keen?" asked Cameron.

"I think a chance to take a swipe at Valknut might pique their interest. But it doesn't look like we've done it in time for today."

"If Jacobs wants you on the high street, it's safe to assume he's going to snatch you? He won't kill you in broad daylight with hundreds of shoppers around to see it."

"I doubt he cares about that. Jacobs is more afraid that MI5 might find him before he gets his chance to take me out. He'll be just as focused on watching out for them as he is on me."

"So why don't we get to him first?" asked Craven, which was a fair question and one that

Kane had pondered himself on the journey north to Swindon.

"Because Jess is in danger, and Jacobs won't be alone. If I take him out, one of his men will gun me down instantly, and Jess with me. Or she might get caught in the crossfire. This is Jacobs' meeting again. He picked this place, so we must assume he has it covered and is happy with whatever measures his team has in place."

"He wants you bad, Jack. That might make him clumsy, force him to make a mistake."

"Phoenix wants Jess as well," said Cameron. "Jacobs took her away from the base when he should have handed her over. That was the premise of the whole thing. Phoenix contracted Jacobs to capture Jess Moore, and the handover was to take place at the army base. His plan was to lure you there using Jess as bait, kill you, and hand her over to the Russians for his pay day. Simple as that. But he didn't. You are alive, and he still has Jess Moore. So, Jacobs now has MI5 on his tail, us, Phoenix, and therefore, Valknut."

"None of that changes the fact that I must walk into the lion's den again. Everything you've both said is true. I still have to meet Jacobs, even though I know he wants me dead. I'm going in. Cameron, Craven, keep an eye on the phone and let me know if you hear anything from Stead or Scooby. I have my earpiece comms in, so we can keep in touch. Frank, do nothing rash. If this all goes tits up, get out of here and get back to Barbara and the kids."

"I know, I know. You don't have to say that every time you walk into a certain death situation."

Kane smiled and left Craven in the Ford Mondeo. He walked for five minutes through the tangle of lanes behind Swindon's main street and turned onto the main drag opposite a phone shop and a Santander bank branch. Kane turned left and wove his way through the throng, sliding past men in colourful shorts and flip-flops, and women in flowing summer dresses. He was warm in his suit jacket and trousers, but the jacket hid the gun strapped to Kane's waist. He only had five bullets remaining in the Glock, so if it came to a gunfight, he was in big trouble.

Jacobs sat comfortably in a pavement café chair, reclining as though he were a gentleman taking a midday coffee, rather than an international criminal and spy. Kane ground his teeth as he caught sight of Jess through the crowd. Her face had a drawn and pale appearance, and her hair hung in lank strips around her head. Jess sat hunched over, eyes flicking from one side of the road to the other like a frightened animal.

Kane wanted Jess out of this, to be home and

safe with her father where she belonged. So, he approached Jacobs slowly to show he meant no threat. Jess saw him first, her eyes widening and her bottom lip quivering. She seemed so vulnerable in that moment, and all Kane wanted to do was scoop her up into his arms and hold her close. Jacobs' cold eyes fell upon Kane, and Kane's former commanding officer smiled.

Jacobs stiffened in his chair, uncrossing his long legs and sitting up straight, barely concealing the feral delight on his face. He saw his chance at vengeance, his opportunity to kill a man he hated, and, in that moment, Jacobs thought he had won, that his dream of slaughter and retribution was about to become a reality.

A blue van pulled up beside Kane, and the car behind beeped its horn in frustration. People turned, surprised by the loud noise from the road beside them. The side of the van slid open to reveal two men in white painters' overalls. They climbed out slowly and kept the van door open. A third man stepped out of the passenger side door with his back to Jack, and he turned, leaving the door open as he moved away from the van.

Kane kept moving, assuming they were workmen here to unload their van and start work inside one of the many shops along the high street. An old lady in a pale blue cardigan pulled her Jack Russell dog away from one painter as it yapped and strained against its lead.

The man at the passenger door of the van kept turning and extended his right arm. It held a silenced pistol. Without hesitating, he fired a shot, the suppressor spitting the bullet from the chamber like the sound of a whip. Kane paused in shock, and the back of Jacobs' head exploded like a watermelon dashed against the wall. Jess Moore screamed as blood and bits of skull spattered her face and shoulders. She raised her hands, shaking and howling at the sheer horror of the execution. The gunman stepped towards her, gun still extended, and fired two more shots, one into Jacobs' throat and another into his skull.

Jacobs slipped from his chair and the surrounding people paused for a moment, stunned and unable to process what they had witnessed. The old woman with the dog screamed and let go of the animal, which ran towards Jacobs and the bloody mess which had once been his face. That triggered the rest of the crowd to run, shouting and screaming in all directions.

Kane surged forwards, shouldering past an overweight man in socks and sandals, and a younger man in a vest and tracksuit bottoms. He barged them out of the way, losing sight of Jess for precious moments, elbowing people as he tried desperately to reach her. He reached the table, but she was gone. Kane turned to see the two painters bustling Jess into their van. Then the gunman was between them, a man shorter than Kane and wearing glasses. Ivanov.

Ivanov recognised Kane and took a step towards him; he had the gun halfway inside his overalls but now drew it again as he saw a chance to kill two birds with one stone. Kane ran at him and barged Ivanov into the van before he had a chance to fully draw his weapon. Ivanov bounced into the van with a metallic bump. The two other men ignored them and pushed Jess's kicking legs inside the vehicle, hopping in behind her and closing the doors. Ivanov drove his knee into Kane's groin and sent a stab of pain surging through Kane's body. He released pressure on the Russian and doubled over. Ivanov grabbed him by the hair, slammed Kane's head into the van and punched him hard in the neck.

Kane fell to his knees, choking and reeling from the attack. Ivanov glanced around at the crowd, snarled at Kane, and jumped into the passenger seat. The van sped off with screeching tyres, speeding along the road ahead and out of Swindon's main street. Kane fumbled in the gutter. Jess was gone, and Ivanov had got the better of him. Jacobs lay dead in a pool of his own blood, and Phoenix had their target in hand. Kane had lost again, but he was still alive.

FIFTY-NINE

"What happened?" Craven shouted, touching his earpiece with his finger, unsure if that even made any sort of difference to the tiny microphone's reception or speaker quality. "Jack, are you there?"

The sound of screaming had burst through Craven's earpiece moments earlier, closely followed by the muffled, crumpled, breathless sounds of a struggle. He feared the worst, that they had taken or killed Jack.

"Cameron, can you see what's going on?" Cameron was on the other end of the radio. Cameron had set up a secure comms line using some sort of satellite-based internet connection which Craven didn't understand, but it worked. He also bashed away at his keyboard, trying to tap into the local CCTV camera video feed.

"Yes, I have it. Jesus Christ."

"What the fuck is going on?"

"Jacobs is dead, and they've taken Jess."

"Jack?"

"I'm here," said Kane, his voice strained and croaking in Craven's ear. "She's gone, Frank. It was Valknut. Ivanov. Phoenix."

Craven slammed his hand into the Ford's steering wheel. "I'm coming to get you."

"No, wait there. Jacobs was just shot dead in broad daylight; the police are going to be crawling all over this place in no time. I'll come to you. There are better exit points from your location."

"We don't want to lose her, though. If they are close, perhaps we can catch them?"

"I have picked up the van on the overhead CCTV cameras," said Cameron. "It's a blue Mercedes Sprinter. I have the plates and I'm following them."

Craven started the engine, his mind turning over faster than the car. After what seemed like an age, Kane came hurtling around the corner, running at full pelt. He opened the passenger side door and jumped in, chest heaving, face sheened with sweat.

"Cameron, we're on the move," said Craven.

"I see you. Head out of town and take the south

road. They have a fifteen-minute head start on you, and are moving fast towards London."

Craven pulled out of the side street and onto Prospect Hill, down Union Street, and left onto Albert Street. He waited at the traffic lights, not wanting to break the red lights and draw attention to the vehicle after being so close to a murder. A line of four Skoda Octavias, marked up in police yellow and blue, hurtled through the traffic lights heading towards Swindon centre, blue lights flashing and sirens blaring. The lights changed and Craven turned right, picking up the pace on the road that would bring them onto the M4 motorway towards London.

"They are still on the M4, heading to London. I'll keep you posted."

"Don't lose them, Cam," said Kane. Craven noticed as they turned onto the motorway that Kane's head was bleeding from a cut just inside his hairline. "If they get away, we have no way of finding Jess."

Craven joined the motorway and sped through traffic, weaving between the right- hand, fastest lane, and the middle of the three-lane carriageway. He pushed the Ford to ninety miles per hour where he could. The motorway was busy, so it was a cat-and-mouse game of speed up and brake as he tried to navigate around slower drivers hogging the overtaking lanes.

"They are turning onto the M25," said Cameron after forty minutes on the M4. "Heading southbound on the ring road, around south London. It's getting busy up there. I've hacked into the motorway cameras and am keeping tabs on them that way."

Craven followed, joining the M25, and then slammed onto the brakes as the motorway turned into a car park. He pulled into the hard shoulder and sped along that inside track for ten minutes, angry drivers stuck in the very congested London traffic beeping their horns as he whipped by.

"We are barely doing forty miles an hour here, Cam," said Kane. "Are they stuck in traffic ahead of us?"

"No, there's a collision ahead of you. It happened behind them. They are turning off, heading north. Biggin airport is close by. I've lost them on the motorway cameras. I'm trying to find another view or a satellite. Head for junction six and follow the signs for the airport."

"What's at Biggin Hill?" asked Craven, wincing as the Mondeo whizzed past cars so close he could have reached out of the window and touched them.

"A small airport, mostly used by private planes."

"Bollocks." Craven swore not only at the high

chance Jess was about to be flown out of the country, but also because cars were diverting into the hard shoulder to avoid the accident ahead, and so he had to slam on the brakes and join the queue. There was no way off the motorway, closed in as they were by large cement crash barriers. Around was nothing but forest, no exit roads or any other way of leaving the motorway to pursue the Russians and Jess.

"She's gone," said Kane, and there was a sadness in his voice Craven had never heard before. He hoped it wasn't true, that they could find a way of saving her.

SIXTY

It took forty-five minutes for the traffic jam to clear, but it felt much longer. Each minute was torturous as Kane checked his watch. Every second seemed to last an hour as the time wasted on the London ring road allowed Ivanov more time to whisk Jess away to whatever fate Phoenix and Valknut had in store for her.

"I have a list of departures from the airport," said Cameron's voice over the radio, but Kane could not process the information. He simply stared out of the window, watching a plane rise into the powdery clouds, as white as snow in a blue summer sky.

"Will you be able to find out where they have taken her?" asked Craven. They took the exit for Biggin Hill airport, but it was too late to stop Ivanov from leaving. Their plane was already in the air.

"I can see from the manifest that their destination was Sochi airport, but they could change that completely once in the air."

"How the fuck did they take off so quickly?"

"They must have had the jet primed and ready to take off the minute they returned from Swindon. This was always their plan."

Kane had nothing to add, but he could sense Craven's eyes flicking to him every thirty seconds to see if he would contribute to the conversation.

"All we can do now then is wait for Phoenix to make the call to Andrew Moore. They now possess the cast-iron threat to kill her unless he sells the football club."

The plane left a trail of dusty cloud in its wake, and Kane wondered if Jess was OK. It was a strange thought, one which left a sour taste in his mouth, robbing Kane of his ability to think any further into the future than the present. She was most certainly not OK, having been kidnapped twice and held by ruthless killers. The car fell silent as both Craven and Cameron ran out of things to say. The vehicle seemed to close in on Kane, weighed down by the expectation of his friends, as if the car were trapped in a junkyard crusher.

"What?" he said, fighting hard to mask his

annoyance.

"What happens to her now?" asked Craven.

"You know what happens to her, Frank. We lost. We tried, but we failed. Valknut has taken her to Russia, where they will use her image and the threat of violence to force her father to sell his club. That's it."

"Andrew Moore has already told them he's going to sell. So why go to such extreme lengths? I just don't understand." Craven's voice was genuine with sorrow and anger, but Kane was too lost in grief to humour his friend.

"Moore can stop the sale until the day funds are transferred, and the deal is done. Jess provides collateral against that. She has a use, a purpose, as a stick to beat Andrew Moore not only into submission but to make sure he completes his end of the deal. Once the deal is closed and her purpose is served, they will kill her. Not gently either, not after going to so much trouble to get her in the first place, and the difficulty they have encountered getting the job done. They have lost comrades here in England, so she will suffer before the end. That is the truth, and I'm sorry for not sugar-coating it for you. They have her, and she will die. Badly."

Kane spoke more harshly than he intended, but every time he blinked, in the momentary darkness before his eyes opened, Kane saw Jess.

Not Jess as she was before: stern, beautiful, intelligent, and warm. He saw the Jess from Swindon—drawn, pale, and terrified. Kane had to wrangle his mind like a bucking bull not to picture her suffering on a Valknut jet. Beaten, tied up, brutalised. Worst of all, were the obvious fears of what the Valknut men would do to her once her usefulness expired, how they would kill her, the suffering Jess would endure before the end.

"Is there no way we can follow them and try to get her back?" asked Craven, glancing nervously at Kane.

Jack rubbed his tired eyes, unable to answer.

"No," said Cameron, and Kane was relieved that his old brother in arms answered Craven's question to spare him the ordeal of manifesting what he already knew. "We know Valknut has training facilities deep inside Russia, on the eastern side of the Black Sea. If they take her there, which they probably will, then to get her out would require a black ops-style incursion. It would take two or three men to go under the radar, to evade the Russian military's state-of-the-art surveillance in that area. A team could go in by water, across the Black Sea, but Russia's Black Sea Fleet patrol that like it's an active war zone. An entry could be attempted by air, but their air defence is second to none, especially around Georgia, Turkey and Ukraine. Perhaps also by land, but border patrols are stringent and access to anywhere within three miles of the Valknut base would be impossible because of satellite and drone patrols."

"So that's a no, then," Craven said, shaking his head.

They were out of options, and out of luck. Jess Moore was lost. As Kane stared out of the car window, he wondered, not for the first time in his life, if he was cursed. Everybody who got close to him died and suffered. His wife, his brothers in arms, Danny and Kim. The curse came for them all. He wondered if it was his involvement, his curse, which had pushed the Wessex Celtic deal to this level of violence and vicious conclusion. Kane slipped into darkness, thoughts of curses and bad luck filling his brain like a swarm of dark bees.

The phone rang, and Craven picked it up.

"Hello?" he said, and there was a pause. "It's for you, Jack."

Kane took the phone absent-mindedly, barely even on the same level of consciousness as Craven, so deep had his melancholy and fear for Jess taken hold.

"This is Kane," he said.

"It's me, Scooby, you miserable fucker. We're on."

SIXTY-ONE

The sun set beyond the skyscraper tower blocks, which rose like oddly-spaced fingers from Dubai's sprawling desert metropolis. McGovern sat hunched over her desk, typing on her keyboard like a squirrel hoarding its trove of nuts and berries for winter hibernation. Mr Hermoth was gone, killed by an unknown enemy in a shocking and brutal assassination in Swindon, of all places.

In her career, McGovern had seen so many hits take place on grainy green night vision cameras fixed to operators' helmets. Slaughter via black and white thermal imagery, or flickeringly dirty satellite video. Targets taken out in the desert, in fortified military compounds in remote mountain regions, drug cartel dens in the deep jungle, or team insertions into central Africa by chopper or high jumps from covert planes. An assassination in Swindon was a bizarre new twist in her career of counter-intelligence.

With Hermoth's death, the Balder Agency folded around her, the tenuous walls and pillars of the company crumbling and shattering like ancient Pompeii before the eruption of Vesuvius. There were only three of the team left in the open-plan space outside McGovern's office. Most had fled after the news spread of Mr Hermoth's death. They took their ultra-valuable, super-powerful laptops and ran from the buildings like ants fleeing a smoked-out nest. McGovern stayed, as had the more hardcore hackers on the team.

Those who remained didn't do so out of any sort of loyalty to the agency. They stayed to flense the corpse of Mr Hermoth's company, scavengers feeding off the carrion left behind. There were assets in secret bank accounts, crypto across several exchanges, and assets held in various countries, which those in the know and with the modern-day superpower of computer hacking could extract, or steal, before the whole thing imploded.

McGovern had a rudimentary understanding of code and systems, but her late-night work wasn't to steal two million dollars of Dogecoin from a dark web account held on a blockchain ending in Syria. She worked to find an out for a dozen Balder agents in far-flung places across the world. They had people in central Africa, the

Middle East and South America who all needed funds, identities and pathways out of their cover positions in the various war-torn, or politically stricken countries in which Balder found itself employed.

The chair creaked as McGovern slumped back into it and kneaded her knuckles into stinging eyes. Another one gone. A female agent struggling to exit a dangerous situation in Yemen, now in a convoy of privately-hired mercenaries who would get her across the border safely. There, she should meet a man in a restaurant who would slip her an envelope with a clean passport and loaded credit card for her to flee to whatever destination she pleased.

McGovern checked her watch. It was late, and also time to think about her own exit. She couldn't go back to the UK and risk being picked up by the authorities the moment she landed on British soil. The investigation into her activities during her time with Mjolnir was still open, and her going missing without leave for so long would not help her situation. She had access to Balder funds and could set herself up with an untraceable offshore account in a bank in the Caribbean. But where to go, and more importantly, what to do? She could go to the Caymans, Belize or Panama and live quietly in tax-sheltered, luxurious surroundings, but what would she do all day? Was her destiny to own a cat and read books alone for the rest of her life?

A shout from outside McGovern's office made her jump. She stood and peered through the glass of her office windows, but could see no sign of any disturbance. McGovern's chest grew hot, her hands shaking. Perhaps it was the office cleaners who came in late at night when the place was usually empty? She crept to her office door, straightening her suit trousers and opening the heavy door half a metre to peer out into the mass of colourful chairs, break-out spaces and white boards.

A shadow moved around a pillar, and a short man in flip-flops ran around a high table used for stand-up meetings. A muffled, spitting sound tore through the office, and the man flew suddenly to his left. Bright red liquid misted the air where his head had been and spattered a white board in crimson. McGovern gasped. It was blood. The shadow appeared, an average-sized man in black trousers and a shirt, glasses on his round face and a silenced gun in his hand.

McGovern retreated, stumbling back into the safety of her office just as the shadow fired again. Another team member fell dead, his body hitting the office carpet like a heavy sack of potatoes. She closed the door with trembling hands and ducked, shuffling towards her desk. She could turn the light off, but it would be too obvious. Perhaps the shadow wouldn't know she was there and just pass the office by?

A scream came from outside the door, and the sound of another body falling. McGovern clasped a hand to her mouth. Death was close, the level of violence she had so often ordered and observed without compunction had come for the Balder Agency in the wake of Mr Hermoth's death, and it was viscerally terrifying to think she might die in her lonely office in a country she barely knew.

McGovern sat on the floor, making herself as small as possible. The door to her office creaked open and soft footprints came inside, like the sound of a wolf's paws on new snow. She held her breath and closed her eyes. The footsteps came closer. McGovern hadn't called her mother, and she should have. Her family wouldn't even know where she was, never mind that she was dead. Bizarrely, McGovern imagined her funeral in the desert with no mourners, just a black casket for a woman with no lasting legacy, no family, no husband, no children, not even a country to call her own.

A whimper escaped her lips, between the fingers held over her own mouth, and McGovern cursed her fear, her loneliness, her weakness and her failure. She gasped a half silent prayer, too quiet to be even a whisper, not to a God she didn't believe in, but to the shadow man, the assassin, come to wipe out the remnants of Balder. *Please, no. Please, no, please, no.*

"Get up," said a voice in a thick Russian accent. She opened her eyes and the shadow in glasses peered down at her, the look on his face impassive, as though he didn't care in the slightest that he had just slaughtered three people in cold blood. "Come with me. Or die."

It wasn't a question. She stood slowly, trying her best not to shake uncontrollably.

"What do you want with me?" McGovern said in an embarrassingly high-pitched voice.

"We can use you. Come," he beckoned to her with his gun, the gun which had murdered her team moments earlier. She hesitated, and he shrugged, raising the gun barrel slightly so that instead of inviting her forwards, the small black cavern inside the suppressor pointed at her face like the entrance to hell.

She stepped forward and followed the man with the glasses, though she knew not if she walked to a new life, imprisonment, torture or death. They wanted the information inside her head—she realised that much. She had value, skills, knowledge. But as she followed the man with the glasses out of the office, stepping around dark, creeping blood stains on the carpeted floor, McGovern wept silently at the misery her selfish, lonely life had become.

SIXTY-TWO

Craven and Kane arrived on England's south coast after nightfall. It was a picturesque drive south through the country's ancient heartland and into the centre of its once all- conquering naval supremacy. As a relatively small island perched on the western edge of what was the old world, it was extraordinary that England had leveraged its vast navy in the 17th and 18th century to rise and become the world's most dominant power. Portsmouth was a key port in that naval and military heritage. South of that historic port lay the Gosport peninsula, pointing like a warning finger from the south coast of a once all-powerful, but now jaded and much-reduced superpower.

"We'll be there in ten minutes," said Kane, excitement in his voice as he sat straight and alert in the passenger seat.

"Were you based here?" asked Craven,

following the road signs that beckoned them on towards Fort Monckton, an army base in a region famous for naval bases. The uplift in Kane's mood following the call from Scooby was infectious, and Craven drove as though awoken from a full night's sleep, rather than at the end of a long, stressful day.

"Sometimes. It's known as the number one training facility. It's where the intelligence services train, and cross-train with the SAS and SBS teams. I trained here for a while when I left the SAS."

"Good memories?" Craven recalled his own basic training back when he was a young and enthusiastic beat copper. Most of his memories of the time were of lots of drinking, waking up hungover and trying to cope with classroom lessons, some physical and combat training, and then more drinking. He doubted Kane's experiences at Fort Monckton bore any resemblance to that.

"Some, yeah. I learned a lot here. It's a big change, moving from the SAS to the Secret Intelligence Service. Some of it is the same. I'd already done a lot of observation work in the regiment, and then obviously I knew how to survive and fight in different terrains, how to clear a building, to be strong mentally. But here at the Fort, or the Rookery, as some call it, I learned about deception, technology, and counter-intelligence."

"So, this is basically where they teach you to be a sneaky bastard?"

"Something like that." Kane laughed despite the desperation of their situation and the plight of Jess Moore. Craven smiled to see a glimmer of light from Kane's dark exterior. "Just up ahead here. Someone will meet us at the gate."

Craven slowed at the entrance to Fort Monckton. The road glowed an ethereal silver beneath the moon, and as he wound down the window, the sigh of the sea washed against an unseen shore close by, and the smell made him take an involuntary deep breath. The gates to Fort Monckton rose from the ground in formidable concrete planes, rising high and impenetrable, like a grey stone castle. Barbed wire and warning signs stretched along the entranceway and up onto the walls, a deterrent for anybody foolish enough to breach such a secure and well-protected location.

A guard in army fatigues stepped out of the guard booth and waved at Craven to slow down. He came to a stop and smiled up at the square-jawed soldier in his mid-twenties.

"Can I help you sir?" the soldier said, in a broad West Country accent which wouldn't have been out of place in a pirate movie.

Kane leaned over the seat to talk to the soldier

at Craven's window. "We are here at the request of Kieran Stead. I think my name should be on the list. Jack Kane."

The soldier cleared his throat and nodded. "Normally I would ask for some sort of identification, Mr Kane, but I understand this is a delicate situation. Please pull over on the left and I will ask Mr Stead to come and collect you."

Craven thanked the guard and pulled the car over as requested.

"What if we go in there and you never come out again?" asked Craven. The imposing walls and razor-sharp wire around Britain's secret services training base suddenly reminded him of their precarious situation.

"Scooby wouldn't let me walk into a trap, Frank. Don't worry."

"Hang on a minute," Craven's eyebrows shot up in surprise. "It wasn't so long ago that the government tried to kill you. Have you forgotten the shoot-outs in Ireland, or the carnage in Manchester?"

"Of course, I haven't forgotten. But that wasn't strictly MI6. It was a black operations division, funded secretly, running separately and with complete deniability by the British Government. This is different. I wouldn't just walk you into a trap."

"Easy for you to say. Did your mate Scooby, which is a stupid fucking nickname, by the way, give you any details about what we are going to do?"

Kane shrugged. "He didn't need to. We are going after Jess, which means I'm going into Russia with one of Stead and Scooby's teams. Going into Russia is normally a big no-no, so this will be an off the books operation, maybe just a handful of operators getting Jess out. You won't go, Frank. I used to do this kind of thing for a living."

"What are you expecting to happen?"

Kane shrugged and shook his head. "High-level covert insertion and rescue mission. Significant chance of small arms fire and casualties. If Cameron is right, Jess is at the Valknut facility in Russia, so we are going behind enemy lines. No cavalry will come over the horizon if we get in a tough spot."

"What if you get caught?"

"We won't be wearing any British insignia, Frank, and Valknut isn't the Russian military. They are a private army, albeit with links to the Russian government. It will just look like a private job gone wrong."

"And afterwards Stead and Scooby will just let you wander off into the distance with the past forgotten?"

"I guess we'll see about that. Here they come."

The gate slowly swung open, barbed wire-topped metal gates opening to reveal a vehicle that looked suspiciously like a golf cart. Kane's old mate Scooby sat behind the steering wheel, and he saluted the guard as he scooted past the guard hut. Kane could hardly conceal his excitement at the sight of his old army buddy. Craven bit his lip. One minute, Kane had been in the darkest place Craven had seen him go to. Jess seemed beyond rescue, and it cut Kane like a knife. Kane had fallen for her. That much was clear. They had tried to save her and failed. But as soon as Scooby called with an opportunity to risk everything in a do or die mission, Kane had brightened like a switched-on light bulb.

Kane jumped out of the car, and he and Scooby embraced with grins and back slaps. What worried Craven more than the risk to Kane's life in whatever crazy plan they were about to come up with was that he suspected it was the thrill of the fight that so illuminated Kane more than the chance to rescue a woman he cared for deeply. He didn't mention to Kane that taking part in something so risky might mean him never seeing Danny or Kim again because he didn't want to burst Kane's bubble. But for a man responsible for two children, Kane seemed always ready to put his life in danger.

Craven shook Scooby's hand and clambered

inside the golf cart as they hummed around the half-open gate and inside the coastal fortress.

"Welcome to Fort Monckton," said Scooby, grinning through the spade of his beard.

"Place hasn't changed a bit," replied Kane.

"It has inside, more gadgets than you can shake a shitty stick at."

"When do we go?"

"ASAP. It wasn't easy to get a green light on this one, Jack. Technically, you shouldn't be getting anywhere near an MI6 and SAS joint operation. You are a wanted man."

"But I am going."

"You are. You seem to have kept a certain level of skill since retirement, and then there's your experience. The top brass doesn't want you along, they want you locked up, or worse."

"But I am going."

Scooby winked and guided the gold cart through a web of efficiently arranged trackways and pavements, travelling alongside sleek training buildings, a shooting range, and the hand-to-hand combat training complex Kane remembered from his time at the facility. To the west and south, the sea crashed above the humming cart's electrical engine, and Kane recalled his sea training, boat work and water insertion training with the SBS, the Special Boat

Service teams.

"Wheels-up in two hours," said Scooby. "Just enough time to get you kitted out and briefed. Mr Craven, you will stay here as our guest until the op is over."

Kane breathed in a chest full of sea air. It was time to go after Jess, but now he wasn't alone. He had the might of the British Special Forces with him, and the weapons and transport he needed to bring the fight to Valknut. For the first time since the Wessex Celtic job had begun, Kane felt like he was on the front foot. He was ready to bring Valknut something they had never seen before. Not a fight against local freedom fighters or poorly-armed infantry soldiers in a third-world country, but a ruthless war fought by highly trained killers. Kane's kind of war.

SIXTY-THREE

Kane knelt in the bow of a black SBS stealth speed boat. The Black Sea shone beneath the stars like an upside-down view of the universe. Stars sparkled and shimmered on the gentle swell, the smell of brine filled Kane's nose, and sea spray flecked his face with icy cold water. He stared hard ahead into the shadowed gap between a Russian Black Sea Fleet patrol ship to a strip of coastline completely shrouded in darkness. A hole of emptiness between the orange glow of villages, and the brighter, flickering lights of coastal resorts.

The boat sliced through the waves like a knife blade, thrumming silently as it raced across the water. Its matte-black military-grade colouring and the strange boxy contours of its stealth shape evaded radar and thermal detection. The boat carried no external fittings, and a small, tight radar dome minimised the vessel's radar cross-section. Panels to the aft contained diving equipment and spare ammunition for the minigun mounted above the vessel's sleek panels.

The whites of Kane's eyes gleamed beneath the starlight, his face covered in camouflage face paint above his black Kevlar body armour, black tactical clothing and boots. He wore an AC100 helmet, which would stop a 9mm bullet at close range, fitted with a camera to the front. Kane carried a Heckler and Koch MP5SD sub-machine gun strapped across his chest with spare magazines in a belt around his body armour. Fort Monckton's armoury contained a vast array of weaponry, but Kane was familiar with the MP5SD and its integrated suppressor, along with its sub-sonic ammunition. The weapon was silent and perfect for the job. The collapsible stock made it comfortable to fire, and Kane had checked and cleaned the weapon on the eastward plane journey. He had a Glock 19 on his thigh, flash bang and fragmentation grenades on his belt, spare ammunition, and night vision goggles on a nearby bench.

Scooby knelt in the bows, similarly clad and armed, with the addition of a Remington Model 870 shotgun strapped across his back. Kane's old comrade stared into the night with flinty eyes, and the spade of his beard jutting towards their destination. Four SBS operators from C squadron huddled in the stealth boat's aft, faces painted and weapons held close, ready for action. Scooby introduced them as Deeney, Davies, Taff, and Beef. They didn't clarify surnames or nicknames. With cold indifference, they said little and stared at Kane. However, he knew they would be fiercely efficient soldiers he could trust. Each SBS and SAS squadron kept a counter-intelligence troop on a black roll. A black roll duty meant that the troop on duty wore all black on operations and could not travel further than two hours from camp at any time. They stood on standby for both domestic and international response.

It was the second day since Kane and the SBS squad had landed at a Romanian Air Force base at Constanta on the Black Sea's western coastline. Since then, they had been surveying the sea and Russia's water patrols. They were searching for an opportunity to cross the politically sensitive coastlines of Russia, Ukraine, Georgia, Turkey, Bulgaria, and Romania, which all bordered the Black Sea. Criminal gangs used the cover of night to engage in illicit smuggling of immigrants, heroin and weapons between the bordered countries and so it was a precarious business slipping between the Black Sea Fleet and the various vessels making crossings at night.

Stead gave Kane and the SBS crew a basic intelligence report of the Valknut base, where they believed Jess Moore had been taken. It was a fortified complex nestled in the foothills close to the village of Molkin in Russia's Krasnodar region. The complex was used as a central training and intelligence hub for Valknut global operations. Various satellite images painted a picture of high walls, guard towers, and a small army inside the walls.

"You must come ashore between coastal villages," Stead had said, while flashing his laser pointer at the pull-down screen projecting a map of the destination. "You will encounter a patrol on that coastline. Eliminate them to set up your exit route. From the coast, it's an hour yomp across pine-forested hills to Molkin. Two of you will stay with the boat, and four will make the extraction."

In Kane's experience, briefings were efficient but impersonal, providing information before the team developed a contingency-filled operational plan based on their collective experience to successfully execute the mission.

"Remember," Stead had said once the projection was over, "your helmet cameras send real-time images back to us for analysis. We want to know the size and layout of the Valknut facility, what kind of capability they have. Jack, you will carry a USB stick in your gear. One of the mission objectives is to get a primed USB into a Valknut network drive. Whether it's a laptop, a PC, a server stack, it doesn't matter. The USB gets us a copy of their data and inserts an undetectable malware programme into their system, allowing us access whenever we choose."

"That's how you got this mission green-lit," Kane had said, leaning in and whispering to Scooby, who had grinned and winked in response. "You want me to get into the IT compound or offices and insert that USB. There will be thorough CCTV in there. They'll catch me on their cameras and find my face on the Interpol database from when I was a wanted man after the Mjolnir issues in Manchester."

"We've wiped your images from the Interpol database, Jack, don't worry."

The memory faded as the speedboat sliced through a larger than usual wave on the glassy sea and salty spray whipped across the deck, splashing Kane with bracing salt water.

"Are you ready?" shouted Scooby above the sound of the stealth boat and the skim of the sea beneath the keel.

"Ready," Kane replied.

"Don't fall behind. We won't wait for you."

Scooby threw his head back and laughed at the sheer madness of it, the joy that comes from fear mixed with confidence and the impending thrill of battle. It was a heady cocktail Kane knew well, and he tried his best not to enjoy the feeling as he focused again on the coastal hilltops as they raced towards him.

Sloping hills and shallow valleys thick with trees appeared from the darkness, where a fortress lay between windswept pines. Jess was in there, held in a private military fortress by ruthless men who wanted to use her and then kill her. She was little more than a business asset to them—a chess piece to push around the board as required. But to Kane, she was much more. Jess was the first woman he had allowed himself to get close to since Sally. The coastline sped closer, a silhouette of jagged hills and rugged land formations above the water. They would be ashore in moments, and Kane hoped he could fight his way into Valknut's fortress and rescue Jess before they killed her.

SIXTY-FOUR

The water splashed cold around Kane's thighs as he leapt from the speedboat to land in the shoreline swell, his boots crunching on the tiny shale stones of the seabed. He moved towards the shore in a controlled crouch, his MP5SD raised and ready to fire as he peered down the sights through the green hue of his night vision goggles. The land rose in shadows of green and black, and behind him, the stealth boat came about to head out to deeper water where Deeney and Taff would wait for the extraction. Kane glanced back at them, water spuming from the aft like a Las Vegas fountain show. They would leave at the allocated time, whether or not Kane and the others returned. He accepted that hard truth and turned back to the shore, ready to risk his life for Jess.

Ahead, gentle waves slopped and lapped against the jagged rocks of Krasnodar's shore.

Kane was in Russia. Danger was close, beckoning him on towards its lethal embrace. Long beaches stretched a mile to the north and south of their entry point, but the hazardous rocks around which they landed posed a danger to boats and were less likely to be heavily patrolled. The grey-green shape of boulders and lichen-covered rocks rose from the surf like the ruin of a collapsed building. Beyond that, a thick covering of dark pine trees littered a mile of coastal flatland before rising steeply onto the slopes of the first of many hillside valleys and promontories disappearing into the distance.

Scooby, Davies and Beef came up alongside Kane, and the four men moved swiftly towards the shore, coming from the water like black-clad figures from a nightmare. The sound of laughter on the shore, accompanied by the caw of a distant gull, stopped them dead, thigh-deep in the cold seawater. The orange glow of a cigarette tip glowed on the shore, and Kane's night vision spied two men strolling along the rocks and the unmistakable shape of rifles slung over their shoulders. Kane fired two sub-sonic rounds, squeezing the trigger, burying the short stock into his shoulder. The weapon bucked with its light recoil and the first patrolman collapsed dead. Scooby fired two rounds from his weapon, and the second patrolman fell.

Kane reached the rocks and clambered over

their chill, slick edges, keeping low and quiet. He was already out of breath from the trudge through the shore water. Davies and Beef moved swiftly ahead of Scooby and Kane, scampering over the rocks like lizards. They secured the coastline and knelt with weapons poised, scanning the treeline and approach paths as Kane and Scooby followed them into the forest's cover. The fresh smell of pine replaced the brine stink, and Kane's boots crunched softly on fallen pine needles as the four men began their tab, or quick march, towards the Valknut base.

"Keep up, and don't get us killed," growled Davies, towering over Kane with a curl on his lip.

After barely twenty minutes of quick marching through the pine forest, Kane was already panting. Sweat rolled down his back beneath the body armour and combat clothing. The straps of his helmet rubbed at his sweat-soaked forehead and the nape of his neck. Scooby maintained pace with the two younger men, and before long, they were little more than green shapes in the distance of his night vision goggles, flitting between the trees like ghosts.

Unseen animals shuffled and shifted in the bracken and fallen twigs, and as Kane trudged up the first hill, his legs burned like they were on fire. Kane steeled himself to the pain, recalling the tricks from his time on SAS selection and in the regiments. He focused on his breathing, forcing his mind to become the master of his body and block out the pain. Each step blurred into a concentrated exercise in pain and fatigue management. Kane counted to three between each breath, head down, cheeks blowing out, and legs powering forward. Jess needed him, and he refused to be left behind in the forest like some raw recruit unfit for duty. Kane vowed to get fit again once the mission was over. If he survived. Lack of endurance had caught Kane out too frequently, rendering him less than optimal for the job at hand. If he didn't address it soon, he would be dead.

After three more hills and what seemed like an age of focused tabbing through the creaking damp forest and across night-darkened meadows, Kane emerged from the treeline to find Davies, Beef, and Scooby kneeling beside a line of wire fencing. Kane slowed his march, trying to master his breathing before he reached the fitter men. His legs trembled from exertion and Kane fought with himself to recover from the forced march and make himself calm enough for combat.

"Some fucking genius idea inviting this useless muppet along," growled Davies, busy using a cutting tool to clip away a section of fence large enough for the men to crawl through.

"Don't worry about him," Scooby replied. "He was running missions like this when your mother was still wiping your arse between episodes of the Care Bears. Hurry up and cut that hole."

"He's your load to carry, Scooby. If shit goes wrong, I'm not dying for him. You should probably take that USB stick. Or give it to me."

"The USB stays where it is. Stop moaning and start cutting."

Kane stayed silent as Davies and Beef clipped away the joins between a dozen wire links. Davies was right. Deniability was the only reason Kane was there. If anything went wrong, the enemy would have Kane's face on which face to pin the blame if Valknut and Russia tried to kick up an international incident about the raid on their territory. Kane was under no illusions about that. He was ready to take the blame and risk his life to get Jess back. Perhaps, if he got the USB stick into a Valknut drive, it might square his debt with MI6, wipe his slate clean, so to speak. His priority was to rescue Jess and get her out of this place alive, but if he could get a brighter future for Danny and Kim—a future without hiding and running forever—then he would take it.

SIXTY-FIVE

Kane ran behind Scooby with his left hand on his old friend's shoulder. Davies led the line and Beef ran behind Kane, his hand laying heavy on the shoulder straps of Kane's armour. They moved like that to maintain control and coordination between the team. Dew soaked through the toes of Kane's boots, which had dried during the quick march across the Krasnodar hills. As soon as he had crawled through the hole in the Valknut compound's fence, adrenaline washed away the aches in Kane's muscles like the tide sweeping kelp from a beach.

A monstrous concrete cube rose from the ground ahead like a gigantic bomb-proof bunker. Like a warning, the Valknut skull insignia glowed on the side of the building through Kane's green night vision. Inside, hundreds of Valknut recruits slept. Jess Moore was imprisoned somewhere inside that formidable fortress, and Kane could imagine how afraid she was. This was not her world; this was Kane's world. She was a businesswoman, used to meeting rooms and negotiations, football matches and cappuccinos. Jess had no exposure to the world's darker side, where death stalked battlefields and men showed their true nature, their desire to dominate others, to murder, torture, and kill. Kane knew that world all too well and as he dashed across an open field, which he thought was most likely a shooting range, flashbacks to old missions circled around his head like unwanted visitors.

If he had the choice, Kane would have preferred to go in alone. To slip inside the fortress unseen and undetected, find Jess and slip away again like a spirit in the night. But he had no way of entering Krasnodar without help from MI6, so here he was. A room full of analysts watched their progress through the team's helmet cameras. Sitting safe and warm in their office, whilst the warriors marched into an enemy fortress crawling with Valknut soldiers on a mission with only a slim chance of success.

The first enemy died as Davies reached the end of the shooting range field. A patrolling guard smoking a roll-up cigarette with an AK-47 slung lazily over one shoulder didn't see the sub-sonic bullet coming as it tore through his skull and spattered his brains over the concrete wall. Security lights around the building flared in Kane's night vision goggles, prompting him to lift them away from his eyes. As the four men reached the grey wall, they skirted around to the south side. Davies found an electrical control box and pranged it open with his knife so that Scooby could attach a small device to the circuits.

"The boffins back at base will do the rest," he said, turning to Kane. "Not like in our day, eh, Jack? We had to cut the wires ourselves. More than once I've thought I was cutting a camera feed only to set off an alarm."

"It's a brave new world," sneered Davies. "Keep the chat to a minimum."

Kane followed Davies east, alongside a swimming pool building and a long barracks in complete darkness. Three more guards died, all killed by accurate and deadly bursts from Davies's silenced MP5. Kane controlled his breathing, his old reactions and skills coming back to him like a comfortable pair of shoes. They entered the fortress through a fire escape. The team in Fort Monckton had already disabled the alarm and security cameras via the electronic device Scooby had attached to the outside fuse box.

"Now we go blind," said Scooby, his boots squeaking on the polished floor inside the building. "We had satellite imagery to show us how to get in, but we do not know what awaits inside this place. Davies and Beef, you work your way around to the west; Kane and I will go east. We have comms on, so if you find any IT hardware hail us on comms and Kane will come with the USB. Once we have the data and the girl, we get out of here. Go quiet and fast, avoid engaging in a gunfight if possible. Our weapons have suppressors, but the enemy's weapons won't. We don't want an entire Valknut regiment closing in on us."

Kane and Scooby turned right along the corridor and marched quickly along a line of closed doors. The signs on the door gave dormitory numbers in Russian. Kane had learned some of the language upon entering the intelligence services. He was a little rusty, but could still pick out the basics. He did not know where to find Jess, only that she would be close to an interrogation room, and they would keep her somewhere secure. There had to be a brig or some sort of prison to house recruits or soldiers who had broken the rules and awaited a court martial. Soldiers were young men in the company of other rowdy young men. In every army in every country in the world, soldiers fought, drank, snuck out of barracks, and got up to no good. So, a brig was a fundamental requirement, especially in a private army like Valknut, where, Stead had mentioned during his briefing, the recruits often came from Russian prisons.

Kane tapped Scooby on the shoulder and showed that he was ready to take the lead. Scooby nodded and did not complain; he had worked under Kane's leadership for years. There was a trust between them. The type of trust that can only exist between men who have fought beside each other in that gossamer thin line between life and death, where each relies upon the other to protect, defend, and fight to the death for him.

The dormitory doors continued, and Kane glanced up at signs above turns in the twist of sterile, shiny-floored corridors. On the communication system in his ear, Davies and Beef made small breathing sounds as they travelled the corridors to the west.

"IT offices located," barked Davies through Kane's earpiece. "The brig backs onto a garage and storage facility on the east wing, and the offices, IT and intel rooms follow on from the brig on the south side."

"Copy that," said Scooby over the comms. "You secure the west wing and stop any of the enemy from coming in that direction. We'll work our way around to the southeast corner."

"Wait," Davies said. "The dorms and recreation rooms are all on that side, so any alarm or danger will come from the east. All there is on this side is a gym, mission prep meeting rooms and a hall for regimental briefings."

"Get over this side, ASAP," said Scooby. "You two can cover our flank whilst we recover the target and get the USB into one of their machines."

Kane turned a corner and two guards faced him, only five paces away. Tall men, clean shaven in army camouflage fatigues, staring at Kane and his painted face and black combat gear with open mouths and wide eyes. They carried brown-stocked AK-47s over their shoulders, but Kane carried his MP5SD before him with his finger poised over the trigger. He fired three short bursts, and the two men shook under the force of the silenced rounds, their clothing tearing and blood gouting from the bullet wounds in dark streams. They slumped dead against the wall and left a red smear on the cream, clean concrete like snails.

A door opened to Kane's left and a pale face popped out, stared at the dead men and cursed under his breath in Russian. Before Kane or Scooby could react, he slammed the door closed.

"Fuck," snarled Scooby. "We have to go in."

Kane nodded, took one step, and kicked the door in. Scooby tossed in a flash bang grenade and as it exploded, Kane went in first, low and fast. Three men coughed to his right, and he shot them in the chest and head, coming from the smoke like a demon. Scooby followed him inside and they swept the dorm clear, taking out seven Valknut soldiers in less than thirty seconds. Those men died silently, fresh from their beds, no screaming or attempts to stop the black-clad assassins. The last soldier, the man from the door, made it to the rear of the long dorm and slammed his hand on a red alarm button. The dawning horror played out on the man's face as he realised that the alarm had not sounded, and he roared in terror at the top of his voice. Scooby shot him through the throat and Kane ran from the room, forgetting the protocol for clearing and securing a room.

"We have to keep moving," Kane whispered urgently. "We don't have time to clean the other dorms." Scooby understood the gravity of the situation, his square jaw tensing.

The soldier's shout had been long and loud, and Kane's stomach turned over with the heat of fear. He and Scooby ran from the room and past the remaining dormitories where the Valknut army slept. They burst through a heavy metal door leading away from the dorm corridor and locked it behind them. The fight was coming. The alarm had been raised by the man's voice, and he had not found Jess.

SIXTY-SIX

Jess Moore woke with a start from an exhaustion-induced deep sleep. She lay on a pallet bed inside a locked, metallic room containing nothing but the bed, a blanket, and a metal toilet. She wrapped the blanket around her shivering shoulders and cocked her head, as though it would make the bangs and shouts which had awoken her so abruptly become clearer.

A panicked voice in Russian yelled down the hallway, and Jess jumped as machine gun fire thundered outside her door, the noise booming and reverberating around her small cell. Jess curled up and covered her ears with her hands. How could things possibly get any worse? A month ago, she would not have dreamed that things could move so fast, so quickly. Or that her life could go downhill so rapidly.

More gunfire erupted, and the door to her cell

shook and banged against its lock. She realised she was whimpering and rocking while sitting on the edge of her bed. Jess forced herself to sit still, staring at the door, her mind tumbling over what fresh terrors were about to come through it.

The lock turned, scratching against its mechanism and then the heavy door swung upon so fast that it clattered against the opposite wall. A figure clad in black and clutching a machine gun stepped into the room. Beneath the helmet and black and brown painted face, Jess realised that there was something familiar about the man who glared at her, dark eyes shining beneath the terrifying camouflage paint.

"Jess," said the man in a familiar voice. "It's me. Let's go." He held his hand out, beckoning her towards him, and Jess began to cry with relief. It was Jack Kane. But what was he doing here? She did not know where here even was, let alone how Kane had found her after flights, cars and an impossibly long journey.

"Let's go, there's more coming," called a gruff English voice from outside the room. Jess ran to Jack, and he held her close for a fleeting moment. She clung to him, the emotion suddenly pouring out of her like a burst dam. She sobbed into his shoulder; the dark fear of death, which seemed inevitable, now punctured by a ray of hope. He had come for her. Jess wasn't sure how Jack had found her or how he was going to get her out, but he was there, and in that moment of hope, it was enough.

"Thank God you are OK," he said, and kissed the side of her face.

"Let's move, Kane," barked a harsh voice from outside the cell.

"Keep close to me," said Jack, cupping her cheeks with his hands and staring deep into her eyes. "Keep your hand on my shoulder."

Jack shifted into an animal-like crouch. He gripped a brutal-looking short machine gun held across his body by a strap in two hands, and brought it up to his eyes. He moved forward in that position, sweeping his weapon across the hall, walking in careful, controlled steps. A heavily-muscled man with a beard waited for them there, dressed all in black like Jack and similarly armed.

Three bodies lay in the hallway outside the cell, slumped and seeping dark blood into the polished floors. Men wearing the uniform of her captors, men Jess should hate, but she still turned away from the horrifying sight of their corpses. She followed Jack, her right hand clutching the harsh material of his bullet-proof vest.

Four soldiers came hurtling around the corner behind the dead men, black guns with brown stocks clutched in their hands.

"Get down!" Jack shouted at her over his shoulder, but before the enemy soldiers could open fire, they shook and toppled, as though electrocuted. Jess realised that a spray of bullets peppered the four men, silent and unseen. They fell to join their dead colleagues, and Jack paused, weapon raised, and the man with the beard knelt next to him, facing in the opposite direction in case another threat came from that direction.

Jess stared down the corridor, holding her breath in case more of her captors came to join the fight, but then released a sigh of relief as two men clad all in black came around the corner, one a large black man and the other smaller with piercing blue eyes.

"Good timing," said the bearded man to the new arrivals.

"Why?" asked the big man, stalking past Jack without even glancing at Jess or Kane.

"Because here they come."

SIXTY-SEVEN

Davies and Beef marched past Kane towards the doors separating the brig corridor from the canteen, kitchen, and dormitories. Beyond that reinforced metal door, shouting thundered around the corridors, accompanied by the sound of boots thumping on the linoleum floor. The shout of the dying man in the dorm room had awoken the Valknut beast, and Kane cursed under his breath.

Jess cowered behind him, her hand gripping his body armour for dear life. He had to get her out of the fortress, but with all the Valknut personnel awoken, that was suddenly even more impossible than before. There could be two hundred soldiers beyond that door, baying for blood, come to kill.

"Bastards are coming," growled Davies. "We'll hold them here. Get the fucking USB sorted, now!" He flashed an angry glance at Kane, ejected the magazine from his MP5, took another from his belt and slammed it into place.

Scooby led the way, picking his steps carefully around the dead soldiers and around the corridor corner. Ahead lay another metal door leading from the brig to the IT rooms and offices. Scooby opened it, and Kane followed him into the open space. To their left stretched a length of windows, and beyond that, three separate spaces. One with four small offices inside, complete with wall-mounted maps and desks, another with an open-plan space with whiteboards and desks for soldiers to meet plus a section of six desks with computers for admin staff, and finally, a dark room with a line of blinking server towers.

"The servers will have USB ports," said Scooby, and Kane nodded in agreement. "I'll hold this door in case the fuckers get through Davies and Beef."

Kane reached up and tapped Jess's slender fingers at his shoulder to indicate that she should follow him along the window towards the server room. To their right was a thinner window with an open atrium space beyond it, where weights, gym and martial arts mats sat still and quiet beneath dimmed night lighting.

Kane opened the door to the server room, and a blast of cold air hit his face like a slap. Servers have to be kept cold so that their processors don't overheat. Kane fished the USB stick from a pocket attached to his belt. He scanned the black towers, green, yellow and red lights blinking and flashing as the machines whirred and buzzed. Electrical wiring in yellow and green coiled like great snakes, bound in thick, satisfyingly organised ropes. Kane found a port and slipped the USB stick in until it clicked. He waited, glancing back and nodding at Jess to show everything was OK.

Gunfire rattled in the distance as the Valknut soldiers fought to breach the door held by Davies and Beef. Kane stared at the USB. It was taking too long, and he tapped his foot impatiently. More gunfire exploded outside the server room, but this time closer. Scooby appeared at the window, firing shots from his MP5. Kane stared at the USB again, willing it to finish its work, chewing at his bottom lip. He should have left the USB and just tried to get Jess out, but the virus it carried and the information that tiny stick currently copied from the Valknut servers were precious to MI6. It could well be his family's key to a better life, a life without fear of pursuit.

More gunfire crackled outside, and Jess screamed as the bursts grew even closer. Scooby's gunfire paused, and he slipped inside the server room to slot a new magazine into his rifle.

"What's taking so fucking long?" he snarled. "They are coming from the east wing now.

Must have skirted around our flank when they couldn't get through Beef and Davies. I'm holding them at the door. They can't get through."

Kane licked at his dry lips and glanced from Scooby to the USB, but its light had not yet turned green. A tiny green light was the signal that the USB had scraped all the information from the Valknut database. A flash of movement caught his attention, and Kane turned, staring through the two panes of glass, one facing out of the server room and the other facing into the atrium. His jaw dropped open because, just at the moment, an RPG, a rocket-propelled grenade, soared across the shadowy atrium towards the server room.

"Get down!" Kane roared and dragged Jess Moore into a crouch. The explosion knocked Kane backwards, the noise ringing in his ears. He forced himself to rise, coughing and struggling to breathe in a cloud of smoke. The window glass had shattered to cover the floor with shards like a sea of broken ice, and the blast had crumbled and broken the wall apart. Scooby rolled on the floor in the doorway amongst the rubble, stunned, but doing his best to recover his senses. The smoke beyond the server room whipped away from a scene of crumbled debris, taken by the wind from the caved-in roof. From that smoke came four Valknut soldiers armed with AK-47 assault rifles, and at their head strode a familiar figure. Valery Ivanov, wearing his glasses, his cruel mouth twisted in an angry snarl.

The USB stick finally blinked green, and Kane snatched it from the server stack, slotting back into the pouch at his belt. Then he raised his weapon and opened fire, as Ivanov, the former Spetsnaz special forces elite soldier, and his men, came to kill.

SIXTY-EIGHT

Kane squeezed the trigger, and loosed a burst of gunfire from his MP5SD; the shots missed Ivanov but dropped a hulking figure beside him. Scooby sat up in the doorway and fired a burst of his own, killing another of Ivanov's men. Scooby pushed himself backwards, leaving a trail of blood from his wounded leg. He looked at Kane and shook his head, pain stretching the features of his face.

A thunderous burst of AK-47 gunfire forced Kane to duck, and he leapt on top of Jess to shield her body. Bullets crashed into the server room walls, even punching into the expensive server towers themselves. Kane waited until the burst of machine gun fire abated, which he knew it would. Firing any machine gun, but particularly an AK-47, results in a recoil that forces the weapon's muzzle to rise, firing bullets in an increasingly upward trajectory. So, just as he had dozens of times before, in battles across the world, Kane waited for the shooter to pause and lower his aim.

The gunfire ceased, and Kane swiftly rose and shot a bearded man in the face. He then fired two more rounds into the man's chest, dropping him dead into the rubble. Ivanov leapt through the ragged gap in the smashed atrium brickwork. He rolled and came up out of Kane's sight, somewhere below the server room window.

"Bastard!" Scooby bellowed, releasing a barrage of fire from his MP5 out of the doorway and along the wall behind which Ivanov hid. Scooby continued to roar incoherently, spittle flying from his mouth as he emptied the magazine. Scooby's injured leg and the rage of battle drove him to empty his magazine and keep clicking the trigger of his empty weapon.

Ivanov appeared in the doorway with a pistol in his right hand. Without hesitation, he fired once, sure and sharp, and shot Scooby in the forehead with a perfectly aimed strike. Scooby toppled backwards with a black hole in the centre of his brow, and the back of his head blown away in a sickening spray of blood and brains.

Kane took a step forward and aimed his weapon at Ivanov, but his enemy already had his pistol poised. Ivanov allowed himself a wicked smile as he watched the realisation dawn in Kane's eyes that he was about to shoot Jess Moore. Kane swallowed and blinked dust from the explosion out of his eyes. He lowered his weapon, taking a chance, hoping to prick Ivanov's warrior pride. Kane unclipped the MP5SD and let it fall to the ground. He reached for his belt, drew his combat knife and beckoned Ivanov to fight.

Valery Ivanov threw his head back and laughed, his eyes twinkling with the thrill, the sheer madness of the fight Kane offered as the fortress rattled with gunfire around them. They had locked horns throughout the operation, two highly-trained soldiers facing off, and now to finish it, to see who the greater warrior was. One would live and one would die, and in that split second decision, it was the only way Kane could save Jess Moore's life. If he fired his weapon, Ivanov would have killed Jess. Now, for them both to live, Kane must kill Ivanov.

The Russian bent and drew his own knife from a strapped sheath around his thigh. It was a long, wicked blade with a serrated edge on one side and a gleaming sharp edge on the other. In a salute to the impending combat, he inclined his head at Kane, changed his grip on the blade, and advanced with the bobbing stance of a boxer.

Kane gripped his knife in his right hand and set himself in a low crouch, light on the balls of his feet. Ivanov feinted with his blade and laughed again as Kane flinched away from the strike. The Russian circled in the opposite direction and suddenly flashed out a savage front kick aimed at Kane's knee, but Kane skipped away.

Gunfire continued to crackle down the hallway as Davies and Beef fought to hold back the larger cohort of Valknut soldiers beyond the door leading from the dorms to the brig. But it was only a matter of time before more of the enemy circled around to the east and found the hole Ivanov had created. Once that happened, the enemy would overwhelm and kill Kane and Jess. So, there was no time to play Ivanov's game. Kane had forced his enemy to drop his pistol with a challenge to fight, but that fight had to be over quickly. Before it was too late.

Kane stepped forward nimbly and lunged with the knife's point. Ivanov swayed away from the attack, but Kane followed it up, punching with his left hand and unleashing a flurry of knife slashes and punches that drove Ivanov backwards. Kane was already breathing hard, but as Ivanov ducked beneath a knife slash, Kane brought his knee up to crash into the Russian's face. Ivanov grunted and stumbled, and Kane swung the knife overhand, aiming to stab down into Ivanov's shoulder, but the Valknut soldier saw the blow coming. He dropped to the floor, rolled and slashed the blade of his knife across Kane's thigh. He moved snake-fast and struck with lethal efficiency.

The blade sliced open Kane's flesh like a red-hot whip, and he could not control the cry of pain that escaped from him. Ivanov sprang to his feet with the agility of a gymnast and Kane lunged at him, furious at being wounded and desperate to end the fight, but Ivanov leapt away. Kane tried to follow but his leg trailed, heavy and stiff, and as he stumbled forwards Ivanov struck again, dragging the jagged edge of his knife across Kane's shoulder and bicep.

Jess cried out in despair and Kane limped away from Ivanov, blood pulsing down his arm to wet his hand and drip onto the floor. Ivanov came on again, a feral look on his hard face as he advanced to slaughter Kane. Kane let him come. Ivanov was younger and faster, and Kane had no hope of beating him in a straight-up knife fight. Ten years ago, before retiring to the witness protection programme, he might have stood a chance against the Spetsnaz fighter, but not now. But the enemy still had to be fought and defeated if Kane and Jess were to have any chance of survival.

Kane set his jaw and limped forward, sagging and leaning as though he might topple over at any moment. Ivanov smiled briefly and then advanced for the kill, knife pulled back and poised to strike underhand beneath Kane's vest, low in the unprotected part of his lower belly. Kane swung his knife lazily, and Ivanov swayed around it and grunted as his knife came forwards. But Kane had exaggerated the severity of his injuries, and at the last moment, he ducked, causing Ivanov's blade to slam into his vest. The vest absorbed the force of the blow, preventing the knife from piercing Kane's body armour. He grabbed Ivanov's wrist below the knife hand and shifted his legs. Kane threw Ivanov over his hip, and as the Russian hit the ground, he spun to come up fighting, but Kane pulled him close again and stamped hard on Ivanov's groin.

Ivanov grunted in pain and tried to twist away, but Kane kept a tight grip on the Russian's wrist, even though his grip was slick with blood from his injured shoulder. Kane dragged Ivanov close and drove his knife point into the Russian's leg as he bucked and fought to get away. Ivanov gasped and Kane kicked him savagely in the face. Kane leapt to his right and rolled onto the server room floor. He came beside Scooby's corpse and tore the Remington shotgun from his dead friend's back. Ivanov snarled and tried to stand, but Kane swung the Remington around, pushing the action lock in front of the trigger with his finger and chambered a shell with a slide of the forestock. A round clicked into the chamber;

Kane released the safety and fired.

Ivanov's neck and chin exploded in a close-range blast of torn flesh and blood. The force of the pump-action shotgun's round threw him backwards against the rubble of the server room wall. Kane sighed with relief and limped to Jess, pulling her up from where she crouched in a corner with her hands over her ears. Ivanov was dead, but there was no time to rest, because boots came pounding along the corridor from the brig doorway. Kane waited and chambered another round in the Remington.

"They are through," gasped Beef as he came running over the rubble.

"Davies?" asked Kane.

"Holding them, did you get the USB data?"

"Got it."

Beef's eyes flickered across Kane's injured shoulder and leg. "We must go up to get out. It's the only way."

SIXTY-NINE

Beef slipped off his rucksack and pulled out a length of rope. He clambered up the edges of jagged rubble, stumbling half a dozen times before reaching the roof above the blown-out window and wall. He fastened the rope to a secure brickwork post and tossed the end down to Kane. Jess raised her arms as Kane secured the rope around her waist. He nodded to reassure her as Jess fixed him with glassy eyes. Beef hauled on the rope as Jess climbed up the shattered breeze block and brick ruins.

The gun battle raged in the corridor, and Kane limped to the doorway to see how close Davies was to making it to the server room.

"Come on, Jack," Beef called from the dark cavity between the server room ceiling and the roof.

"We can't leave Davies," said Kane as he peered

around the corner. Davies took quick steps backwards, letting off small bursts of fire from his MP5. Ahead of him, the metal door stood wide open and sprung from its hinges. Gun barrels poked through the space as the Valknut soldiers fired at the retreating man in black.

"Run, Davies!" Kane called.

"Get out of here," Davies shouted in reply. "We can't all make it. The second I stop firing, they'll swarm us. Get the girl and the data and go."

Davies had scorned and insulted Kane since the mission began, and now the SBS soldier was ready to give up his own life so that Jack and Jess could live. Kane's heart swelled, and he wanted to run out into the corridor and stand with Davies, make a last stand worthy of legend. But his leg was useless, and it dragged behind Kane like a dead weight. His shoulder screamed with pain, and Kane's left arm was out of action. A bullet whipped through Davies' calf, and he dropped to one knee, firing back at his enemies. Davies reloaded and another bullet crashed into his body armour.

Davies roared in pain, clicked a fresh magazine into place and returned fire as a hail of bullets came from the enemy to thud into the walls and floor around him. Kane pulled a fragmentation grenade from his belt, yanked the pin free, and tossed it down the hallway towards the enemy.

He fired the two remaining shells from the Remington and limped back to the rope, where Jess's pale face peered at him from the gloom above.

Kane grabbed the rope and let Beef haul him upwards, whilst in the corridor, Davies roared his war cry, a hero's shout to shake the very fortress. Davies charged at the Valknut soldiers firing his MP5 as he went to die so that Beef, Kane and Jess could live. Kane left a bloody smear on the crumbling walls as he reached the roof, and Beef clicked on his torch, leading them south in the dark roof cavity above the brig.

"The garage and storage area are this way," Beef called out in the gloom, where his torchlight illuminated steel roof beams in the space between the ceiling and corrugated iron roof panels. "We won't make it back to the sea on foot. We need transport."

Jess hooked her arm around Kane's torso and supported him as he limped through the darkness. Loss of blood and his wounds caused Kane's vision to blur and his breath came in ragged gasps. Beef stopped and knelt, tearing at the ceiling tiles with his combat knife to make a hole he then dropped through. Gunfire crackled in the distance as Davies fought valiantly to the death, and Kane's heart burned with both admiration and regret as the bullets stopped and Davies met his end, fighting for his country and the regiment he was so proud to serve.

Kane lowered Jess through the space, though his wounds screamed at him to stop, to lie down and rest for a while. He knew that feeling well, his mind playing tricks on him, wanting his body to stop fighting against the knife wounds, to rest and repair. But to stop was to die, and so he grimaced as he lowered Jess into Beef's arms and then jumped down after her. He found himself in a long, hangar-like garage filled with jeeps and other military vehicles, all daubed with the fearsome Valknut skull.

Beef jumped into the closest jeep, and Jess climbed into the back. Kane slid into the passenger door and gasped as the gash on his leg touched the seat to send a pulse of blood cascading down his leg. Beef started the engine, and the jeep roared to life. He gunned the accelerator, and they sped through the garage, racing towards a set of white roller-doors.

"Seatbelts on," Beef growled. "Brace yourselves."

Beef didn't stop to open the doors. He smashed through them, and the impact almost threw Kane through the windscreen, only his seatbelt saving him from that fate. They careened out into the darkness, and guns blared around them, accompanied by shouting voices in the darkness. Beef drove the jeep at full pelt through the grounds of the Valknut fortress, speeding across the shooting range and bursting through the fence at the exact point the team had entered through the clipped wire opening.

Behind them, vehicles roared to life as Valknut made ready to pursue them across the hills and valleys of Krasnodar. Beef kept ahead of them, driving in grim silence across rough tracks, skirting the forests beneath the shimmering moon. Kane reached backwards with his uninjured arm and Jess grabbed his hand, gripping it with the strength of the desperate. He couldn't turn to check on her. Kane's wounds throbbed and tore at him, blood seeping from his shoulder and leg. The fight with Ivanov had almost killed him, but they were alive and free. Kane carried his survival tin with his kit, and though his wounds were deep and painful, he knew that once they reached the stealth boat, he had everything he needed to stem the flow of blood. As the jeep raced across the tree line, headlights bumped and flashed to the east as Valknut pursued them in the wrong direction. Beef had cut the jeep's headlights the moment they had left the fortress, relying on moonlight alone to guide him towards the Black Sea, where Deeney and Taff waited with the stealth boat.

Kane squeezed Jess Moore's hand. She was alive, and he closed his weary eyes. It had been a desperate mission. He had come within a hair's breadth of dying and of losing Jess forever. Kane thought of Danny and Kim at that moment. He owed them more than a present at the airport on his return home. He owed them time, and they needed and deserved a better father.

SEVENTY

"They made it!" Craven cried out, and slapped Kieran Stead on the back. The MI6 man did not appreciate the gesture, straightening his jacket and rewarding Craven with a withering, side-eye look of disgust.

The screens in Fort Monckton's mission room blinked and flickered with green computer code. A large screen on the wall showed satellite imagery of vehicles in shadow speeding towards the Black Sea coastline. To the place Kane and the survivors were twenty minutes earlier.

"De-brief in one hour," said Stead, and a young soldier in army fatigues saluted and went to pass the order around the mission room.

"When do they fly home?" Craven asked.

"The boat will return to our base in Georgia, and we'll get them home tomorrow."

"And we can go free?"

Stead raised an eyebrow. "You can go once they return."

"Are you going to wipe Jack's slate clean?"

"It doesn't work like that, Mr Craven. Kane knows too much, has done and seen too much. He is still both an asset of the British Government, and a threat to its national security. So, he is friend and foe."

"But you said if he got that USB thingy that this would all be over?"

"Over for now, Mr Craven. But never truly over. Not for Jack Kane."

Stead left the mission room, and Craven stared after him. They would leave Kane alone for now, but for how long? Craven sat down heavily in an office chair and kneaded stinging eyes with his broad knuckles. He couldn't wait to get back to Barb in Spain, to have some quiet time with her. To rest and support her. To just live. Kane would go with him. Kane and Jess Moore were close, but Jack had to return to his family and Craven hoped his friend would take some time to be with his children and live in peace. But there would always be people who need help, the type of help only Craven and Kane could offer, and Kane could not stay away from action for long.

AUTHOR NEWSLETTER

Sign up to the Dan Stone author newsletter and receive a FREE novella of short stories featuring characters from the Jack Kane series.

The newsletter will keep you updated on new book releases and offers. No spam, just a monthly update on Dan Stone books.

Sign up to the newsletter at https://mailchi.mp/danstoneauthor/sgno14d1hi for your FREE ebook

Or visit the author website at https://danstoneauthor.com/

ABOUT THE AUTHOR

Dan Stone

Dan Stone is the pen name of award winning author Peter Gibbons.

Born and raised in Warrington in the North West of England, Peter/Dan wanted to be an author from the age of ten when he first began to write stories.

Since then, Peter/Dan has written many books, including the bestselling Viking Blood and Blade Saga, and the Saxon Warrior Series.

Peter now lives in Kildare, Ireland with his wife and three children.

Printed in Dunstable, United Kingdom